Linwood Barclay is an international bestselling crime and thriller author with over twenty critically acclaimed novels to his name, including the phenomenal Number One bestseller *No Time For Goodbye*.

Every Linwood Barclay book is a masterclass in characterisation, plot and the killer twist, and with sales of over seven million copies globally, his books have been sold in more than thirty-nine countries around the world, and he can count Stephen King, Shari Lapena and Peter James among his many fans.

Many of his books have been optioned for film and TV, and Linwood wrote the screenplay for the film based on his bestselling novel *Never Saw It Coming*. Born in the US, his parents moved to Canada just as he was turning four, and he's lived there ever since.

He lives in Toronto with his wife, Neetha. They have two grown children.

Visit Linwood Barclay at www.linwoodbarclay.com or find him on X at @linwood_barclay.

Also by Linwood Barclay

Whistle
I Will Ruin You
The Lie Maker
Look Both Ways
Take Your Breath Away
Find You First
Elevator Pitch
A Noise Downstairs
Parting Shot
The Twenty-Three
Far from True
Broken Promise
No Safe House
A Tap on the Window
Never Saw It Coming
Trust Your Eyes
The Accident
Never Look Away
Fear the Worst
Too Close to Home
No Time for Goodbye
Bad Luck
Bad News
Bad Guys
Bad Move

LINWOOD BARCLAY

NOT A WORD

HQ

ONE PLACE. MANY STORIES

HQ
An imprint of HarperCollins*Publishers* Ltd
1 London Bridge Street
London SE1 9GF

www.harpercollins.co.uk

HarperCollins*Publishers*
Macken House, 39/40 Mayor Street Upper,
Dublin 1, D01 C9W8, Ireland

This edition 2026
1
First published in Great Britain by HQ,
an imprint of HarperCollins*Publishers* Ltd 2026

Linwood Barclay asserts the moral right to be identified as the author of this work. A catalogue record for this book is available from the British Library.

HB ISBN: 9780008555801
TPB ISBN: 9780008555788

This book is set in 10.4/15.5 pt. Sabon by Type-it AS, Norway

Printed and bound in the UK using 100% Renewable
Electricity by CPI Group (UK) Ltd

FSC www.fsc.org
MIX
Paper | Supporting responsible forestry
FSC® C013604

For Neetha

"You can't ever tell anyone about this. They wouldn't understand. It's very complicated."

"Okay."

"And if you ever did tell anyone . . . and this might be the worst thing of all . . . you know what would happen?"

"No."

"I wouldn't love you anymore. You wouldn't want that, would you?"

"No."

"Okay, then. Now give us a kiss."

ONE

Reece

"Tell me how you came to find them."

"I went into the room," I said, "and saw them on—"

"Let's go back a bit. What were you doing before you came over here?"

"Sorry," I said. "I'm kind of rattled."

"I get that. It's okay. Just start at the beginning."

Here was this detective, giving me advice on how to impart information. I was the one who was supposed to know how to do this. Spin a tale, let a narrative unfold. Present the facts in a logical order. But I was jumping straight to the conclusion, the denouement, as it were.

"Right, right," I said. "I'd decided to drop by."

"What time would this have been?"

She was patient, this detective. She'd told me her name, but I'd already forgotten it. McCain? McCabe? Something like that. Again, not like me, who was supposed to be good at this. Remembering names, getting the spelling right. But right now, I could barely remember my own. Chartwell, I'd said when she'd asked. That a first or last name? Last, I'd told her. When

I realized she was waiting for my first name, I'd had to think about it for a second. Shock does strange things to your brain.

"Reece," I'd said, and spelled it, lest she think I shared a name with a famous actress. And then the detective had asked what my father's name was. "Brent," I'd said. "Brent Chartwell." And, knowing what her next question would be, I'd said, "My mother's name is—was—Catherine."

We'd been inside the house when we'd traded introductions, but now we were sitting outside on a decorative white wrought-iron bench. One of those pieces of garden furniture you admire but don't often sit on, too uncomfortable. But Mom liked those kinds of touches, things that looked nice but had no real practical use. Like fancy flower-shaped soaps you leave in a bathroom but never actually use.

Now, outside, I said, "Around half past one. I'd had lunch at my place, was trying to come up with a strategy, having lost my job recently, but really wasn't feeling it, and—"

"Feeling it?" Detective McCain or McCabe said.

"Needed to clear my head. Go out of the house, grab a coffee or something, and I found myself driving over here."

"Why?"

I shrugged. "I had an excuse. Couple of books I'd borrowed from Dad, thought I might as well return them."

"You do that regularly? Drop in, unannounced?"

"They're my parents."

The detective waited for me to say more.

"Dad's the one I've always talked to when I'm looking for a sounding board. I've been wondering about what to do next."

Her puzzled look seemed to require some explanation.

"I worked for WorldWide." One of Canada's major television

networks. “Wrote copy for the midday and evening newscasts. WorldWide’s been hemorrhaging money, ad revenue collapsing, people getting their news off their phones instead of TV, and when they did a huge round of layoffs they went after the news division big-time.” What I didn’t bother getting into was that newscasts with two anchors now had one. There was less local coverage, more segments from south of the border. The noon news broadcast was axed entirely, replaced with reruns of *Hawaii Five-O*. But I figured this detective was more interested in what had happened here than a failing network’s program schedule.

I said, “I got a decent package when they laid me off but I need to find something else.”

“So you’d come to ask your father for money?”

“No,” I said somewhat defensively. “I just wanted his advice. He had a good business sense.”

“So you live nearby? Here in Yorkton Hill?”

“Yeah, other side of town. About ten minutes away. Sunnydale.” It was the name attached to our part of town.

The detective nodded. “We could almost be neighbors,” she said. I didn’t know whether she was trying to be affable, or really did live near us, and didn’t ask. Anyway, she was still interested in why I happened to be here.

“Okay, so, dropping off the books, that was an excuse, but you wanted to pick his brain about your career.”

I nodded. “More or less.”

“And didn’t call ahead.”

Another nod. I thought I’d made that clear.

“So you drive over and get here when? Half past one? Notice anything when you arrived?”

I shook my head. "Car was in the drive."

Detective McCain or McCabe wrote something down in one of those spiral reporter notebooks. I took a moment to size her up. About forty, I guessed, five eight, black hair with a few gray streaks running through it. Not striking in any way, I thought. A plain, oval face. Businesslike.

"That's your father's car? The Lexus?"

"Yes."

"Where's your mother's car?"

"She doesn't drive." Still using present tense. "There's an old Plymouth Barracuda in the garage. A '72, I think. Dad had a car like that when he was in his twenties. Found one in mint condition, got it fifteen, sixteen years ago."

The crazy things you think of at the strangest time. I wondered how I'd dispose of the cars when Dad couldn't sign over the ownership.

"That's your car behind the Lexus."

She was looking at the eighteen-year-old blue BMW sedan in the driveway. I nodded.

There were three other cars at the curb, two of them marked police cars, one a black, unmarked vehicle, the one the detective had shown up in. A couple more cars were parked farther down the street including a Toyota Corolla that looked as old as my car.

"So after you got here what happened?"

"I rang the bell. Waited a few seconds, rang it again. Then I tried knocking. And when neither of them came to the door, I thought maybe they were out back. They like to sit out there, look at the pond."

"Pond?"

"There's a couple of acres back there, and part of it's a pond that's got trees around most of it. There's a gate, which is locked so kids don't get onto the property and end up drowning, and I looked over it and they weren't out there, so I came back around to the front, figured, maybe they went for a walk, although that seemed unlikely. They're not big walkers. And out here, you want something as simple as a coffee, you have to drive."

"So why didn't you leave?"

I sighed. "For one thing, the car was there, so it seemed like at least Dad would be home. I knocked again, no answer, so then I just tried the door and it wasn't locked. Thought I could leave the books just inside. When I stepped in, I called out."

The detective was still making notes, glancing up regularly. "Go on."

"Nobody answered. That made me, I don't know, a little anxious. I mean, my parents, it's not like they're at death's door or anything. They're still active, travel, do things, but they're at an age where things can happen unexpectedly. A sudden heart attack, a stroke, you know." I shrugged.

"But so far as you knew, their health was okay."

I nodded.

"No bad news from the doctor? For either of them? Something that might have precipitated an event like this?"

I knew what she was getting at. I'd heard of older couples, one of them gets a terminal diagnosis, they decide to check out early. Maybe the person's spouse doesn't want to go on living, either, if they're going to be alone.

"If there was, they hadn't shared it with me."

I was starting to feel overwhelmed again, the enormity of what had transpired starting to sink in. You know you're going to lose your parents one day. But not like this. Not both of them at once.

"I just can't . . . I can't believe they're . . ."

"You need a minute?" the detective asked.

I nodded, but managed to say, "I'm sorry, I don't remember your name."

"Detective McCabe. Janice McCabe."

I tried to commit it to memory. Said it to myself three times.

"Coffee's here," she said.

McCabe had sent someone to fetch it. A uniformed officer approached bearing two red paper cups from the country's most popular coffee place. Although their outlets were everywhere, there wasn't one close to my parents' house.

"Black, right?" the cop said to me.

I nodded. I pried open the small opening on the plastic lid and took a sip to test how hot it was. It was lukewarm, evidently having cooled down on the trip here. I gulped a mouthful.

"It's a lot to process," McCabe said, putting down her notebook and taking a sip of her own coffee. She gave me another few seconds, then said, "When did you decide to go into the bedroom?"

I put the coffee down next to me. "I walked through the ground floor first, called down to the basement, and when I got no response I went upstairs. Their room's at the end of the hall and the door was partly closed and I thought, did I pick a bad time to come? Were they having a nap, or, you know, something else?"

McCabe got the drift.

"I start deliberately making noise, clearing my throat, saying things like, hey, I'm here, you guys okay? Stuff like that."

"Go on."

I was starting to get the shakes again, picked up the coffee and took a sip. Maybe caffeine wasn't what I needed right now.

"Even before I got to the door, there was some kind of . . . there was a smell. I don't know how to describe it. It was almost like metal, like copper or something. I'm never going to forget it."

"You pushed open the door."

"They're both in the bed, the covers kind of pulled up halfway, although I could see they weren't wearing anything, and my mom . . ."

"Take your time."

"She's sort of turned away, her back to me, and there's blood all over the back of her head. And Dad, he's just sitting in the bed, up against the . . . the . . ." I was losing my words.

"Headboard?" McCabe said.

"Yeah. Headboard. And his arm is hanging down the side of the bed, and there's a gun on the floor there, a few inches down from his fingers. The top of his head, it's all . . . there's this painting hanging on the wall over the bed, a seaside thing, with a lighthouse, they bought it years ago when they were in Cape Cod, and there's . . ."

"Okay," McCabe said.

I nod. "It's . . . everywhere, blood all over the painting, like he must have put the gun under his chin and . . ."

"Okay."

I closed my eyes tight, picturing it, but trying to substitute the image for something else. No luck there. It was a photograph imprinted onto my brain I'd never be able to delete. I knew it would be there when I went to sleep that night. Maybe every night, for the rest of my life.

"I didn't even know my father had a gun," I said. "He's never been, like, the kind of guy who'd own a gun. He wasn't interested in them, didn't collect them, nothing like that."

"Had your parents been having troubles?"

"Like?"

"Arguments? Anything we'd classify as domestic violence? Had they been talking about a separation, a divorce?"

I shook my head slowly. "I mean, every marriage has its ups and downs." And for an instant, I thought about my own. The kinds of disputes Diana and I had, often rooted in how I'd been treated by these two people in that upstairs bedroom who were no longer with us. "To be honest, for as long as I can remember, they'd kind of been going through the motions."

It hit me, at that moment, that if someone were to have asked me whether I thought my parents were still intimate, once I recovered from the question, I would have said no. Not because they were older, but because I didn't have the sense their relationship was particularly loving. I was trying to remember back to a time when I thought it was. My parents lived under the same roof but in many ways had separate lives, their own friends, different interests. I kept these thoughts to myself as McCabe continued with her questions.

"Do you know whether your father ever hit your mother? Threatened her?"

"No," I said emphatically. "No. I never saw anything like that."

"You never saw your mother with a black eye or something and she said she'd walked into a door?"

"I'm telling you, *no*."

"How about money troubles? Were they going through any financial difficulties?"

I shook my head, but my mind was elsewhere. I was thinking of all the people I needed to call. My father's brother, Frank, who lived out in Vancouver. Mom's older twin sisters, Amelia and Geraldine, who'd never married and shared an apartment in Gatineau. And finally, and most importantly, my brother, Holden.

Holden needed this news like Florida needed another hurricane. His life was fucked-up enough already. This could send him into another downward spiral; I'd have to find him, tell him in person before he heard about this from anyone else. I'd call Diana with the news, and let her break it to our son, Gage, if there wasn't a chance for us to do it together. Gage thought the world of his grandfather, and this would hit him hard.

And god, the arrangements that would have to be made. What did you tell people in a case like this? *Oh hey, Dad just killed Mom, then turned the gun on himself, we're having a service next week, can you make it?*

"What did you do when you saw them?" McCabe asked. "Did you enter the room? Did you touch them?"

"I took a couple of steps in, thinking, should I take their pulse? See if they're breathing? But it was so obvious, and then, I started to feel . . ."

"Feel?"

"Like I was going to be sick. I ran into the bathroom, and I threw up."

She nodded understandingly, closed her notebook, slipped it into her jacket. "I'm going back in for a moment. You stay here, okay?"

"Sure, yeah."

"I have more questions."

I nodded resignedly.

"And let me give you one of these before I forget," she said and handed me a card that had her name and a phone number on it.

She got up from the bench, gave me a mournful smile, and went back into the house, leaving me there in a daze. I slowly turned and looked to the street. The police had strung up that yellow tape like you see in the TV shows, blocking traffic in both directions, making people turn around and go the other way. This wasn't a high-traffic area. My parents' place was on the outskirts of Yorkton Hill, where the lots were bigger, the homes older, the neighbors spaced well apart. The Chartwells had lucked out, scoring a place that bordered a pond that led to a nearby creek that eventually found its way to the center of town, and beyond that, Lake Ontario. So this was not exactly what one would call waterfront property, but it gave the place where I grew up some distinction.

By comparison, Diana and Gage and I lived in a relatively new suburb where the lots were small and if you wanted water in your backyard, you got one of those plastic pools that looked like a turtle and was small enough to bring home on the roof of your car.

Yorkton Hill was about a thirty-minute commute west of Toronto, what they called a bedroom community because so many people drove or took the train to jobs in the city and only came back here to sleep. In Toronto, a couple found dead in their bed might not even make the evening news, but in Yorkton Hill that sort of thing wasn't supposed to happen. On average, its residents were better educated, had a higher standard of living. More one-percenters than other communities.

I guess that meant we were supposed to be happier too.

I got up. I needed to move around, but I wasn't heading back into the house. I couldn't go in there. I didn't know when I'd be able to. I'd have to at some point, of course. The place would have to be cleared out, put on the market. I didn't want to live there, and I was pretty sure Holden wouldn't. He'd be more interested in the windfall its sale would produce, and then the bets would be on how quickly he could blow it on meth or crack or whatever it was he was on these days.

My mind went over the detective's questions, particularly those about whether my parents had been having any serious problems. I'd said no, but clearly I'd had no idea what was going on between them. What signals had I failed to pick up on? What could have been going on right in front of me that I was too blind to see, that could have led to something this tragic?

I left my half-finished coffee on the bench and walked out onto the lawn, turned and looked back at the two-story house where I'd spent so much of my life. My parents had bought this place when I was eight, when Dad was making a fortune working for that pharmaceutical giant. I'd never lived here again after I'd left to attend university in Kingston, where I'd met and fallen in love with Diana. We got married and set up house much sooner than we'd planned. That can happen when somebody gets pregnant.

My cell rang. I felt the simultaneous vibration of it in my sports jacket pocket. Diana, I was betting. I didn't feel ready to break this to her yet, but there was never going to be a good time. I reached into my pocket to answer, but I was so on edge I fumbled the phone and dropped it onto the grass.

"Fuck," I said under my breath. I leaned over, picked up the phone, and looked at the screen, then felt my heart stop as I saw the caller ID. It wasn't Diana's name on the screen.

MOM.

I blinked a couple of times, not believing what I was seeing. I slid the bar across to take the call and put the phone to my ear.

"Hello," I said tentatively.

"Hey," said a familiar voice. "You at home? Can you drop by the house and see if your dad's okay? I've been calling and he's not picking up."

TWO

Yorkton Hill Police Detective Janice McCabe did another walk-through of the house before returning to the upstairs bedroom. The coroner was there, and once she was done, McCabe could have a closer look at the bodies, move them as necessary, then have them sent to the forensic science center in Toronto.

A nice house, she thought to herself. Nicer than what she could afford on her salary. She had not yet asked the son, Reece Chartwell, what his parents did for a living, or if they were both retired. She had the sense Brent Chartwell was, given that Reece believed he'd find his father home on a Friday.

McCabe found on a console table in the front hall the two books Reece had brought to return to his father, both hardcovers. A Richard Russo novel, *Everybody's Fool*, and an early John Irving, *A Widow for One Year*. So that part of his story checked out.

Judging by the house and the furnishings—tasteful, modern, leaning toward minimalist—it was clear the Chartwells had money or, at least, had had it.

She took out her phone, opened a browser, and did a search on Chartwell's name. Up came a Yorkton Hill–based consulting firm called Chartwell Strategies. Scanning information about the company, she learned the firm run by the Brent Chartwell who lived at this address had wound down operations two years ago.

Consulting evidently had been good to him. McCabe wasn't surprised. She'd seen enough of politics and the business world to know everyone was terrified to make decisions and happily threw hundreds of thousands of dollars at consultants to make choices for them. Then, when things went south, they could always blame the consultant.

Not that any of this had much to do with the matter at hand. This investigation, at least so far, did not look overly complicated. Husband shoots wife, turns gun on himself. And while Janice McCabe liked to solve life's mysteries, her job here was simple. Who did it? That gun on the floor, a 9mm Beretta just inches away from Brent Chartwell's dangling arm, was a glaring clue. It might be nice to know why he did this, but even if she learned his motivation, it wasn't as though she could charge him with anything.

Nearby residents might be shocked when they found out what happened here, but it wasn't anything McCabe hadn't seen before. Behind some of this idyllic community's closed doors lurked drug dealers, white slavers, child pornographers. But they were careful not to bring attention to themselves. They had Mercedes and Range Rovers in their driveways, kept their lawns cut, didn't have wild parties on Saturday night.

It wasn't likely this case would keep her up at night. Truth was, if McCabe could put her head on a pillow right now she'd be as dead to the world as those two upstairs. Her fourteen-year-old daughter, Moira, had ignored her ten o'clock curfew and didn't respond to her mother's texts asking where she was and why she wasn't home. When you're a cop, and all too aware of the trouble a teenager can get into, there's no sleep until that kid's home. Shortly after eleven McCabe had pulled on her clothes, slid her sockless feet into a pair of Skechers, grabbed her car keys, and headed out. She found Moira, close to midnight, on the back deck of a friend's house where the smell of pot was wafting through the air.

Lost track of time, Moira'd said. *Forgot I'd muted my phone.* The interrogation that followed once they got home went on till well past one. And the weekend grounding would begin that evening.

Still, McCabe thought, bringing herself back to the moment now, due diligence was in order. She'd want to know, for example, where Brent Chartwell got that gun, whether it was registered, why he'd believed he needed one.

In the kitchen, she noted a half-full carafe in the coffee maker. She put the back of her hand to it, feeling it for warmth. Stone-cold. There were a few dishes in the sink, but otherwise the place was tidied. She opened the fridge, looked inside. Plenty of provisions there. A just-opened container of half-and-half. An open bottle of wine, a temporary cork in the top, stood upright in the door. Some leftover lasagna on a plate under plastic wrap.

Do you save that bottle of wine, cover up unfinished pasta, when you're planning to end it all?

Maybe. Especially if you're the wife and don't know what's coming.

McCabe looked out the window over the sink to the backyard and beyond. Saw the pond and woods Reece had referred to.

How tranquil.

In the hallway out of the kitchen was a door to the basement. Down there, McCabe found no surprises. A large sectional couch, a huge screen on one wall, a home theater projection system hanging from the ceiling. In the center of the room, a pool table, balls perfectly set up in triangular form, waiting for a game.

There was a basement bathroom and utility room, where McCabe found a washer and dryer combo. She lifted the lid on the washer and found a load of washed, damp clothing. The dryer was empty.

Janice McCabe said, "Hmm."

If gender stereotypes were in play here, and Catherine Chartwell did the laundry, this was more evidence to suggest she didn't know what plans her husband had in store for her.

Back upstairs, she passed the uniformed officer standing in the front hall, making sure no one entered who shouldn't be there. McCabe asked him, "Williams, right?"

"Yes, Detective. Williams." She nodded and walked into the living room.

There were shelves built into one wall and stuffed with books. A lot of nonfiction. Political bios of a couple of Canadian prime ministers, four books by that Woodward guy who helped bring down Nixon decades ago and had written about all the presidents who'd come after him, a celebrity memoir or two, including that doorstopper by Barbra Streisand. Fiction by Margaret Atwood, more novels by Russo and Irving. Half a dozen art books, stored sideways because they were too big to fit upright in the shelves. Small items of Inuit sculpture.

Family photos.

McCabe examined those. All displayed in sleek black frames with white matting, they featured the Chartwells, some with only the couple, others with two young men McCabe presumed were their grown children. She recognized Reece. There were the Chartwells at a wedding. Chartwells at the beach. The couple at a restaurant table, champagne flutes raised, celebrating some occasion. McCabe told herself she might be reading too much into them, given the scene in that upstairs bedroom, but there seemed, despite the physical closeness in these pictures, a kind of distance between the Chartwells. As though they were strangers who'd been asked to stand next to each other by the photographer.

They weren't together in all the photos. There was one of Brent Chartwell with some buddies standing on a golf course green. In another, Catherine Chartwell sat on a dock, dangling her feet in the water, her jeans rolled up to her knees.

McCabe picked that one up, took a closer look.

She was an attractive woman. Dark blond hair with a hint of red in it, high cheekbones, bold eyebrows. Something in the eyes that suggested a fierceness, McCabe thought. A mole dead center in her right cheek. Not much of a smile, not unlike the pictures where she was paired with her husband, as though she was tolerating having her photo taken but wanted it to be over with.

McCabe put the picture back. Time to see whether the coroner was done.

She mounted the stairs to the second floor, catching the coroner on her way out.

"Well?" she asked her.

"We'll know more later, but looks pretty straightforward,"

she said. "Woman died of a gunshot wound to the head, ditto the husband. Bagging his hands for GSR. They're all yours."

McCabe gave her a nod and entered the room, taking in the scene for a second time. It was as Reece had described it. He'd said he hadn't touched anything, had bolted from the room to be sick. She couldn't blame him there.

She stood for a moment, puzzling it out. If you're angry enough with your wife to shoot her, and then take your own life, do you do it in bed? Incidents of domestic violence could take place anywhere in the house. The bedroom, for sure. Bathroom. Plenty occurred in the kitchen, where there was access to knives.

McCabe wondered whether she was overthinking it. Why not in bed? Maybe the part that bothered her was that they were both naked. It implied intimacy, which didn't exactly match what had happened here.

Maybe anger wasn't the motivation. Technically a murder-suicide, but more like a suicide pact, perhaps. If you were each going to down a bottle of sleeping pills, you could do the deed simultaneously. But if you opted to use a gun, someone had to go first. So she'd have had to know it was coming and opted not to protest. McCabe imagined those final seconds between the first and second shot. That moment after Brent sees what he's done to Catherine and then has to put that gun under his chin and pull that trigger a second time.

Something seemed off.

The woman had been shot in the back of the head. If the husband had shot her while sitting in the bed, she would more likely have been hit in the temple. If she'd been trying to talk him out of killing her, she'd have been looking at him, and taken the bullet head on. Face, neck, or chest.

Perhaps, at the last second, she'd had second thoughts. Her body's position suggested she was starting to roll, like she was headed for the floor on that side of the bed.

McCabe looked down at the Beretta on the floor. The outstretched hand. Her eyes went up to the bedside table. There was a cell phone sitting there, face down, pinning a small piece of paper with some writing on it. Next to it, a pen.

With her gloved hand, McCabe moved the phone, and as she turned it over the motion prompted a series of unread texts to pop up. She'd check those in a moment, but first she wanted to look at the paper. Across the top: FROM THE DESK OF BRENT CHARTWELL. Below that, a short note, handwritten:

I am so sorry for all the hurt I have caused. I did this. I bear all responsibility. Brent

She set the note back on the table, then looked at the four unread text previews on the phone. They read:

Might be late (90 min ago)

Going to a gallery after the lunch (1 hr ago)

Are you there? (50 min ago)

Is everything okay? (30 min ago)

All four were from "Cath."

McCabe looked at that name for several seconds, then walked around to the other side of the bed to get a better look at the woman, still on her left side, facing the wall. McCabe put a gloved hand on her shoulder to turn her onto her back, her head rolling onto the blood-soaked pillow to allow McCabe to get a better look at her face.

"Hmm," she said again.

She went back down to the living room and retrieved the photo of Catherine Chartwell sitting on the dock in her swimsuit. She took it back to the bedroom and held the picture not far from the dead woman's face.

Where was the mole?

There wasn't one to be found on the cheek of the woman in this bed. Which meant she'd either had it removed, or this woman was not who everyone had, up to now, assumed her to be. And if she really was Catherine Chartwell, how was she sending texts to her husband after she was already dead?

She didn't want to bring Reece back up here to ascertain whether this woman was, in fact, his mother. Not with the father's body still here, his brains splattered across that painting. With her phone, she took a close-up photo of the dead woman's face she could show to the son.

McCabe went back downstairs, past Williams, and out the front door.

Reece Chartwell was not sitting on the wrought-iron bench. McCabe scanned the yard but didn't see the man anywhere.

The BMW was gone.

"Where's the guy?" she asked Williams, nodding at the bench.

The uniformed cop said, "He left."

"When?"

Williams shrugged. "Five, ten minutes ago? He wasn't supposed to stick around, was he?"

THREE

Reece

"Mom?" I said, my voice no more than a whisper.

"Yes. Can you do it? Can you check on him? You're closer than I am, unless you're not at home." Her voice was breezy, chipper even.

"Mom, where are you?"

"It's Friday," she said. "You know what I do on Fridays."

I had no fucking clue what she did on Fridays, and even if I did, it wasn't likely I would remember it in my current state of mind. When I said nothing, she reminded me.

"It's my arts lunch. I've told you about that. It's—"

"It doesn't matter. Where—"

"All of us on the Yorkton Hill Arts Council? We meet for lunch every other Friday?"

"Is that where you are now?"

"I just stepped away from the table, yes. I wanted to ask your father to check my datebook."

"Your datebook." Mom was old-school. She wrote appointments and important dates down, on paper, with a pen. She didn't keep anything like that in her phone.

"It's in the drawer in the kitchen. He knows where. I wanted him to look ahead to early August. A group of us were talking about going to that inn on Fogo Island. In Newfoundland? But I can't remember if that's when Sheila's daughter is getting married. I thought he could check, but he must have muted his phone. I tell him over and over again not to do that. He mutes it overnight and then forgets to unmute it when he gets up in the morning. I don't know how many times I've reminded him about this but he doesn't listen."

I wondered why she didn't just try the house. My parents had resisted giving up their landline, thinking it would be essential should some apocalyptic event occur.

But then she said, "I tried the house phone too. You'd think he'd have heard *that*."

"Which restaurant?" I said.

"What?"

"What restaurant are you at?"

"Benjamin's."

"Stay there. I'll come get you."

"Why would you—" She cut herself off, then asked, "Has something happened?"

"Just stay there."

"Go by the house first and check on your father."

"I'm *at* the house."

A pause at the other end. "Why didn't you say so? Tell him to check his phone. He'll see the texts I sent." There was an edge in her voice that was verging on panic.

"I'll come get you."

"Reece!" she said sharply. "Tell me what's going on."

What was I supposed to say? *Dad killed some strange woman in bed and then shot himself.*

And then I thought, maybe she *wasn't* some strange woman. She might be someone I knew, would recognize, but from the back, with hair color pretty much the same as my mother's and matted with blood, I'd jumped to a conclusion that didn't seem like much of a jump at the time. It was also very possible that, even if I didn't know who the woman was, my mother did.

"If something's happened to your father, tell me."

"Yes, there's been . . . an incident," I said.

"Put him on."

"I can't."

I could hear an intake of breath. "Oh my god," she said.

"I can be there in just a few minutes." There was a short *whoop* from the street, as though someone had accidentally hit a police siren for half a second.

"What was that?"

"Mom—"

"Was that a police car? A fire engine? Has there been a fire at the house?"

"There hasn't been a fire."

She went quiet for a moment, as though working up to a question. I wasn't surprised when it came, straight out.

"Reece, is your father dead?"

"Mom," I said evenly, "let me come and get you."

Another extended silence so lengthy I thought maybe I'd lost the signal. Finally, she said, "I'll be out front," and ended the call.

I put the phone back into my pocket and turned to look at the house. The front door open, that one uniformed cop stationed there, Detective McCabe somewhere inside. Should I tell her about the call? That my mother was not the woman in that bed, that I'd just spoken with her?

That would prompt a dozen questions, and while I attempted to answer them, my mother would be standing out in front of Benjamin's. It made more sense to get her first, bring her back, and let McCabe ask whatever she wanted of the two of us.

I headed for my car. There was a cruiser half blocking the end of the driveway, so as I was opening the door of my aging BMW, I called out to the officer behind the wheel, "Can you back up so I can get out?"

"McCabe give you the okay?" he asked.

I nodded.

The cop keyed the ignition and backed up far enough that I could squeeze past. Once I was on the street, I put the car in drive and was on my way after that same cop raised the yellow tape to let me pass.

My car was too old for Bluetooth so I took the phone back out of my pocket and with one hand on the wheel and one eye on the road ahead, I brought up my wife's number, tapped the screen, and held the phone to my ear. I knew there was a chance it would go to voicemail. Diana was at work in the Yorkton Hill municipal offices, where she was probably sending out tickets to people whose vehicles were caught on camera running red lights. A leading source of revenue for the town.

Her cell rang twice.

"Hey," Diana said. "'Sup?"

"I dropped by Dad's and . . . Jesus, I hardly know where to begin."

"What's happened?"

"There was no answer at the door, so I went in, and . . . he's dead."

"Oh, honey, god no! A heart attack?"

"No." I almost said *I wish.*

"An accident?"

She was probably remembering an incident a few years ago, when Dad slipped getting out of the tub and threw out his back.

"Nothing like that," I said. "The circumstances are . . . they're complicated. Mom wasn't home. She's at some lunch."

"This is horrible, I'm so sorry. What can I do?"

"I don't know. I think . . . I guess I'm in shock. On a whole bunch of levels."

"You want me to go pick her up?"

"No, I'm going for her now. Can you get Gage from school?"

Our fourteen-year-old son would be devastated by the news. His relationship with his grandfather was a close one, closer than with his grandmother. They shared an interest in anything automotive, and Dad had often taken Gage with him to classic car rallies, dealerships to see newly released models, drag races, monster truck shows. I'd never had that same level of enthusiasm, maybe because when I was a kid, Dad was away so much, he didn't take the time to indoctrinate me in his passion. But when Gage came along, whenever Dad came over, he'd tell Gage to check his coat pocket for a surprise, which was invariably some toy car.

It would be hard enough for Gage to lose someone this special. But trying to explain how Grampa had died was going to be particularly difficult. I had no idea how I was going to come to terms with it myself.

"There is no school today," Diana said.

I'd forgotten. This was a so-called PD day, one of two or three throughout the school year when teachers were in "professional development" sessions designed to make them better at their jobs. It was also why we'd given him slack after he'd stayed out late the night before, since Thursday was not a school night this week. He'd promised to be home by midnight, but when he woke us with a text after eleven asking if he could have an extra hour, we relented. There were days when we worried we were being too lenient, days when we worried we were too strict. It was hard finding a balance.

"I don't know where he is," Diana continued. "Probably with Joey, or at Bashir's playing *Minecraft* or *Fortnite* or god knows what."

"Call him, tell him to come home, tell him there's been . . . an incident, with his grandfather. Details to come. And whatever you do, don't bring him to my parents' house."

"How bad *is* it?"

I steeled myself to deliver the news. "It looks like Dad was having an affair and he and . . . this other woman, whoever she is . . . were upstairs and he shot her and then he shot himself."

Diana's gasp was audible. I could picture her at her desk, sitting there, her mouth open, trying to take in all that was packaged into those few words. If I had ever, in my life, delivered more stunning news to anyone, I couldn't think what it would have been.

"Okay," she said. Diana had always been one to put aside overt reactions and start dealing with the facts. "I'll head home, try to find Gage." She paused, then asked, "What about Holden?"

It was my turn to go quiet. After a few seconds, I said, "Leave him with me. I'll try to reach him."

"And just when he's been running on an even keel," Diana said. Yorkton Hill was right on Lake Ontario, and sailing was big here. Diana's family had owned a sailboat—nothing special, barely a twenty-footer—when she was a kid, so the *even keel* expression came naturally to her.

"So far as we know," I said. Holden had been out of rehab—I'd lost count how many times—for a few months and seemed to be doing okay these days. But I hadn't talked to him in two or three weeks, and a lot could happen in that time. With Holden, a lot could happen in twenty-four hours.

"Once I've got Mom, I'll track him down. Maybe *she'll* be the one who wants to break it to him, once she knows the details, but I don't know. She's gonna be a mess."

"So she has no idea—"

"Only that something's happened to Dad. But I think she's guessed it. She asked me if Dad was dead and I wouldn't give her a straight answer."

"You don't know who the woman is?" She quickly added, "Was?"

I shook my head, even though Diana couldn't see me. "At first . . . I thought it was Mom, until she phoned me."

"My god, what a clusterfuck."

That was the understatement of the year.

"I'm so sorry," Diana said. "I'm just . . . I can't believe it."

"Yeah, ditto. I'm almost at the restaurant, gotta go. Love you."

"Love you," she said, ending the call.

I dropped the phone in one of the cupholders between the seats. I'd made good time getting across town. Benjamin's, a waterside restaurant with beautiful views of the lake, was now only a couple of blocks away.

When I got there I stopped out front in a No Parking zone and hit the flashers. I'd expected Mom to be waiting, but I couldn't see her out front. I jumped out of the car and ran inside, stopping just inside the door, scanning the room for her. Had she decided to hit the ladies' room first?

There was a young woman standing at reception. "Hello. Do you have a reservation?" she asked.

"I'm picking up someone," I said. "My mother. She's here with some others from the arts council?"

"Oh, yes, they're just finishing up." She pointed. "They have that table over there? By the window?"

I looked, spotted four women, two still seated, two getting to their feet and collecting their purses. My mother was not among them.

"Did you see a woman standing here in the last five minutes, like she was waiting for someone? Catherine Chartwell?"

The woman recognized the name. "Oh, Mrs. Chartwell. I did see her when she came in, but I've been away from my post here for a few minutes."

I made way through the tables until I'd reached the women. I recognized one or two of them, but did not know any names.

"Hi," I said urgently. "I'm Reece Chartwell, Catherine's son?"

They all smiled as one, their gleaming teeth reminding me of four Cheshire cats. "Oh, we've heard so much about you," said the woman closest to me. "So nice to finally meet. So sorry about you getting, what do they call it? Downsized?"

Mom had clearly been filling them in on my job situation. Nice to know I'd been fodder for conversation.

"Have you seen her? I'm her ride."

Another one of the women spoke up. "She left, must have

been five, ten minutes ago?" She looked at her lunch partners, who nodded a confirmation.

"Thanks," I said, turned and went back outside. No sign of her.

I got in the car, grabbed my phone from the cupholder, entered her number, put the phone to my ear. Her cell rang. And rang. And rang. Finally, voicemail.

"Hello. You've reached Catherine Chartwell. I can't take your call right now but please do leave a message after the beep."

I waited, then said, "I'm here. Where are you?"

Christ.

FOUR

"Well, it's a good thing you two aren't prison guards."

Janice McCabe had summoned the cop who'd been watching the door to the house and the officer who'd moved his cruiser so Reece Chartwell could leave the scene in his BMW.

"Like, if a prisoner told you, hey, the warden said I could leave, you two would say, oh, okay, that's cool, can I help you pack? Can I get you an Uber?"

Williams, the one who'd been on the door, said, "He was just sitting out there. It wasn't like he was in handcuffs or anything. You didn't tell me to keep him—"

"It didn't occur to you to check?" McCabe asked. "Our only witness, so far, to what happened here?"

Williams said nothing. McCabe turned on the other uniformed officer. "What's your excuse?"

He tipped his head toward Williams. "When he didn't stop him, I figured it was already sorted out."

Williams gave his colleague a sharp look.

"It's like having twin Inspector Clouseaus," McCabe said. "What was he doing before he left?"

"He was talking to somebody on his phone," Williams said.

"You hear any of the conversation?"

Williams shook his head.

McCabe turned on the other officer. "What do you think would be a good thing to do now?"

He blinked a couple of times, then said, "Find him?"

McCabe nodded. "And to think I was worried you weren't on the ball."

As she turned to go back into the house, she could hear the cop mutter "bitch" under his breath. She stopped, spun around, and said, "I'm sorry, did I hear you say you've got an itch? Mosquito bite, maybe?"

The cop, his face flushed, turned and said, "It was nothing."

McCabe returned to the upstairs bedroom. Earlier, she'd spotted a purse hanging off a chair by its strap and assumed it had belonged to Catherine Chartwell. Maybe it did, but recent developments had led her to think otherwise.

She opened the purse, looked inside for a wallet or something smaller that would hold a Social Security card, driver's license, or credit cards. She found a pale blue wallet, opened it, and extracted a Visa card in the name of Leah Kennard. Next, a driver's license. Leah was born on April 15, 1972. McCabe did a quick calculation in her head. The deceased was fifty-four years old. The photo on the license matched, more or less, the woman in the bed. The license showed that Ms. Kennard lived at 231 Galen St. McCabe knew the street and believed that address was part of a stretch of semidetached houses. Before making detective, she'd patrolled all corners of Yorkton Hill in a cruiser, knowing the town as well as her own house with the lights off.

McCabe pocketed the driver's license and continued searching the purse. A lipstick tube, other makeup items, a plastic pill container that held what looked like a mix of Tylenols and Advils, tissues, a pair of reading glasses in a slipcase, a pen. Loose change in the bottom.

A ring with several keys attached, including one with a Toyota fob. She recalled seeing a Corolla on the street. McCabe pocketed the keys.

There was an iPhone in a cream-colored plastic case adorned with pale pink roses. McCabe pressed the home button, and up came the security screen, asking for a six-digit passcode or touch ID. She decided to give the woman's birth date a try, using the year and month. 197204. No luck. 041972. Again, no luck. Tried the day and the year: 151972. McCabe decided to try one more combination before the phone locked her out: 197215.

Bingo.

McCabe let out a breath of satisfaction as the screen filled with apps. If that last code hadn't worked she'd have tried putting the dead woman's thumb on the home button and was glad that hadn't been necessary. And now that she had the passcode, she could get back into the phone whenever she wanted.

She tapped the texting app first. Leah'd had a lot of different conversations underway. Someone named Jerry had asked if she was enjoying her day off, and could she stay late on Monday? Leah had replied with a thumbs-up emoji. There were exchanges with someone named Billy—McCabe wasn't sure, scrolling through the most recent messages, but she believed Billy was a woman—who was sending Leah photos and short video clips of a toddler, probably no more than two years old. Leah's replies ranged from He's so cute to Awww! to Love him so much!

There was a long thread between Leah and someone identified only by a phone number that went back several months. It struck McCabe as odd that a person she texted with that often wouldn't have been assigned a name.

She read a sampling of exchanges, with the unidentified party going first:

I can't see you this weekend.

Y not?

Not a good time. Next week better. R u ok? Do you need anything?

I don't like to ask you've been so generous already. Don't think I'm not grateful

The most recent exchange had been earlier that day.

I need to c u

Maybe tomorrow

Today. Feeling pretty down

OK. C at arts lunch, gone till afternoon

McCabe had a hunch. She got out her own phone, entered the number of the person Leah Kennard had been texting with, tapped on it and waited.

She heard a low-level buzzing sound. It wasn't coming from the phone on the bedside table, but from somewhere else in the room. McCabe let it keep ringing until she found a phone in a pair of slacks tossed onto the floor on the man's side of the bed.

She declined the call.

So Brent had a second phone. Didn't want his spouse picking up his regular phone and reading texts with his mistress.

Speaking of the wife.

Now that it appeared certain Catherine Chartwell was not the deceased, McCabe very much wanted to find her. If those two numbnuts hadn't allowed Reece to leave the scene, she could have asked him, once she'd told him his mother was not the woman in that bed, where to find her.

So, McCabe thought, almost smiling to herself. Now we've got ourselves a potboiler. A cheating husband. A mistress. A betrayed spouse. Maybe, for all McCabe new, a cuckolded husband.

There was a word you didn't hear every day.

It didn't have to mean that this still wasn't a slam dunk, but it did prompt McCabe to think of one of her favorite, and most apt in her line of work, clichés:

The plot thickens.

FIVE

Diana popped her head into the office of her department head, a woman named Sheila. She could see from Diana's expression that she was in some distress.

"Family emergency," Diana said. "I'm gone."

"What's happened?" Sheila asked. "Is there anything I can—"

Diana kept on walking. She hurriedly crossed the municipal building's parking lot, phone in hand, bringing up Gage's number on her cell. Once in her car, she tapped it and let it ring five times before it went to voicemail. She ended the call without leaving one and then entered his number again. If he was ignoring her, repeatedly calling would send the message to pick up.

Four rings into the second call, he answered.

"Yeah?"

"You home?" she asked.

"Not exactly."

What the hell did that mean? Diana wondered. You were either home or you weren't.

"So you're *almost* home?"

"Kind of heading that way." She thought she could hear the

wheels of his skateboard rolling along asphalt. How did he do that? Talk on a phone and whiz along on that thing at the same time? As dangerous as she considered his skateboard to be, at least he hadn't yet saved up enough money to buy one of those one-wheel gadgets, a self-balancing electric skateboard with a single wheel that he'd been eyeing online.

"Got something else to do first."

"Do it later. Where are you? I'll pick you up."

"Aren't you at work?"

"Your dad called. There's been some kind of trouble with your grandfather."

A pause. Then, "What kind of trouble?"

She didn't hear the skateboard wheels now. He must have stopped.

"It's not something I want to get into on the phone so—"

"Are you there?"

"Where?"

"At Grampa's?"

"No. I—but your father called and—"

"Dad's there?"

"He was. He—"

"Tell me what happened."

Diana was starting to feel she couldn't hold the truth back. "Gage, I'm so sorry, but your grandfather passed."

Nothing.

"Gage?"

Nothing.

"You hear what I said? He's passed away."

She was already regretting telling him this way. She wanted to be able to look into his eyes, to take him into her arms if he started to cry. He liked to think he was an adult, that he didn't need to be treated like a kid anymore, but he was still fourteen, and he hadn't lost anyone this important to him yet. She tried to picture him now, his face cracking, eyes welling up with tears.

"Gage?"

"I'm here."

"You okay?"

"Seriously?"

"I know, I know, stupid question. Where are you?"

"Just . . . around. I'll be home soon."

"Are you su—"

"Where's Grandma?"

"Dad's gone to get her."

"Grandma didn't find him?"

"No, she wasn't—"

"How did— I mean, how did anybody—"

"Your dad dropped by."

"Shit," Gage said.

Any other time, Diana might have called him on that kind of language. If there was ever a time to let something slide—

"I gotta go," Gage said.

"Gage, wait, listen, why don't—"

He was gone.

"Damn it," Diana said aloud. *I should have waited.* Now he was out there, dealing with his grief alone, tears marring his vision as he rode that goddamn skateboard down busy streets.

Her phone rang.

"Yeah?"

"She's not here." Reece.

"Wait, what?"

"She didn't wait for me. She's gone."

Diana's mind raced. If she were Catherine, what would she do?

"I bet she went home. Didn't want to wait for you."

Reece considered that. "Maybe."

"I got Gage."

"He's with you?"

"I got *hold* of him. On his cell."

"But he doesn't know yet—"

"I told him."

"Over the *phone*?"

"I didn't get into details, but I told him his grandfather was dead."

"Over the *phone*?"

"You *told* me to let him know." Her voice bristled, but she was also feeling defensive.

"No, look, I'm sorry. I'm just— I feel like my head's gonna blow up. I'm going back. I'll call if I know anything."

From across the street, sitting in a coffee shop close to the window, Catherine Chartwell had watched her son arrive at Benjamin's, run inside, then emerge a couple of minutes later. He had that exasperated look on his face she knew so well.

She'd ordered a tea as an excuse to hold the table while she decided what to do, but she would have liked something much stronger.

Reece was back in his car now, on the phone. Hers sat on the table and started to buzz. She hit the button on the side to mute it, watched as it rang several times before going to voicemail. She didn't need to listen to it. She knew what the message would be.

Where are you? Why aren't you here?

Because I'm not ready, she would have said. But that would have prompted even more questions from her son, so it was easier to not answer.

Let him stew.

She didn't know what, exactly, she'd be facing. Didn't know how it had gone down. She hadn't been provided those kinds of details. But she knew her husband was dead.

Just *knew* it.

If there was even a sliver of good news, it was that she hadn't been home when it happened. And not to suggest anyone would, but no one was going to think she had anything to do with it.

She was at lunch with her arts council friends.

Catherine had witnesses.

And if anyone were to ask them, they'd say Catherine was her usual self. Chatty. Happy. Engaged.

Like she didn't have a care in the world.

That was Catherine all over. Feeling one way, pretending to be another.

SIX

Reece

Diana was probably right.

Mom wouldn't have wanted to wait for me. She'd have grabbed a cab or an Uber and raced home, and if that was what she'd done I suppose I couldn't blame her.

The only other place I could think she might have gone would be my brother's, but why head there when she didn't yet know, with certainty, what had transpired on the home front? Maybe my failure to answer her question about whether Dad was dead as much as told her he was. Maybe she wanted to get to Holden's place so that they could face the bad news together.

She'd always been more protective of him than of me. Maybe *protective* was the wrong word. Where Holden was concerned, Mom was more anxious, more fretful. Holden was the family land mine. Take one wrong step and he might go off.

How to put this. Holden had been, for as long as I could remember, the "problem child." Of the three men in my mother's life—Dad, Holden, and me—it was Holden she'd always worried about most, and not without reason, I suppose. As he came into his teens, he became disruptive, troubled. Drinking at fourteen, and it wasn't long before he moved on to more serious stuff. In my later teens, I'd done my share of drinking and had episodes of getting high, like plenty of dumbass kids, but Holden was more hardcore, trying just about everything by the time he was twenty.

He'd been in and out of rehab between his early twenties and now more times than I'd had my teeth cleaned. Every time he'd come out, there'd be renewed hope on the part of my parents that this was the time it would stick, and it would, for varying periods of time. But they were always waiting for the other shoe to drop, knowing today might be the day he'd be back to sticking a needle in his arm, doing a line, smoking meth from a crack pipe, looking for any way he could to stop the pain. Not the physical kind, but emotional. Holden's private demons were exactly that. Locked away. No matter how hard I might have pried over the years, he kept things to himself.

Even when Holden was getting top-notch care at Sharnwood, Mom fretted about how it reflected on Dad and her. More than once I heard her speculate that Holden's counselors had probably concluded that his parents were all to blame, that they'd fucked him up somehow.

Dad wondered if maybe that wasn't true.

He was as concerned about him as Mom was, maybe more, but it was different with him. His concern was driven largely by guilt. He'd come to believe Holden's addiction problems were some kind of karma, a cosmic retribution for the work my father had done for Wiffel-Smith, the pharmaceutical giant.

You may have heard about them.

There was a time when you couldn't turn on the TV without seeing a commercial from Wiffel-Smith, whose corporate headquarters could be found in the suburban sprawl northwest of Toronto, but whose primary market was south of the border. They hawked their remedies for everything from restless leg syndrome to bowel disorders on all the major networks, but their most famous, or infamous, as it turned out, was Oxy-Mirac, a so-called miracle (hence its name) pill to treat chronic pain. The miracle turned out to be miraculously addictive. It was abused by countless thousands, all with help from dodgy doctors willing to write prescriptions in return for perks and kickbacks from the company. A great many of those who got hooked on Oxy-Mirac only beat the habit by dying.

Dad was one of their top salespeople back in the late '90s, traveling all across North America. While the Wiffel-Smith higher-ups and marketing geniuses were willfully blind to the international crisis they were creating—or could see what they were doing and just didn't care, seduced by making hundreds of millions of dollars—Dad was clear-eyed enough to see there would one day be a reckoning. He didn't want to be around when that happened, so he quit, and sold all the shares he and Mom had put into the company when they were at their highest point.

Quitting may have eased his conscience some, but his windfall was tainted. He used that stock money to launch a successful consulting enterprise, but I knew it haunted him that his later successes were built on the money he'd made from the suffering of others.

Holden, he had come to believe, was payback.

Dad and Mom, over the years, had spent tens of thousands trying to get Holden clean—much of it at the Sharnwood Clinic right here in Yorkton Hill—and while I couldn't fault them for wanting to do everything they could to help him, their actions had often been a source of friction between Diana and me.

"*They spend a fortune trying to set your brother straight, but they don't have a dime for you,*" she'd said. And pretty recently, too, since I'd lost my job.

"*It's not like they're giving him money to buy a Corvette,*" I'd countered.

"*No, it's more like they're throwing it into the wind or setting it on fire for all the good it does.*"

Diana wasn't as cold as that might make her sound. She was sympathetic, to a point, where Holden was concerned. And when he wasn't in the throes of some addiction, she liked him. Holden was a likable guy. He was funny. (He was an excellent mimic and did dead-on impressions of our parents he was smart enough not to perform in front of them.) He took an interest in others, and if you were moving from one house to another, he was the first one there helping to lift boxes or maneuver a couch down a flight of stairs as long as there was pizza and beer. Especially beer.

He cared about those less fortunate than himself, and there were times when it was hard to find someone who fell into that category. But once when I was with him in the heart of the city, he struck up a conversation with a homeless guy, his hand outstretched looking for change. I kept on walking, because I'm the kind of asshole who often pretends those people are invisible. When Holden caught up to me, I noticed he was no longer wearing his jacket, and I inquired.

"He was cold," Holden said.

Like our father, Holden had always taken an interest in Gage, right from the time he was a baby. He reveled in his role as uncle.

And Gage loved him in return, although if I'm being honest, we didn't encourage the relationship, and I felt my own guilt over that. You didn't want your son hanging around with an addict—current or recovering—even if he was the kid's uncle. It had been a source of friction with Gage, who accused Diana and me of not being supportive, that Holden couldn't help being the way he was, and we should be ashamed for not understanding that.

That stung. The truth has a way of doing that.

Gage saw in Holden the qualities we sometimes overlooked. That concern for people who were down and out. An interest in the broader world when he wasn't under the influence. When Gage, an aspiring idealist, learned Holden was taking part in a rally to fight a Yorkton Hill decision to let a developer build on parkland, Gage not only wanted to join him, he questioned why we weren't coming too.

"You think he's a bad influence," Gage once said to us, "but he's made me care about things that matter."

If only Holden could be *that* Holden all the time.

For all those reasons and more, I thought Mom might be headed his way. But it was worth checking first to see if she'd gone home. I took from my pocket the card that Detective McCabe had given me. I entered the number of her cell.

"McCabe," she said upon answering.

"It's Reece Chartwell."

"Who said you could leave? Where are you?"

"I found out something."

"I've got two officers I'd like to write up because you—"

"My mother's alive."

I guess I was expecting some sign she was shocked. But instead, she said, in a calm voice, "I know. How is it *you* know?"

I wanted to ask her the same thing but decided to answer her first. "She phoned me, said she'd been trying to reach Dad and couldn't. How'd *you* find out?"

"Get back here."

Questions worked one way with her. "Has my mom shown up there?"

"No."

"I told her I'd pick her up—she was at a lunch with friends—but she left before I got there. Thought she might have gone back to the house."

"No," McCabe said again. Pissed. "I want you here. Now." Her tone softened. "Look, Mr. Chartwell, I know this is all a shock, that maybe you think you have more important things to do, but your presence here is needed."

"Soon," I said. "If she shows, call me." She didn't need to ask my number. I was now in her call history.

"Mr. Chartwell, I'm serious. Get back—"

I ended the call.

Holden lived on Bakerton Street, in one of Yorkton Hill's less flashy neighborhoods in the west end. Yorkton Hill had its reputation as one of the country's wealthier towns, but not everyone lived in a house like my parents'. There were still plenty of people here who didn't commute into the city on a daily basis, people who lived and worked right here, many of them in older parts of town that hadn't yet been remade into fancy enclaves where every house came with a Wolf stove and a Sub-Zero fridge. That's where Holden lived, in a simple, one-story, two-bedroom home that, if it could speak, wouldn't have said no to a new roof and a fresh coat of paint. He rented, paying his landlord with the occasional odd jobs he got. Last I'd heard, he was helping out a guy who put up drywall. You gave Holden a task, he could do it, so long as he wasn't on one of his downswings.

While Holden's part of town had a different feel than ours, which was more of a transition neighborhood, it wasn't far. A five-minute drive, an hour's walk. I parked on the street when I saw his old blue Honda CR-V sitting beside the house and walked slowly to the front door. As I knocked, I thought I heard a banging noise, like someone slamming the back door of the place. I took a few steps to peer around the corner to see whether my brother had seen me coming and decided he didn't want to talk to me, but if he'd taken a runner, I didn't see him.

Before I could get back to the front door, it opened.

"Hey, little brother," Holden said dreamily. Dressed as always in faded jeans and a T-shirt, this one bearing a map of Canada with the words "Not For Sale." He was just under six feet, and thin enough that even small sizes seemed to hang off him. His arms were ropy and his hair brush cut short.

I knew instantly he was high. The euphoric tone, the dilated pupils. I felt a wave of disappointment wash over me. Here we were again. When things went south, I usually heard from one of my parents, asking if I'd seen him lately, had I noticed any changes in his behavior. The fact that they'd not been in touch suggested Holden's slide was recent.

"Hey," I said. "How's it going?"

He smiled broadly. "Top of the world. What's up?"

"Was by this way. Thought I'd pop in." I climbed the two steps to the door. "Don't suppose Mom's here, is she?"

He blinked a couple of times. "Why would *she* be here?"

"I was supposed to meet her at something, but she kind of stood me up. Was wondering if she came by here."

"When were you talking to her?"

"Like, fifteen minutes ago."

He started to shake his head but stopped abruptly, as though the motion hurt. "Can I come in?" I asked.

"Uh, yeah, sure. Why not? Enter!"

Holden held the door open and followed me inside. The first thing I noticed was a dusty trace of white powder on the coffee table and an uncoiled twenty-dollar bill that looked as though it had been used like a nasal straw earlier. Holden scooted past me, swept the table clean with the edge of his hand and tucked the bill into his pocket.

He laughed nervously. "I know that might look bad, but it's not what you think."

"Whatever," I said. "I'm not here checking up on you."

"You sure?" he said, eyeing me suspiciously. "They didn't send you to spy on me? Because I've been doing real good lately, and this was just a little pick-me-up to celebrate. It's not like it's going to turn into a regular thing."

Like we'd never heard that before.

I looked around the room. Holden, even straight, was not someone you'd ever accuse of being under the spell of Martha Stewart. The place was its usual mess. An open pizza box on the couch with one cold slice left, CD cases scattered across the floor. Like me, he'd grown up with CDs and had never cottoned on to streaming his music. There was a beer bottle on an otherwise empty bookshelf, empty Coke cans here and there, a jacket hanging off a chair. A video game console and two controllers on the coffee table across from a wall-mounted screen.

"Whatcha celebrating?" I asked.

He adopted an exaggerated expression of puzzlement, like he couldn't exactly recall. But after a moment, he said, "You ever think you've fucked up big-time, then realize, okay, maybe you still did, but not as bad as you first thought?"

"Maybe."

"Like, you think you left your wallet someplace and you're kicking yourself over it and thinking about the credit cards you gotta cancel and then you get home and find it on the kitchen table?"

"Did you think you'd lost your wallet?"

"That was just as an example, a *for instance*, if you will," Holden said. He waved his hand in the air. "Doesn't matter what it was. But I'm in a better place now than I was earlier."

"Good to know. Was someone here? Thought I heard the back door slam."

"Putting out the garbage," he said. He glanced at the pizza box. "Missed some. You're welcome to that last slice if you want it. It's from last night but I could nuke it for a few seconds."

It was a genuine, if unappealing, offer. Holden was always one to share. I shook my head.

He studied me for a moment, like he was trying to get me in focus. "Would you like to take a seat?"

"That's okay. But why don't you sit down."

"Well, okay," he said agreeably, moved the pizza box to the floor and plopped down on the couch. Removing the box revealed a pair of panties on the coffee table.

"Well, how did *those* get there?" Holden said with mock shock, scooping them up and stuffing them between the sofa cushions. He grinned at me sheepishly. "The toppings they put on pizza these days. Better than pineapple though."

“That who I heard leaving when I got here?” I asked.

He shrugged.

I went back to what I’d been talking about a moment earlier. “The thing is, in your . . . current state . . . can you get help right away if you need it? Like, those places Mom and Dad sent you, can you turn up at the door and they have to let you in?”

“Like home?” he asked, smiling. He closed his eyes for a moment, concentrating, then said, “Home is the place where, when you have to go there, they have to take you in.”

“Robert Frost,” I said.

Holden pointed, made the sound of game show buzzer, and said, “We have a Final Jeopardy winner, ladies and gentlemen. You always were a literate fucker.”

“I was asking seriously, about you getting help. If you have to go back, will they take you? Is there a referral process or anything? Or could you go in there today?”

“It was just one line,” he said, looking down at the coffee table where the powder had been. “Just some shit I had left over from a long time ago. Saving it for a rainy day. You don’t have to make a federal case out of it.”

“I thought you were celebrating. But now today’s a rainy day?”

“Figure of speech,” he said, waving his hand again.

“Thing is, I’ve got some bad news that might set you back.”

Holden suddenly looked very serious. “And what might that be?”

We both heard a car pull up out front and come to a stop. Holden rose from the couch and peered over my shoulder through the grime-covered living room window.

“Oh shit,” he said.

He embarked on a more thorough brushing off of the coffee table, grabbed something in a small plastic bag, and ran for the bathroom, presumably to flush it away.

I went to the window and saw what had him concerned. A Yorkton Hill Police cruiser had turned in toward the curb, blocking my car. An officer I recognized was checking it out, standing out back of it and reading the license plate.

"I've got a feeling he's not here for you," I said.

SEVEN

Gage didn't want to go home.

He didn't want his mom or dad trying to comfort him. He could guess the kinds of things they'd say.

We're here for you.

Let it out.

It's okay to cry.

We know how much your grandfather meant to you.

He didn't want to hear it. They were always trying to make things better, or telling you that all the shit in your life wasn't as big a deal as you thought it was, that they knew high school was tough, but this too shall pass. Like, if people were texting crap about you, you were supposed to just let that go, that there'd always be people who made themselves feel better by putting other people down. How in the long run, this stuff didn't matter. Gage thinking, he should try that on his dad. *Sure, WorldWide canned you, but hey, walk it off, you'll find another newswriting gig any day now.* Yeah, right, they tried to dismiss his concerns, but flunk a test, well, that was a whole different thing. Fail a course, you'll have to go to summer school, you'll never get accepted into a university and if you're lucky, maybe you'll get into a community college, but more likely you'll be stocking shelves at Walmart your entire miserable life.

Not that he hated his parents or anything. They were okay. It was just that there were things he couldn't talk about with them. But he could always talk about stuff with his grandfather. Brent Chartwell was pretty cool for an old guy. He'd seen it all, done it all, and it wasn't like he'd rat Gage out if he told him stuff he couldn't bring himself to tell his parents.

"We all make mistakes," his grandfather would say. "God knows I've made plenty."

While his grandfather didn't go into details, Gage had an inkling of what some of those mistakes were. There was his uncle Holden, of course, who was a constant concern, and his grandfather had given hints that he felt some responsibility there.

But Gage liked his uncle Holden. When he wasn't going through one of his rough patches, spending time at that Sharnwood place getting his head screwed back on straight, he was cool to hang out with, often without his parents' knowledge. Watching movies, playing video games, but also really *talking* about things. How corporate self-interest controlled the flow of information. How critical thinking was a thing of the past, and if you repeated a lie often enough, people believed it. When he wasn't high, Holden was a thinker, and in that way, a role model for Gage.

He also told Gage not to make the same mistakes he'd made. If Gage asked to take one small drag off a joint, Holden would say no and give him shit for asking.

Drugs were kind of a family cross to bear. Gage knew his grandfather had worked in Big Pharma at one time, and it was a period he'd not been proud of. Lots of people got hooked on some pain pill and a whole lot of them died. His grandfather'd actually talked to him about it a few times, almost like confessing. One of his biggest mistakes, he'd said, working for that company. And although he never said it outright, Gage got the idea one of his others might have been marrying his grandmother.

Gage's mother sometimes referred to Catherine Chartwell as a "cold fish." Gage thought that was a nice way of calling someone a bitch, and his grandmother could be one on occasion. Bit of a control freak. Wanting everything just so. He got on okay with her, but when he went over to their house it was his grandfather he wanted to hang with.

Two years ago, when Gage was twelve, a couple of his dumbass friends dared him to steal some shit from a 7-Eleven. They'd create a distraction—pretend to get into a heated argument over some girl while over by the cold drinks aisle—and give Gage the opportunity to walk out with a couple of bags of Doritos under his jacket. He didn't want to do it, but when they accused him of being a pussy, he caved. But the shopkeeper was no dummy. He'd seen kids run games like this before and was wise to them, and he grabbed Gage by the arm as he was walking out the door.

Called the cops.

Gage's so-called friends bailed, leaving him there to face his fate alone. A Yorkton Hill officer showed up, put Gage in the back of his cruiser—at least he wasn't handcuffed—and let him sweat it out there for a while. The doors wouldn't open from the inside and he couldn't put down the windows, which was too bad because there was what looked like dried vomit on the floor by his feet and his own stomach was starting to heave. The cop left him there for about twenty minutes while he was in talking to the shopkeeper. When he came out, he said his parents would be called, that they'd have to come down to the station for a chat.

The cop let Gage make the call himself, and instead of calling his mother or father, he called Grampa.

He explained tearily what he'd done, that he'd been caught. "On my way," Brent said.

"Please don't tell Mom and Dad," Gage said.

"We'll see."

When Brent arrived, no one challenged him about whether he was the boy's father. Sure, he looked a little old to be his dad, but you never knew.

Gage and his grandfather and the arresting officer sat at a table in an interrogation room. Gage had not yet wet his pants, but he was close. He was already wondering whether he would be sent to prison. Could you go to jail for stealing Doritos? What would happen to a kid his age, locked behind bars with grown men? Gage had seen prison movies. He knew what could happen.

"There are a number of ways we can proceed," said the officer, whose name was Glidden, like the paint. "Given that Gage here is only twelve, and has no previous record of getting into trouble, this would typically fall into the area of the Youth Criminal Justice Act of Ontario."

Criminal, Gage thought. *I am so dead.*

The cop said a bunch of other words, like felony and misdemeanor and rehabilitation and how old a kid had to be to get sent to jail and Gage wasn't taking in any of it because all he could think about was what might happen in the prison shower, but his grandfather was listening very closely, and being super-respectful and thanking the officer for his time, and asking whether it would be appropriate to take Gage back to the 7-Eleven and apologize to the store manager.

When Gage walked out of the station with Brent, he'd never been happier to see the light of day. He wasn't exactly sure what had happened.

"You got off with a warning, and now we're going to the 7-Eleven and you're going to tell them how sorry you are. Honest to god, nearly throwing your life away for a bag of Doritos."

Gage didn't think anything was to be gained by saying it was *two* bags of Doritos.

"What the hell were you thinking?" Brent asked.

"My friends dared me."

"Oh well, now I understand," he said as they got into his car. "Good thing your friends didn't dare you to jump in front of a bus. At least then all I'd have had to do was scrape you off the grille."

"I'm sorry."

"You should be."

"You gonna tell my parents?"

His grandfather didn't answer right away. "I should," he said, starting the engine. "Let's discuss it once you've made your apology."

Brent had driven to the station in his old Barracuda. Any excuse, Gage figured, to take it out for a spin, even getting your grandson out of jail. They drove straight to the 7-Eleven. Brent accompanied him as they went inside. Listened while Gage told the guy behind the cash register that he was sorry, that he would never steal from him again.

"No kidding," the man said. "You're banned from this store. I never want to see your sorry ass in here again."

Gage nodded.

Something hanging on the wall behind the register had caught Brent's eye. He said to his grandson, "Wait in the car. I'll be right out."

Gage got in the Barracuda, watched as his grandfather made some purchases. He came out of the store, tossed a bag into the back seat. Gage caught a glimpse, saw a new phone in a clear plastic clamshell container.

"This is your one get-out-of-jail-free card," Brent said. "Literally. I won't tell your mom or dad about this episode. But pull a brain-dead stunt like this again, don't call me. Call your folks. I won't save your ass a second time over something this stupid. Understand?"

"Yes."

"That doesn't mean I won't be there for you if you get in trouble again. Sometimes things happen that aren't our fault. This? Today? That's all on you. But there's something you need to know. Your grandpa would give his life for you if he had to. I love you. Just don't grow up to be an idiot."

"Okay."

That was Grandpa.

If only that episode had scared him off ever doing anything stupid again. But sometimes, when you were Gage's age, the first lesson didn't stick. Not the second or third either. God, as recently as the night before he'd nearly got caught being somewhere he shouldn't have been. Took off seconds before shit hit the fan.

Too bad his timing wasn't always that good.

After the call from his mother, Gage rode his skateboard to the center of town, where Fifteen Mile Creek wandered through. This was one of Gage's favorite places. Hanging in the park by the creek, listening to the water flow past, watching the tiny ripples. He picked up his skateboard, tucked it under his arm, and walked across the grass to a picnic table not far from the water's edge. He perched himself on the tabletop, his feet planted on the bench, and wondered what it would be like to be on a raft and ride the creek all the way down to the lake. Wouldn't it be great if, instead of that lake, the creek took you to some wondrous, magical place where there was no bullshit? Where everyone was decent to each other, where they didn't pretend to be something they weren't, where the people who meant the most to you didn't suddenly die and make you feel like you wanted to kill yourself?

Something to think about, as you put your head in your hands and bawled your eyes out until your chest hurt.

EIGHT

Reece

The officer who'd tracked me down to my brother's house instructed me to drive straight back to my parents' place. He'd be following, in case I decided to be a wise guy and take a left when he took a right.

"McCabe is some pissed with you," he said as I came out of Holden's house and headed for my car. I had a sense she might be just as pissed with him, since he was the one who'd moved his car, allowing me to get mine out of the driveway and leave the scene. "Don't do anything stupid like trying to lose me on the way back."

I had no wish to be part of a police pursuit and told him not to worry. The one who was most relieved was Holden, who'd clearly feared this cop was going to come inside the house and find more of what he'd brushed off that coffee table. At the same time, he was puzzled the police were here for me.

"What'd *you* do?" he asked. "You're the *good* son. You probably don't even have unpaid parking tickets."

I could understand his confusion. I hadn't even had a chance to tell him our father was dead. There was no way I could break it to him now and then just leave.

"I'll be back later," I told him. "Okay? You gonna be here? You working today?"

"I'll double-check my calendar, but I don't believe I have any pressing engagements," he said as I headed out the door.

McCabe was waiting for me outside my parents' house when I returned. After reaming me out for leaving, she asked, "Do you know a Leah Kennard?"

"No," I said.

She showed me a driver's license in Kennard's name, with her picture on it. "Recognize her?"

I took a close look without touching it. "No," I said again. "If I've ever seen her before or met her, I don't remember."

"Where's your mother?"

"I don't know."

"She called you?"

I nodded. "After you and I talked, my cell rang, it was her, saying she'd been trying to reach my father. Wanted me to come by the house, see if everything was okay. Told her I was already here."

"What else did you tell her?"

I tried to recall our conversation, what I'd said exactly. So much had happened in the last couple of hours that I was feeling overwhelmed.

"I said . . . I didn't tell her Dad was actually dead, but when she asked me point-blank, I didn't answer, so I think she's figured it out."

"You went to pick her up."

"At Benjamin's." McCabe nodded. Everyone knew Benjamin's. "But she didn't wait. I thought she'd come back here, but you hadn't seen her, so I went to my brother's, but she hadn't gone there either."

"You've called her since?"

"Couple of times."

"So where do you think she is now?"

"I have no idea. I'm guessing she's in shock. She knows something bad's happened and the longer she puts off coming back here, the longer she doesn't have to know *how* bad."

McCabe couldn't send her minions out to find her the way she'd had them find me, unless they had some way to track her location from her cell phone. Mom didn't drive so there was no car to hunt down. While McCabe figured out what to do about that, she pursued a different line of questioning.

"Did you know your father was having an affair?"

"I don't know that he was." She gave me a look she might give a three-year-old. Without saying a word, she was asking if I had some other explanation for the scene upstairs. "Okay, I get how it looks and I can't think of any explanation other than . . . my dad was seeing someone else." In the world of euphemisms, I am willing to admit that "seeing" was pretty lame.

"No inkling? Nothing?"

I shook my head. "Look, I'm still reeling, okay? I haven't been given a chance to shed so much as a single tear yet because you've got a job to do, and I get that, but I'm trying the best I can here. I didn't know my father was seeing someone else, I have no clue who that dead woman in bed with him is, and if you'd told me a week ago that he was cheating on my mom I would have—"

I stopped myself short.

"Would have what?" McCabe asked.

I found myself, in that moment, reassessing everything I had thought to be true. Slowly, I said, "I would have thought that maybe it was possible."

"And why's that?"

"Because . . ." I was finding it hard to put into words. Not because I didn't know what the words were, but because saying them out loud made them real.

"Because I don't know that they were ever really happy," I said. "At least, not for as long as I can remember." I shook my head slowly. "I guess my dad was fooling around, must have felt like shit about it, shot this woman and then shot himself. I've got to find a way to *live* with that. To help my *mother* live with that. To explain that to my son, who adored his grandfather, who looked up to him, who saw him as a role model."

"He left a note," McCabe said.

"He what?"

"Your father left a note. On the bedside table, under his phone. Written on personal stationery, a notepad with his name across the top."

She took out her phone, showed me a photo she'd taken of the note. It read: *I am so sorry for the hurt I have caused. I did this. I bear all responsibility. Brent.*

I was a tire that had just run over a nail. Slowly deflating, the life slipping out of me.

"Jesus," I whispered.

"Is that your father's handwriting?" McCabe asked.

My eyes were getting misty and I had to blink several times to be able to bring the photo on her phone into focus. "Can you make it bigger?"

McCabe used two fingers to magnify the image.

"Yes," I said.

"You're sure?"

"That's his handwriting. I'm sure of it."

McCabe exited her photos app and put the phone away. "You mentioned a brother," she said.

"Holden. Older than me. By a year."

"Any other siblings?" she asked.

"No."

She had her notepad in hand. "Give me your mother's cell number."

I complied.

"If she doesn't turn up here soon, and you find her before I do, let me know immediately," she said. "What occurred here might seem straightforward, but I'll still need to speak with her. We'll be looking into Leah Kennard's death as a homicide and I'd like to find out what your mother can tell us about her."

Dad died a murderer. We could put something on his headstone. *Loving father, indifferent husband, mistress killer.*

"If I hear from her, I'll tell her to get in touch," I said.

McCabe nodded solemnly. "You can go," she said.

This time, I followed orders. I headed for home, still in a daze from the events of the morning. Before I got there, Diana called me.

"Gage hasn't come back," she said.

NINE

Galen was a dead-end street. Detective McCabe slowed to a stop out front of 231, the address that was on Leah Kennard's driver's license. It was a semidetached, the middle of five connected, two-story homes, none more than twenty feet wide, and each with a driveway about half that size. Of the lot, the Kennard address was the most well-maintained. No flaking paint, a small flower garden below the front window.

There was no car parked out front, but that wasn't a surprise. She'd found the dead woman's Toyota Corolla down the street from the Chartwell home and had used the key from her purse to unlock it.

The car yielded no useful information. No discarded fast-food wrappers, nothing in the ashtray, the floor mats free of gravel and dirt. Even the trunk was empty save for a spare and a couple of reusable grocery bags.

McCabe didn't yet know whether Leah lived alone or shared this place with others, so she rang the bell, steeling herself to deliver bad news to next of kin. Waited ten seconds and rang it again. Finally, she tried knocking, hard. No one came. She peered through a narrow pane of glass in the door, shielding her eyes with her hand. No movement inside.

With one of the other keys from Leah's set, McCabe was able to open the front door and step inside.

"Hello!" she called out, just in case. Her voice echoed through the house.

She opened the front hall closet. There were half a dozen light jackets or heavier coats in there, all sized for someone of Leah's build. No men's coats. On the floor, three pairs of shoes, including one pair of Reeboks, and some boots. McCabe was betting the woman lived alone.

The furnishings in the small living room were simple and functional, the stack of magazines on the coffee table perfectly stacked and lined up with the edge. The kitchen counters were free of clutter, not unlike Leah's Toyota. The stainless steel sink was empty and clean. The dishwasher's light was on, indicating a completed cycle. Many items in the refrigerator or cupboard were labeled low-fat, sugar-free, or made without artificial preservatives.

You try to live a healthy life, McCabe thought, *and then someone comes along and shoots you in the head*. The poor woman should have treated herself to a dozen Krispy Kremes the day before.

McCabe slowly worked her way through the first floor, looking for anything that jumped out at her, and came up empty. She climbed the stairs to the second floor, where there were two bedrooms and a bathroom, although one of the bedrooms appeared to be a combined exercise and storage room. Business boxes were stacked neatly along two walls, and in the center of the room was a basic treadmill, without a screen or other fancy electronic gadgetry.

She went into the bathroom, opened the medicine cabinet, and found, mostly, what she would have expected. Various over-the-counter pain medication and ointments. One antianxiety drug that was also used to treat depression. McCabe made a note of the doctor who'd prescribed it.

McCabe entered the bedroom, opened the top drawer on the bedside table. There was a plastic jar of fruit-flavored Tums, some earplugs, an eye mask, a charger cable for an iPhone. Nothing much out of the ordinary, except for a small photo album.

About the size of a paperback novel turned sideways, she opened it and found, on the inside cover, three words, done in calligraphy. Maybe that had been one of Leah's hobbies. The words were: *My Boy Tom.*

What followed were several pages of snapshots of a white male over what appeared to be a span of several years. In some, he looked no older than a teenager, while in others he was, McCabe guessed, in his midthirties. There were a couple of him when he was probably no older than ten. Unmistakably the same person, although in some his hair was long, or he was sporting a beard. In others, shorter hair, clean-shaven. In the later pictures, he was thin, with lank brown hair.

All the pictures appeared to have been professionally processed. The older ones undoubtedly were shot with an actual camera, the roll of film taken to a retailer to be printed. But some of the pictures looked more recent, the cars in the background more current. Those, McCabe guessed, were taken with a phone, then emailed to a photo shop to be printed out on the proper paper.

In all the pictures, this young man was alone. Some of the

snapshots were smaller, oddly sized, suggesting the rest of the picture, which presumably had featured other people, had been discarded. At least a dozen of the pictures had been edited with a pair of scissors.

In her pocket was the phone she'd found in Leah's purse. Having broken the passcode, she brought up the home screen and tapped on the photos app. Up popped hundreds of pictures. McCabe started scrolling through them quickly but found none of the person whose images filled the album. That led McCabe to think these pictures had been taken by someone else and given to her. That, or she'd taken the pictures with a device other than this phone.

McCabe took the album with her—it was small enough to tuck into her purse—and exited the residence, locking the door on her way out. She went first to the house on the right, rang the bell twice, but no one answered. She tried the place on the other side of Leah's, figuring her closest neighbors would be the most likely to know anything about the woman.

At the second door, someone answered.

It was a curly-haired girl, no more than six or seven years old.

"Hi," McCabe said, looking down at the child. "Your mom or dad or any adult home?"

The girl said nothing, turned and walked back into the house. A moment later, a thin woman in her late twenties in a Springsteen T-shirt and frayed jeans appeared. She brushed some hair away from her face as she eyed McCabe with curiosity.

The detective displayed her badge, introduced herself, and asked the woman for her name, which was Elaine Turcotte. McCabe said, "I'm seeking information about your neighbor, Leah Kennard."

"Yeah? She done something wrong? Because she's good people," Elaine said, turning every few seconds to check on her daughter, who was seated at a kid's desk-and-chair set, making circles on a sheet of paper with an orange crayon.

"You know where she works?"

"Uh, she works at the walk-in clinic? The one on Proctor? She works the desk, runs the office, stuff like that?"

"Is there someone there named Jerry?" McCabe was thinking of the text she had seen on Leah's phone, asking if she could work late Monday.

"That'd be Dr. Fielding," she said. "Gerald Fielding. He runs the clinic."

"And does she have a friend named Billy?"

"Billy?"

"Someone who has a young child."

"That might be a cousin or somebody."

It would be easy enough to find out, McCabe thought. Billy's number was right there in her text exchanges with Leah.

"Does Leah live alone?"

"Just her." She paused, then added, "Most of the time."

McCabe tilted her head slightly, waiting for Elaine to expand on that.

"She's had a couple of boyfriends, but no one permanent."

"So, not married? No kids?"

"No, and no." Elaine was getting impatient with the questioning. "Seriously, is she in some kind of trouble?"

"Just making some inquiries."

Elaine gave her a dubious look, but said, "Not married, though there was a guy who lived there for a while. She kicked him out, thank god. There's an older guy, too; he comes by occasionally.

I mean it's not like I'm hanging out by the window all day. I've got my hands full with work and looking after my daughter but we talk sometimes."

"Are you and Leah close?"

"More or less. She bails me out if I can't get home from work in time to meet Shana when she gets out of school. I work part-time at Walmart, which gives me a lot of flexibility, but it doesn't always work out. We look out for each other. If she's ordered something from Amazon and isn't home I'll grab it off the step before someone steals it. She babysits Shana when I'm in a jam. I'm on my own here."

McCabe could identify.

She had her phone out, brought up a picture. "You said there was an older guy who comes by sometimes. This him?"

Elaine looked at a shot of Brent Chartwell that McCabe had taken from one of the photos in the house. "Yeah."

"When did you first start seeing him around?"

Elaine had to think. "I've been living here for seven years and I don't remember seeing him back when I first moved in. Year, year and a half, maybe two. More recent."

"Ever talk to him?"

"Just hello or goodbye if I happen to be out front. He's not a big talker. Not rude or anything, just comes and goes fast. Seems a little embarrassed when I spot him. Nice car. Got some old classic car too. Decent dresser. Definitely doesn't buy his clothes where I work."

"Leah tell you about him?"

Elaine shrugged. "She said she knew him from a long time ago, that they kind of reconnected. Bumped into each other or something, whatever. He's a little older than her, but hey, I don't judge."

The detective took the photo album from her purse, opened it up so Elaine could see the pictures, turned a few pages for her to look at.

"Do you know who this is?"

She shook her head. "No idea. That Leah's?"

McCabe managed a nod. "She ever mention someone named Tom?"

"No," Elaine said, her tone indicating the conversation was coming to an end. As McCabe returned the album to her purse, Elaine added, "What's actually going on here?"

McCabe sighed. You could only hold things back for so long. "Ms. Kennard died this morning."

Elaine's jaw dropped. "Oh god no." She said it loud enough that her daughter raised her head, looked their way, eyes wide.

"Sorry."

She glanced back, saw that her daughter was still engaged with her crayons, and stepped outside, leaving the door open a crack.

"What happened? Did she have a car accident?"

"It's a homicide."

Elaine put a hand to her mouth. "Someone *murdered* her?"

McCabe sidestepped the question. "We're trying to learn all we can, and we want to get in touch with next of kin. Do you know whether her parents are still living?"

Elaine needed a moment. "She never mentioned parents." She shook her head slowly, then stopped, a thought occurring to her. "Was it the guy she kicked out? Did he kill her? It wouldn't surprise me for a minute."

"What was his name?"

"Roy. No, that's not it. His name was Ray."

"You remember a last name?"

She bit her lip, struggling. "He lived there long enough that he was getting mail, and sometimes they deliver to the wrong house, so I'd get his stuff and walk it over, put it in their mailbox. Stanhope. Ray Stanhope."

McCabe had her notebook out, asked how to spell that last name, wrote it down. "And he moved out when, again?"

"Around the time . . . that the old guy started showing up. They had fights about it, her and Ray. I could hear them going at it through the wall. These places are supposed to be soundproof, but you make enough noise, your neighbors are gonna hear it. Especially when someone screams."

"And you heard Leah scream?"

"Ray hit her, at least once. One time, Leah was wearing sunglasses when we had a week of rain. So he must have popped her in the eye."

"Were the fights about this other man she was seeing?"

"You couldn't always hear the actual words, just the noise, you know? Maybe the odd snippet. This other guy was married and Ray was saying she wanted him for his money. Leah threatened to call the cops on him, but I don't think she ever did. You're the first one I've seen around here."

Something else occurred to her. "I remember one day, the new guy shows up in his fancy car, and Ray is coming out the front door, and they start to get into it. Ray's in the guy's face, pointing a finger at him, the older guy's looking pretty freaked out, starts backing up, but then Leah comes out and starts screaming at Ray to leave or she really will call the cops this time. So he heads off but he's telling them to fuck off and giving them the finger. He was kind of scary, Ray was."

"Has he been around lately?"

Elaine shook her head. "If he has, I haven't seen him."

"You know where he lives now? Works?"

"I don't know where he lives. But he was always driving Toyotas. Not the same one every time. I think he might work at the dealer and that's how Leah met him. Went in there for service."

Ray Stanhope was worth talking to, McCabe thought. He might provide some insights into what was going on between Leah Kennard and Brent Chartwell.

Elaine, clearly having made up her mind about Stanhope, said, "I hope he fucking rots in hell."

TEN

Reece

Diana was out the door the moment I pulled into the driveway and standing by the car as I got out. Her shoulder-length dark brown hair, which she normally kept pinned back, was falling across her face, a clue, as if I needed one, that she was anxious.

"He's home," she said, brushing her hair away from her eyes.

I sighed with relief. Her earlier call that Gage had not returned had had me on edge from the moment I'd left McCabe.

"Family room," she said.

Even though I knew he was back, it was a relief to see his skateboard on the floor just inside the front door. I found him slouched on the couch, feet on the coffee table, remote in hand, scrolling through the channel guide, as if on a quest to find just the right show. The constantly changing feed seemed to have a hypnotic effect on him. Like a lot of boys his age, Gage was all arms and legs, as if his torso hadn't had a chance yet to catch up with his growth spurts. If he'd been standing, we'd have been able to look at each other eye to eye.

"Hey," I said, putting my butt down on the table, resting

He kept on going. "It's pretty obvious that's why Grandpa was fucking somebody else."

The comment was so raw, so shocking coming from our son, that it stunned Diana and me into a brief silence. Like we'd been slapped. The kid was grieving, but he was pushing my limits.

Gage, sensing he'd not only crossed a line but leapt right past it, said, "I'm just saying, that's all."

"Enough," I said, recovering my ability to speak, but with an edge in my voice.

"Sorry," he grumbled.

"We're all trying our best to deal with this," I said.

"Where were you?" Diana asked him.

Gage rolled his head around in her direction. "Around."

"Around where?"

"The mall. With Dan. He was looking for shoes. Got something to eat at Five Guys."

"Where were you when I called?" she asked.

A shrug. "Heading home. Like I said. God, it's like an interrogation room around here."

Not something Gage would have any familiarity with, I thought. But he did watch plenty of cop shows.

Diana said, "I'm not interro— I was just asking, okay? And while we're at it, what about last night?"

"Last night?" he said.

"Where were you?"

"I was out."

"You were supposed to be home by midnight."

"I texted that I'd be late. You said okay."

Diana glared at me, as though it had been my decision to let him come home an hour later, even though we had discussed it. Well, as much as you can really discuss something when you were fast asleep seconds earlier. Gage had texted Diana, who woke up, saw the message, nudged me awake, and said, "What do we say?"

"It's fine," I'd said, just wanting to put my head back onto the pillow. So Diana had texted back to say it was okay, but now it was all on me.

And why were we fighting about this now, anyway?

"I just think there need to be some more rules around here," Diana said. She was generally pretty cool under pressure, but suddenly she looked as though she'd hit the breaking point. "It's all been too loosey-goosey. Everyone does whatever they want no matter how it affects others. Come and go as you please. Stay out all night. From now on—"

"I *didn't* stay out all night. I came—"

Diana wasn't done. "From now on you'll do what we say and you'll be home when we say you're to be home and—"

"Jesus!" Gage said. "What's this got to do with Grandpa—"

"Hang on," I said.

But now Gage and Diana were talking over each other, no one actually listening.

"Hey," I said. "*Hey!*"

They both stopped and looked at me. I raised my palms as I tried to bring the tone down a notch. I had a vague sense what was happening here. Something unthinkable had happened, we were overwhelmed, feeling powerless. And Diana had channeled all that frustration and anxiety into trying to control something, anything. At this moment, it was Gage.

"Look, we're all on edge, and right now, we need to lean on each other, not start tearing each other apart."

Diana turned and walked out of the room.

Gage and I looked at each other, neither of us knowing what to say. I broke the silence. "I've got people to call, I guess. Arrangements to make."

Some of those arrangements might be more my mother's responsibility than mine, but would she be in any shape to make them once she knew the details of what had happened? Would she even want a funeral for my father? How obliged would she feel to give my father a proper send-off when his final act was one of betrayal and jaw-dropping scandal?

"You okay?" I said to Gage.

"No."

I nodded. "Me neither." I sighed. "I'll talk to your mom. She's just stressed. It'll be okay." I didn't know whether I believed that, but I couldn't think of anything better to say.

"Are the police all done with this?" he asked.

"No. They've got to do a full investigation."

"Why?"

I thought, *Seriously?*

"It's . . . a murder, Gage. Due diligence and all that."

"But they found a note. Grandpa said he did it. It's obvious." He shook his head, then asked, "And where *is* Grandma, anyway?"

Good question.

And at that moment, as if on cue, my cell phone rang. I pulled it from my pocket, saw that it was my mother. I answered.

"Take me home," she said.

ELEVEN

Catherine had known she couldn't sit in the coffee shop forever. Eventually, she'd have to return home. Her phone kept buzzing. Reece, of course. And another persistent caller, the ID blocked. Catherine assumed that would be the police. Messages had been left but she did not check them.

Catherine had always put off getting bad news as long as she could, even when it came to small things. When the monthly Visa bill arrived in the mail, she wouldn't take it out of the envelope for a couple of days, fearful of how much she might have spent and forgotten about. So when it came to family crises, the longer you avoided the truth, the longer you deluded yourself into believing things couldn't be better. The whole Schrödinger's cat thing.

She'd finished her tea in the coffee shop across from Benjamin's. While drinking it, she had shredded her paper napkin into a hundred tiny pieces. She swept them into the empty paper cup and snapped the plastic lid back on. *Don't like to leave a mess*, she said to herself, and then laughed quietly.

Catherine reached into her purse for her wallet, set it on the table, and opened it up. She removed a department store points card from one of the sleeves, then dug her finger in, looking for something.

She withdrew a yellow Post-it note, no bigger than a pack of matches before it had been folded over once. The note was worn and dirty, as though it had been hidden in that sleeve for a very long time.

Catherine managed to unfold the note, its one sticky edge adhering to itself. Written on it in faded ink was a phone number.

She punched the number into her phone, put it to her ear, and waited.

It rang once, twice, a third time. When it got to five rings Catherine was ready to give up, but just then someone answered.

There was a moment of silence, and then a man's voice said, "Hello?"

"It's me."

"I have caller ID."

"I wasn't even sure you'd still have this number. I wasn't even sure you'd still be alive." When he said nothing, she said, "Brent just died."

"Condolences. Still at the same address? I'll send a card."

"I need to see you."

"A bit soon to start dating again."

"There's nothing funny about this."

"Forgive me."

"I *do* need to see you."

"I can't imagine why."

"Someone knows."

No funny comeback this time. After a few seconds, he

said, "If someone knows, someone talked." Another moment's silence. "I see."

"You see what?"

"Brent couldn't keep a secret any longer. My god, Catherine, do I have to clean up after you again?"

"Why would Brent say something now? It couldn't have been him."

"Well, that only leaves one other person."

"No, it had to have happened some other way. But someone's figured it out."

"And you know this how?"

"Can I just see you? I don't want to do this over the phone."

She thought she could hear a sigh at the other end. "I'll call you later," he said, and he was gone.

Catherine still had the phone in her hand when it buzzed. That blocked number again. She didn't feel she could put this off any longer.

"Hello," she said.

"Catherine Chartwell?"

"Yes."

"This is Detective Janice McCabe, with the Yorkton Hill Police."

"I've been expecting your call."

"Tell me where you are. I'll send an officer to pick you up."

"It's okay. I'll call Reece. He must be frantic by now."

"No, let—"

Catherine ended the call, brought up Reece's number, and tapped the screen.

"Mom," he said.

"Take me home."

"Where are you?"

She told him. "But I want you to tell me, right now, how bad it is."

And so he did. Brent, dead. This other woman, dead. And who was this woman, Catherine wanted to know. Reece gave her the name McCabe had revealed to him.

"Do you know who she is?" Reece asked.

"No," she lied.

The police believed it was a murder-suicide, her son told her.

Jesus, she thought. She wasn't even on her feet yet and felt dizzy. This was an unexpected turn of events.

Leah Kennard.

"Mom?"

She managed two words. "Which way?"

"Which way what?"

"You said . . . a murder-suicide. Which way?"

Matter-of-factly, her son said, "Dad shot her. Then he took his own life."

Catherine went several seconds saying nothing. Then, just before ending the call, she said, "I'll be out front."

TWELVE

Reece

Mom was ashen-faced when she got into the car. She took her seat, closed the door, put on her seat belt. Didn't so much as glance at me, just stared straight ahead through the windshield, and said nothing.

I didn't see the point in asking whether she was okay. I didn't know whether to pepper her with any other questions, either, although I had plenty. But soon enough she'd be bombarded with them from McCabe.

"Will they still be there?" she asked.

"The detective, I'm sure, because she wants to talk to you. And there are plenty of other police on the scene. Cars on the street, police tape strung up."

Mom looked pained, no doubt thinking about the shame of it all. She said, "I wasn't talking about them."

Oh, I thought. *The bodies.*

"That depends," I said. "They'll have to do whatever it is they do. Take pictures, study the scene. But I think they . . . I think they'll be taken away pretty soon. I don't think they're keeping them there for you to see them. I was able to identify Dad. They might want a more formal identification, later, at, you know, the morgue." I didn't want to say the word, but it seemed we were well past the euphemism stage.

Mom barely nodded.

Tentatively, I asked, "Did you know Dad was seeing somebody?" She'd already told me on the phone she didn't know who Leah Kennard was, but she could still have known, or at least suspected, Dad was seeing another woman.

She pressed her lips together tightly for a moment, still didn't look my way, and said, "Your father's personal life was his business, not mine."

I took my eyes off the road long enough to shoot her an *Are you kidding me?* look.

"You knew?"

"I'm not saying that. People are people. Nobody's perfect."

"But if Dad—"

"I don't want to talk about it, Reece."

"The *police* will want to talk about it."

"I'm sure they will."

Then, for the first time, concern crossed her face and she looked my way. "What about Holden?"

"I went to see him, but I didn't have a chance to tell him what happened to Dad," I said. "The police tracked me down there—I'd left the scene, when you called me, without their permission—and I had to go. But unless someone else goes by Holden's in the meantime, I don't think he's going to be finding out any other way."

"How was he?" she asked hesitantly.

I knew what she was really asking. "He was . . . you know."

"High as a kite?"

"Maybe not that high. But kinda."

"And you're sure he doesn't know?"

I nodded.

She nodded resignedly. "I'll have to send him away again."

"I know you keep trying that, Mom, but it never takes. Like you said, people are people. Nobody's perfect."

"What, I should give up on him?"

"People have to want to change. You can't force them. Maybe it's time for a different approach."

"And what would that be?"

She had me there.

We turned onto my parents' street. There were still a couple of cruisers out front, the yellow tape still strung up around the perimeter of the yard. The street crime tape was down now, though, and now there were two TV news vans there. One from CP24, the all-news cable station, and, ironically, WorldWide. This definitely wasn't a news story I'd be writing up for them. A couple of female reporters with cameramen were being held back behind the yellow tape. I knew the one from WorldWide and kept my head down in the hopes she wouldn't recognize me.

"I'll go see Holden after I've talked to the detective," Mom said.

"I'll wait, take you over."

"I don't know how long they're going to want to talk to me."

"I'm okay waiting. I can—"

"I'll get an Uber. Or maybe the police will drive me."

"What else can I do? Do you want me to get in touch with Heffernan & Sons?"

The town's best-known funeral directors.

"I know my responsibilities and obligations," she said curtly, still staring straight ahead. Her voice sounded almost robotic, like she'd gone into some kind of self-induced trance as a way to get through this. "If there's anything I need I will let you know."

I pulled the car over to the curb, got out quickly, intending to come around in time to open the door for her, but she was half out by the time I got there. The uniformed cop who'd found me at my brother's place greeted us and said Detective McCabe would be back shortly.

"I rushed back and she's not here?" Mom said. Of course. Now that she'd finally turned up, she'd *rushed.*

"Is my husband still in the house?" she asked.

The cop shook his head. "No, ma'am. The bodies have been removed."

"Then I'll wait inside."

"No, ma'am."

"I can't enter my own home?"

"If you could just wait for the detective."

"May I even set foot on my own property?"

The cop nodded, lifted the yellow tape to allow her to duck under. I followed. She walked across the front lawn, paused briefly to look at the open front door, then went around the side. The gate to the backyard was open. The police, out of a sense of thoroughness, must have wandered the entire property looking for who knows what.

We walked beyond the deck, across the yard, and stood by the edge of the pond.

It was maybe the size of half a dozen swimming pools, surrounded by woods on three sides, and no more than five feet at its deepest point. We'd wondered why it never dried up, but Dad had explained that it was connected by an underground channel to the creek that eventually wound its way to the lake.

Holden and I thought it was cool when we were kids, having our very own pond, although a pool might have been nicer. The pond wasn't much good for swimming. The bottom was soft and mucky. If you walked out into it, you'd be up to your knees in no time. But as kids, we made the best use we could of it, incorporating it into our adventures. Dad bought a small wooden rowboat, barely six feet long, that Holden and I and our friends would use to paddle out to the middle and pretend we were in Lake Ontario or even the ocean.

We each had a fishing pole, but we never caught a damn thing and gave up over time. The pond was not stocked with fish, although one time Dad brought back some live perch he'd caught on a fishing trip with friends, dumped them into the pond, and said maybe we should give it one more try. We didn't hook into any of them, but it wasn't long before they were floating sideways on the surface.

That little rowboat was still here, pulled up a few feet from the water, a rotted reminder of the past. There'd been discussions over the years about junking it. The paint had mostly peeled from it, the wood graying, the paddles—one of them in two splintered pieces—left in the bottom. My parents had either become sentimental about it or just couldn't be bothered to have it taken away, but to make it less of an eyesore Mom had scattered topsoil in the bottom and planted flowers, some of which grew high enough to be seen from the deck.

It struck me as oddly peaceful, standing here with my mother, away from the squawk of the police cars, the yellow tape, the officers milling about out front.

"We should have had a pool," Mom said, as though reading

my mind. "I asked your father so many times to have one put in, but he'd say, we've got the pond. He loved to sit on the deck and look at it, said it was like having his own private lake. He was never much of a swimmer anyway. He just liked the view. I think it was just a breeding ground for mosquitoes."

I said nothing.

"I wonder what the new people will do with it. Fill it in? Could you do that? If you had enough dirt?"

"New people?"

"I can't live here," she said. "Not anymore. Where your father shot his whore and then himself?"

I took her point.

"I'll get it on the market as soon as I can. Stay in a hotel until I've found another place, rent an apartment. See what's for sale at the Yorkton Towers."

The most expensive condos in town. Right downtown, overlooking the harbor, where the town's one-percenters kept their yachts and sailboats.

She paused, and I wondered whether she was waiting for an offer of temporary accommodation with Diana and Gage and me. It was on the tip of my tongue, but I couldn't quite spit it out. There was enough tension in the house now. I saw us moving into a rough patch with Gage. Bringing Mom into the mix wouldn't help. And there was no way she'd stay with Holden, even if he offered. A "pigsty," I'd once heard her call his place. Let her get a hotel if that was what she wanted.

We heard someone approaching from behind and both turned. I recognized Detective McCabe and introduced Mom.

"Sorry for your loss," McCabe offered.

"About time someone said it," Mom replied.

THIRTEEN

Before Detective McCabe had returned to the Chartwell home, she'd gone to the local Toyota dealership in search of Ray Stanhope, Leah Kennard's former boyfriend who'd lived with her, for a period of time, at her Galen Street address.

She parked between a new Camry and a Prius hybrid and went into the showroom, heading straight for reception. She didn't introduce herself to the young, blond woman when she asked where she could find Stanhope.

"Parts," the woman said.

The parts department was adjacent to the service area, where McCabe found four people waiting for work on their vehicles to be completed, leafing through old issues of *Toronto Life* and *Canadian Living*. She went to the parts window, tapped a bell to get someone's attention, and waited until a short man in a red polo shirt with a Toyota emblem stitched to it approached.

"Can I help you?" he asked.

"Looking for Ray Stanhope," she said.

"Hang on."

He turned and called out, "Ray! Someone to see you!"

A burly guy who stood about six two came out from behind some metal shelving. He was fiftyish, had a full beard, and weighed in, McCabe guessed, at two seventy easy.

"Yeah?" he said.

She flashed her ID. "Detective Janice McCabe, Yorkton Hill Police. Is there someplace we could talk?"

"What's this about?" he asked, his eyes narrowing.

She said, "Maybe someone's office, or outside?"

He muttered something that sounded like "just a sec" and vanished from the window, presumably to find a way to join her on the other side. But when almost a minute had passed, McCabe started to think he wasn't coming.

She ran out the closest door and saw Stanhope striding toward a pickup truck. He was getting behind the wheel and closing the door when McCabe started running his way, shouting: "Mr. Stanhope! Stop!"

McCabe was fifty feet away as he started the truck and put it into gear. She stood in the vehicle's path and drew her weapon, aiming it directly at the man behind the windshield.

"Stop!"

The truck braked to a stop. Stanhope, wide-eyed, his fingers still gripping the steering wheel.

"Step out of the vehicle with your hands where I can see them!"

The door opened and Stanhope slowly got out, arms in the air. The man McCabe had encountered at the parts counter had come out. "What's going on?" he shouted.

"Go back inside, sir!" McCabe said, and when the man didn't immediately do as he was told, she repeated the order. He complied.

To Stanhope, she said, "Lie down with your arms above your head!"

He looked incredulous. "On the pavement? It's all oily and shit." McCabe stood there with the gun trained on him and said nothing. "Okay, okay."

Stanhope went down, stretched out his arms. McCabe straddled him, holstered her weapon, pulled out a pair of handcuffs, had Stanhope put one hand behind his back, cuffed it, then ordered him to bring down his other hand, and cuffed it. She patted him down for a weapon, found none, then reached into the truck and turned it off.

He was too heavy a man to grab under the shoulders and haul to his feet, so she ordered him to do it on his own. It was a struggle, a bit like watching an upended turtle right itself, but he finally managed it and when he did, McCabe turned him toward the truck, leaning him up against the front fender.

"Am I going to find any weapons in there?" she asked him.

"No," he said. "Shit, I think I dislocated my shoulder."

"Why'd you run?"

"I wasn't running. I just didn't want to talk to you."

"And why's that?"

"Look, the other guy started it."

"What other guy?"

"I didn't get his fucking name. I don't know how the hell he knew mine. Louis rat me out?"

"Louis?"

"Runs the place. He show you my credit card receipts? Isn't that a violation of my rights? Should've paid cash."

"Why don't you tell me your version of the story," she said.

"I'm having a beer, minding my own business, when this guy, he says, 'Hey, I thought Chris Farley was dead.'"

McCabe had to think. Farley, Farley. "The *Saturday Night Live* comic?" Stanhope did bear a passing resemblance to the late performer.

"I ignore him at first, minding my own business, but then he says, 'You ever heard of Weight Watchers?' Like, I'm the only heavy guy in the bar? I don't even know this asshole and he's making cracks at me, so yeah, maybe I got a little pissed off and I might have hit him."

"Might have?"

"It all happened so fast. I spun around, had the beer bottle in my hand, and it kind of crashed into the side of his head. But it's not like it broke or anything. The bottle, I mean. Not his head either. No blood. He just went down. But I waited to see if he woke up, and he did, so I figured he wasn't dead."

"Which bar was this?"

He turned around, looked at her, puzzled she didn't already know this.

"Village Idiot."

A bar named after its clientele, McCabe thought.

"Where'd you go after you left the bar?"

"Home."

"And what time'd you get into work today?"

"Seven thirty. You don't believe me, ask Terry."

"Mr. Stanhope, I'm going to remove your cuffs. Try not to do anything else stupid."

He was quiet while she freed him. He turned around, rubbed his wrists, rolled his head on his shoulders.

"So, like, did the guy file a complaint or something?"

His brow furrowed. He waited.

"Tell me about Leah Kennard."

"Oh, man," he said, shaking his head. "What shit from the distant past is that bitch dredging up?"

"When's the last time you saw her?"

"I don't know. Got to be a year, at least, but even then, I didn't talk to her. She was here getting her car fixed. I saw her waiting. But I didn't say shit to her. We were *done*. Look, I admit, there was this one time, we kind of got into it, and maybe I kind of—it wasn't even like a hit, more just a slap—and it was really more like an accident, and I'm sorry about that, but there was blame on both sides. I was basically defending myself. What am I supposed to do when she starts swinging a frying pan at me?"

"When's the last time you actually talked to her?"

"When she kicked me out."

"When was that?"

"Couple years ago. What's this about?"

"Do you know a Brent Chartwell?"

He nodded. "Oh yeah. He's the rich asshole she was seeing when she broke up with me. Married guy."

"You must have been upset."

"I thought we had a good thing going for a while there. Ups and downs and shit, but it was okay. But you could never make her happy so it's just as well it's over. You have to move on, right?"

"Leah ever talk about how she got along with him?"

"Far as I know she's still seeing him."

"Who's Tom?"

"Tom?"

"She has a photo album full of pictures of someone named Tom."

"I have no— What's this about, anyway?"

"Leah's dead."

His shock appeared genuine. "Dead?"

McCabe nodded.

Stanhope's entire frame seemed to sag. "Oh shit, that's awful. Are you serious? She's really dead?"

"She is."

"What happened?" His face sagged and his eyes were starting to mist.

"She was shot."

His mouth opened.

"Oh man. Oh Jesus."

He lost it, put his hands over his eyes. His large frame seemed to shrink as he bent over in despair. "Oh man," he said again. When Stanhope took his hands away McCabe saw genuine tears.

"Shit shit shit," he muttered. "I really loved her." He lifted his head, fixed his eyes on McCabe through his tears, and asked, "Who did it? Who shot her?"

"Our investigation is continuing," she said gently. "Did you keep in touch at all? Did you know what her relationship with Mr. Chartwell was like?"

"It was *him*?" he said. "*He* did it?"

"That would surprise you?"

He thought a moment, shook his head. "I mean, he doesn't seem like he'd have it in him. You arrested him? He confessed?"

"No," McCabe said. "Mr. Chartwell is also deceased."

Stanhope blinked the tears out of his eyes, as though trying to see McCabe better. "What? Someone shot the both of them?"

"At this time, it doesn't appear anyone else is involved."

She let that sink in. Watched Stanhope put the pieces together. He slumped against the truck, using it to prop himself up. "Oh man," he said quietly.

McCabe asked whether Leah had any nearby next of kin. Stanhope said her parents had both passed, that as far as he knew, she had nobody. He took some persuading, but McCabe got him to agree to come to the morgue within the day to make a positive identification of the body. And she'd still see if she could track down an actual relative to do the same.

Back in her car, McCabe tried Catherine Chartwell again. This time she reached her, but the woman hung up before she could get her location, and McCabe could only hope she would find her at the house by the time she got back there.

She found her in the backyard, with her son. Dismissed him politely, because she wanted to question Catherine alone. They each took a seat on the back deck.

"You were at a luncheon?"

"Yes. The arts council. I'm a member."

"What time did lunch begin?" the detective asked.

"Half past eleven. I can give you the names of the other women who were there. They'll confirm I was with them the whole time."

McCabe blinked. "Thank you. I might get back to you on that."

"I just thought . . . when things like this happen, you want to know where everyone was."

"Of course. Can you tell me, when did you leave the house?"

"Around ten."

"Isn't that kind of early? How long would it take to get to Benjamin's? Ten minutes tops?"

"I wanted to wander around the downtown first. I thought I'd pop into Angela's."

McCabe knew it. High-end ladies fashion store. Not that she ever shopped there on her salary.

"Did you speak to your husband before you left?"

Catherine nodded.

"I told him I'd be back midafternoon."

"And Ms. Kennard had not arrived before you left?"

Catherine gave the detective a sharp look. "You must be joking."

McCabe smiled apologetically. "I always ask what might seem like stupid questions. Sometimes I hear something I'm not expecting. So she arrived after you had left."

"Clearly."

"Did you know Leah Kennard?"

"I didn't . . . know her. It's possible we might have met at some point. But it's not an encounter I remember clearly." She bit her lip, as though that would help her recall.

"She's not someone your husband worked with?"

"No," Catherine said quickly.

"Was your husband retired?"

"Yes, mostly."

"Mostly?"

"He had his own consulting firm that he wound down in recent years but he still did the occasional assignment if someone begged him hard enough and was offering enough money."

"He'd always worked in this field?" McCabe asked.

Catherine hesitated before answering. "Years ago, he worked for Wiffel-Smith."

"The pharmaceutical company? The one that got in trouble over—"

"Yes. That one. They made Oxy-Mirac before they were forced to pull it off the market. It was very unfair. It was an excellent pain reliever. But people abused it, just like with other drugs, or alcohol, but you don't see them banning vodka, do you? All that trouble happened after my husband left."

"What did he do for them? Was he a researcher, a scientist?"

"Sales. He was very good at it." She said it with some pride. "He traveled all over Canada and the United States. But he decided he'd had enough. He could see what was coming. All the legal problems."

"You tried to reach your husband while you were out?"

"I wanted him to check something in my datebook," Catherine said. "I tried his cell and then the home phone. And texted him. I couldn't raise him so I asked Reece to go by the house but he was already here."

A pause, and then, "Did she look like me?"

There you go, McCabe thought. *Sometimes I hear something I'm not expecting.*

"What do you mean, Mrs. Chartwell?"

"This woman. Did she look anything at all like me?"

"That . . . seems like an odd question, Mrs. Chartwell."

"I'm sorry. I was just . . . wondering."

"What?" McCabe walked on eggshells as she asked, "That maybe your husband, even when unfaithful, wanted to be with someone who resembled you?"

"Something like that, I suppose."

McCabe pondered whether that would be flattering in some strange way. She said, "Her hair color, maybe. And it was about the same length." She waited a beat, then asked, "You're not suggesting Ms. Kennard was shot by someone thinking she was you? Your husband could hardly have made that mistake."

"No, I'm sorry, it was a ridiculous question," Catherine said. "Do you have any more questions or can I go tell my other son what's happened before there's a news crew at his door?"

FOURTEEN

Reece had departed, so Catherine accepted McCabe's offer of a ride to her older son's residence.

McCabe said, "Tell me about Holden."

"I'm worried how he'll take this," Catherine said.

"Reece appears to be handling it as best as can be expected."

"Holden is not Reece."

"What makes them different?"

"Holden has had a more difficult time. We support— My husband and I have supported him as best we can, but as I'm sure you're aware, there are no easy solutions to addiction."

McCabe's eyebrows rose a notch. "No, there aren't."

"He's more fragile than Reece, more unpredictable. I don't want him to end up back in rehab, but if he needs it, I hope he won't fight me when I urge him to go there." She paused, then said, "Don't misunderstand. He's a good son. He has a good heart."

"Does he have a job?"

"Occasionally. He's been helping someone with house construction lately. Up here, on the right. That little blue SUV in the drive."

McCabe slowed the car, brought it to a stop. "Thank you,"

Catherine said, got out, and went to the front door. She glanced back, said, "Do you have to talk to him?" She had a pleading look in her eyes.

"At some point, but not right now," McCabe said.

Catherine smiled a thank-you, went to the door, and knocked. When the door started to open, McCabe drove off.

Holden, tears already forming, threw his arms around her. "Oh, Mom," he wept. "I'm so sorry. I'm so sorry."

Catherine put her arms around him, wanting to comfort him, but also miffed. *Reece came by*, she thought. *He broke the news. That was for me to do.*

"It's okay," she said, patting his back. "Everything's going to be okay." She pulled back, far enough to look into his face. "Reece was here, wasn't he?"

Holden nodded.

"Well, Mommy's here now," she said.

"I'm so sorry," he said again.

"I know. Me too. So you know . . . what happened. Your father, that woman."

Holden slowly nodded.

"It's a horrible thing. A horrible, horrible thing," Catherine said.

Once inside, with the door closed, Holden began to sob.

"It's okay," his mother said.

Holden doubled over, his back heaving as he wept. Catherine wrapped her arm around him, guided him to the couch. "I know, I know. It's hard to believe," she said soothingly.

"Everything's gone to shit," he said between sobs. "It's all gone to shit."

"No, no, we'll get through this," she said, sitting down next to him. "You know I'm here for you. You have to be strong, you have to—"

He jumped up from the couch, startling her. The sobs had stopped as though a switch had been flipped. His cheeks still lined with tears, he managed a smile and said, "I have an idea."

". . . Okay. What kind of idea?"

"We should take a trip."

"A trip."

"A round-the-world trip!" he said, waving his hands in the air. "Maybe a cruise! Book a couple rooms on one of those big ocean liners that stops in ports all over the world! What do they call them on a ship? Are they still rooms? Don't they call them cabins?" He laughed. "That's crazy. A cabin is something you find in the middle of the woods, not on a ship. But that's what they call it, right? So we'd get two cabins, maybe one with windows or a little balcony off the side so you can look at the ocean and—"

"Holden."

He'd begun pacing back and forth, arms still waving. "We should go for a month. Maybe two! I hear some people, they live on these ships—mostly older people, but whatever. They just go on one cruise after another, they don't even have a permanent address, but with the net, they can still pay their bills or their insurance or taxes or whatever it is that people have to do even if they're not really living anywhere, so—"

"Holden, stop, listen to—"

He took both her hands in his and brought Catherine to her feet. "What do you think? I know there's probably stuff you have to deal with, wrap things up, but couldn't you get someone else to do that? I bet Reece would do it. He can figure out all that shit! That would allow us to get away sooner."

Holden gave his mother a short, abrupt hug, then ran down the hall to his bedroom, shouting the whole way.

"I've only got one bag! I'll need to borrow one, maybe two. We'll have to go back to your place and get lots of suitcases. Bring as much stuff as you want because we don't know how long we'll be gone." He paused a second, thinking of something. "Will they have laundry facilities? On the ship? And food! Don't they have these like twenty-four-hour buffets where you can eat your face off?"

He had all the drawers of his dresser open and was tossing socks and underwear onto his unmade bed. He stopped, briefly, looking at what he'd selected, then turned to his mother and asked, "What do you think the weather will be like? If it's mostly hot, I'll want shorts and tees, but if it's a long cruise we'll be hitting all kinds of weather, and—"

"Holden!"

He froze, stared at her wide-eyed.

"Holden, please, just . . . stop. What have you been taking?"

"Taking?" He laughed. "*Taking?*"

"Whatever it is, you need to let it get out of your system, to come down from this. I understand wanting to go away. I'd love to run away from all this, but we can't just pack up and go on a—"

"Of course we can," he said, pointing a finger at her. "That's always been your problem. You're wrapped up too tight. Come on. This is *exactly* what we need. *Both* of us. Put all this shit behind us, forget about it, start over."

"You can never start over."

"Why not?" He said it in a pleading, desperate tone. "Clean slate. It's exactly what we need to do."

"If only that were possible. We can't run from our problems."

Holden suddenly became quiet, focused. "How is that any different than burying them? Hasn't that always been your policy?"

"You need help, Holden."

"Help?"

"You're in shock. *I'm* in shock. Your father . . . what he was doing, what he did, it's unimaginable, and we may never come to terms with it. But we have to figure out how to deal with it, and sailing away on some cruise isn't the answer. Maybe one day, when you're not in the shape you're in now, maybe that's something we *should* do. But not now, not today. I'm deeply worried about you."

"I'm fine, honestly. Actually, seeing you right now, pretty great."

"There's something I have to know."

His eyes were darting about the room, as though following an invisible fly.

"Holden, I need you to look at me."

He tried to focus on his mother. "Yeah."

"You didn't break your promise, did you?"

His eyes narrowed. "What do you mean?"

"Holden, please. Don't pretend you don't know what I'm talking about."

"No," he said firmly, acknowledging he did, indeed, understand her meaning. "No, I wouldn't do that."

"Because . . . there have been some strange developments lately."

"Yeah, well, no kidding."

"I don't mean what happened today. Before today."

"What are you talking about?"

"I've had some phone calls," she said.

"What do you mean, phone calls? From who?"

"*Anonymous* phone calls. From someone who seems to know things they couldn't possibly know."

Holden shook his head furiously. "Don't look at me. You think I'm nuts?"

She didn't want to answer that one directly. "Well, someone had to have said something."

Holden's face lit up. "Dad."

"What about your dad?"

"That's why he did it. That's why he shot himself. He'd talked about it, and . . . and the guilt overcame him!"

Catherine did not look convinced. "I don't think so, Holden." She sighed, took her phone from her purse, and started looking through her contacts for a number.

"Who are you calling?" he asked.

"I want to get you some help."

"You calling Sharnwood?"

She raised a finger in the air.

"Are you? Because I'm not going! I'm not!"

"Hello?" Catherine said into the phone. "Yes, could you put me through to Dr. Memphis, please? It's Catherine—"

"I won't go back there," Holden said, pushing past his mother as he left the bedroom, heading back to the living room.

"—Chartwell? Holden's mother? He's had a relapse at a very difficult time and needs— Holden, stop!"

She took the phone away from her ear and went after him. The front door was open. She ran out in time to see him get into his Honda CR-V and take off down the street.

She shook her head in frustration, then put the phone back to her ear. "I'm back, is the doctor— Yes, I'll hold." She waited a moment, then, "Hello, Dr. Memphis? Catherine here. It's Holden . . . yes, he was doing well for a while, but we've had a family tragedy and . . . okay, that's good to know. I'll bring him in . . . but he's going to take some convincing."

FIFTEEN

1999

"God, I can't believe it," Brent Chartwell shouted. "What a party! You ever seen anything like this?"

Catherine, elegant in a sparkling, floor-length red gown, had to admit she had not. "What must this have cost him?" she replied, raising her voice to be heard over the band that had set up on a temporary stage.

Brent laughed. "Whatever it was, it's just a drop in the bucket. Graham's raking in more money than God."

"Thanks to you," she said, slipping her arm around him.

"Thanks to a lot of people," Brent said, growing hoarse as the evening progressed.

They were standing out on the lawn to better enjoy the band, having emerged from under the massive tents that had been set up over the dining tables, their stomachs filled with lobster and caviar and risotto and champagne.

Graham Wiffel had hired Chicago, the jazz rock band that had burst onto the scene in the late sixties, for a private engagement. They'd set up out in front of the Wiffel mansion and were in the middle of belting out "Saturday in the Park," having already performed "25 or 6 to 4," "Does Anybody Really Know What Time It Is?" and "If You Leave Me Now." Brent and Catherine had done a slow dance to that one, Brent whispering into her ear how much he loved her.

"Saturday in the Park" could not have been more appropriate. This venue felt like one, with its expansive lawns and towering trees, but it was actually Wiffel's private estate, a rambling ten acres in the rocky Bruce Peninsula, on the western shore of Georgian Bay, a more than two-hour drive north of Toronto.

The property had been in the Wiffel family for generations, but recently, Graham had renovated the main home, expanding it from ten thousand to fifteen thousand square feet. There were four guesthouses, each with ten rooms, on the property now—Brent and Catherine would be staying in one of them that night—plus a tennis court and two swimming pools, even though the estate was on some of the cleanest, bluest waterfront to be found anywhere in the country. Guests who didn't make the cut to stay on-site were in motels and B&Bs in nearby Wiarton and Owen Sound.

The last three years had been especially good ones for Wiffel-Smith. (The "Smith" was a nod to the other founder of the pharmaceutical giant, Isaiah Smith, now deceased, his half of the empire subsumed by Wiffel more than a decade ago.) Their new wonder drug, Oxy-Mirac, was being heralded by medical journals around the world as the greatest advance in the treatment of pain since aspirin. It certainly didn't hurt that Wiffel-Smith had made major contributions to these journals, as well as to key people at various federal agencies in countries around the world who had influence over which drugs were approved and which were not.

Brent guessed there were more than two hundred people at this party, which was being held to celebrate the company's year-end results. Top salespeople like himself were in attendance, of course, but so were doctors from across the continent who were true believers in what Oxy-Mirac could do and were prescribing it for patients who'd found no relief with other pain medications. GPs, specialists, heads of clinics and hospitals, so many of them here, taking a much needed break from the pressures of their jobs to accept Graham Wiffel's gratitude and largesse.

Brent recognized several in the crowd. There was a doctor from Vancouver, Arthur Kilgallen. Brent had first dropped in on him two years ago, getting to know all he could about him beforehand, that his wife's name was Julie, he had two children named Jeremy, eleven, and Sally, fourteen, he enjoyed boating, his father had served in the military. Sally was learning to play the violin, and Jeremy had won a local spelling bee championship. Most important of all? Kilgallen liked Kentucky bourbon. Never show up without a bottle of Bondstone Triple Oak.

And over there, nuzzling the neck of one of several "hostesses" whose services Graham had engaged for these festivities, was Oscar Winsome, who ran a clinic outside of Buffalo. Married to Lisa (clearly *not* accompanying him on this trip), father to Ian, who had at one point expressed concern that a few of his patients taking Oxy-Mirac were finding their pain gradually returning. Not a problem, Brent had said. He shared with Winsome several new studies by Wiffel-Smith that had concluded it was perfectly safe to increase the dosage without any addictive side effects.

"They're just building up a slight tolerance," Brent had explained. "Totally expected. Prescribing three pills a day instead of two should correct that." He brought his voice down to a whisper, and with a sly grin, said, "And I meant to mention, you remember Tandy, from the convention we had in Chicago? She's very much looking forward to seeing you again next time you're in town."

Next, he spotted Miriam Blade, formerly of the Federal Drug Administration south of the border, who had not been terribly supportive of approvals when she worked there. Now she was a Wiffel-Smith consultant and a believer, making three times what the FDA had paid her. Between them, she and her husband were able to afford to send their son, Jason, to Yale. Brent would have to say hello at some point before they left, tell her how happy they all were that she'd come aboard.

You got to know these people. You became their friends. You insinuated yourself into their lives. You learned what their appetites were, and fed them.

Those doctors couldn't write those scrips fast enough.

"Oh, there's the big man now," Brent said.

Graham Wiffel was making his way through the crowd. When he spotted Brent, he smiled, showing off those perfect teeth of his. Midsixties, lean and tanned from a recent trip to his place in the Bahamas, thinning hair and piercing eyes. He extended a hand, and when Brent took it, he drew him in, hugged him, patted his back.

Looking over Graham's shoulder, Brent noticed another man, standing two steps away. Unassuming in a black suit, narrow black tie, he had short black hair and glasses with thick, black rims. Maybe five six, five seven tops, a little soft around the middle. Brent caught the man's eye, and there was an almost imperceptible nod between them.

"How's my number one guy?" Graham asked Brent.

"Just great, sir, just great. You've met my wife, Catherine?"

He turned to her, took her hand and kissed it.

"Oh my!" Catherine said, laughing. "Aren't you the charmer!"

"This is a very talented man you have here," he told her. "This guy could sell shit to pigs!"

Brent chuckled nervously. That analogy didn't sit well with him, but Graham could be a bit earthy at times.

"He's something, no doubt about it," Catherine said, beaming.

"And how are the boys?" Graham asked. "Holden? And Reece?" The boss followed his own teachings. Get to know your people. Draw them in close.

"They're great," Catherine said, unable to hide how impressed she was that the big man knew their sons' names. "I really can't thank you enough. We're going to be able to provide them such a wonderful future."

Graham smiled. "That's what I love to hear. Well, I gotta keep mingling. Everyone wants to kiss the ring!" Another laugh and he began to move on. The short man in the black suit followed and as he passed Catherine he flashed her a quick smile.

"Such a lovely man," Catherine said of Graham once the boss was out of earshot.

"Yeah, he's something."

"What?" she said, detecting a tone in his voice.

"Nothing, nothing. You're right. He's a great guy."

"He's changed our *lives*, Brent," Catherine said. "Everything we have, we owe to him. I grew up with nothing. I never dreamed I'd live a life as nice as the one we have now." She scanned her surroundings. The beautiful people partying, the band, the majestic mansion that dominated the landscape. "It's like a dream, you know? But it's not. We're not going to wake up from this. It's our *life*. And did you notice, he knew the boys' names?"

"He's good at that," Brent said. "Probably had them whispered into his ear two seconds earlier by Crane."

"Crane?" Catherine asked.

"His shadow."

"The little nerdy guy with the glasses?"

That made Brent laugh. "Yeah, him."

"Is Crane a first or last name?"

"Last. Don't ask me his first name. No idea."

"Is that his job? To whisper the right name into Graham's ear at the right time?"

"A little more than that. He oversees security."

"Him?" said Catherine.

"Appearances can be deceiving. He makes sure Graham's safe. Not a bodyguard exactly, but I wouldn't be surprised if he's packing."

"No," she said, aghast. "I didn't see a gun."

"You're not supposed to."

"Why does Graham need someone like that?"

"You get to where Graham is, you need a bubble around you. Protection. Someone could, I don't know, kidnap him, figuring they could charge a hefty ransom. Maybe someone with a bone to pick with Wiffel-Smith. You never know when you're at his level. There've been death threats. Even I've had the odd run-in with people."

"When?" Catherine asked, startled.

"On the road, checking in on all these clinics, some strung-out addict nut thinks you've got a trunk full of Oxy-Mirac, wants to rip you off."

"When did this happen?"

Brent shrugged it off. "It was nothing, really."

"You've never told me about this."

"I don't want you to worry about every little thing that goes on when I'm traveling."

She grabbed his arm. "I want to know. Right now."

Brent sighed. "Okay, but it's going to sound worse than it actually was. I was coming out of a clinic in Cleveland, and the waiting room was standing room only, people getting scrips for Oxy-Mirac, and I came out of the doctor's office—a briefcase in my hand—and this one guy follows me out, thinks maybe I've got samples in that case, and he pulls a—"

"Oh my god."

"It's okay. Just listen. He's kind of wild-eyed and he pulls this gun and tells me to hand him the briefcase but this doctor, who ran the clinic? He was no fool, and he had security there and before I've even got my hands up this guard comes over and whacks this guy in the back of the knees with a nightstick and he goes down like a sack of bricks."

"What if that guard hadn't been there? You could have been shot. You could have been *killed*."

"Yeah, but he *was* there, and the cops were called, and they hauled that guy away and charged him and it all turned out okay. I was just glad I didn't have to go back and testify. The guy's lawyer arranged a plea, he got sent up for six months or a year or something."

Catherine had paled. "You should have told me this before."

"It was nothing. No sense having you worried every second I'm away."

"What about at home?" she asked. "People might think we have Oxy-Mirac samples there, someone could break in. What about the boys? Are *we* safe?"

"Of course we are. Come on, let's not get into it now. Let's get some more of that Dom Perignon."

"I'm not done talking about this," she said.

He steered Catherine toward the tent. A mid-thirties, blond woman in a glittering silver gown was heading his way. Staggering more than walking, a nearly full flute glass in hand, some of the champagne spilling over the top as she approached on six-inch heels.

"Brent!" she called out, still thirty feet away. "Look at you!"

"Evelyn Corby," he whispered to Catherine. Now that the band was on a break, he could actually speak in a softer voice. "I don't think you've met."

"I'd have remembered," Catherine said.

"Sales, like me, works coast to coast, but actually lives not too far from us, other side of Yorkton Hill. Think maybe she's had a bit too much to—"

"Knew I'd find you eventually," Evelyn said, having closed the distance between them. She almost fell onto him, placing a hand on his chest to steady herself. She flashed Catherine an exaggerated smile. "You look like an actual spouse, not one of those hookers Graham hired." She grinned. "No offense." A pause. "I think."

"I'm Catherine," she said, extending a hand. "And yes, I'm Brent's wife."

"A pleasure," Evelyn said, raising the flute to her lips and taking a drink.

"Looks like you're enjoying the party," Brent said with a hint of disapproval.

"Immensely. Having a wonderful time. Nothing like an open bar to take your mind off your troubles."

Brent glanced at Catherine, as though seeking guidance about whether to ask. "Troubles?" he said.

"Just a little death in the extended family is all," she said, licking her lips.

"Oh, I'm so sorry. Someone close?"

"Nephew." She wavered slightly, had another drink. "Miles. Twenty-eight. Computer programmer, a real whiz." She snorted. "I always called him when I couldn't get my printer to work."

"That's terrible," Catherine said. "So young."

"Yeah, right? Completely unexpected. Miles was playing hockey, some asshole the size of a Zamboni slammed him into the boards, fucked up his shoulder big-time. He went to all these doctors, looking for something to take the pain away. Enter Aunt Evelyn to save the day! She's got just the answer. A miracle cure! And even better, she's got the inside track on where to get what you need."

"Evelyn," Brent said quietly, leaning in, "why don't we go in there and sit down?"

"Hmm?" she said.

He nodded in the direction of the tent. "Maybe have a seat, get some coffee into you?"

He went to take her drink from her, but she swung her arm away, champagne spilling over the rim. "But I haven't finished my story," she said. "It gets better."

"Maybe you could tell it to me another time and—"

"No, no, you need to hear it now. So I had some sample packs

I gave Miles, and he gobbled them down like M&Ms. Did the trick, too, right? But I had to go and tell him about this doctor I knew who could help him out if he never needed a renewal on a prescription. This doctor, very good friend, might even be here tonight and if he is I'll rip his fucking face off. Because see, not only did Miles go see *that* guy, he found three or four *other* doctors who were happy to help him out. Wolfing pills like I downed those shrimp at the bar." She had distracted herself with the mention of shrimp. "Did you have any of those jumbo ones? Best shrimp I ever had in my life. Big as horseshoes."

"Evelyn, this is not the place," Brent whispered.

"No wait, listen, then I get the call. From my niece—boy, does she ever love me now—who hadn't heard from Miles for a while, went by the house to check on him, and he was out cold. She can't get him to wake up, so she dialed nine-one-one and they came and tried their best but . . . he's gone."

Evelyn went quiet for a moment, knocked back the rest of her drink. Brent and Catherine said nothing.

Evelyn, dismayed that her glass was empty, tossed it. It shattered on the flagstones. She fixed her gaze on Brent.

"You living the good life?" she asked. "I sure am. I treated myself. A Boxster. Little Porsche convertible. All my life I dreamed of getting a car like that. Putting the top down, feeling the wind in my hair. You know what I've been thinking of doing to it? Dousing it with high-test and tossing a match to it. I wonder if that would make me feel any better. What do you think, Brent?"

"Where are you staying, Evelyn? In one of the guesthouses?"

"As a matter of fact, I am. They had me fill out a little form, pick what I wanted for breakfast. I chose the fruit plate."

“Let us walk you there,” Catherine offered. “Get you all tucked in. In the morning, things will look better.”

She smiled. “They treat you so well, don’t they? Get you hooked. Not on Oxy-Mirac. That’s for the other suckers. They get *us* hooked on the money. The perks. The trips to Hawaii when you shoot past your quota. Do you know what my father made a year? No, of course you don’t. I bet, his best year, he might have made twenty, twenty-five thousand. You know what I pulled in last year? Half a mil. Half a fucking mil. It’s like they shot that money right into my arm. Think I saw our grand pooh-bah go by a minute ago. Should go say thank you.”

Brent and Catherine exchanged worried glances. He said, “I don’t know about you, but I really *could* go for a coffee. Why don’t we—”

Evelyn swayed one last time, fell into Brent’s arms, and passed out.

SIXTEEN

Reece

It was closing in on ten o'clock on the longest day of my life.

Earlier, I'd called Mom to ask whether there was anything she needed after her meeting with McCabe. Help with funeral arrangements? Hire someone to go into the bedroom she'd shared with my father and make it look like nothing had ever happened there? (I'd watched enough TV and read enough Elmore Leonard to know there were businesses that provided such a service.) Or, very simply, be there for her? Did she want to come over and have dinner with Diana and Gage and me?

Before I could get to any of those things, Mom lit into me.

"You should have let me tell him," she said.

"I'm sorry, what?"

"Holden already knew," she said accusingly. "I went to his house to break the news to him, because you can never know how he's going to react to these things, and it was really the kind of thing he should have heard from me and not his brother."

"Mom, I—"

"Never mind. What's done is done." A pause, and then, "Do you know where he is?"

"Home, I guess," I said.

"Well, he's *not* home," she said, like it was my fault.

"Then I have no idea. Has something happened?"

"I was making arrangements to admit him to Sharnwood and he got very upset and took off. He needs to be reassessed and go back into treatment."

"He probably needs us more than a bunch of guys in white coats right now."

"Sharnwood is *not* a psychiatric facility," Mom said defensively. "They don't wear white coats."

"I'm just saying." She was getting under my skin, but considering the circumstances, I didn't want to be short-tempered with her.

"If he shows up at your house let me know immediately."

"Okay, I will. Is there anything else we can do for you? Why don't you come here, we'll have dinner, we can start figuring out—"

"Thank you, Reece," she said icily. "I need to be alone right now. I'm going back to the house, going to gather together what things I can without having to go into . . . you know."

I didn't know how she'd manage that. Anything she might need would be in the bedroom or adjoining bathroom. As if reading my mind, she said, "Or I may just have to buy what I need for now. I'll get a room at the Marriott." And suddenly, she thought of something. "I have to let people know."

"Can I do some of that for you?"

"I'll get in touch with Amelia and Geraldine." Her older sisters. As far as I knew, Mom wasn't all that close to them, but still, she'd have to tell them. "Oh god, and Frank."

My father's older brother, in Vancouver. "You want me to handle that?" I offered.

"Would you?" she asked. She'd never been close with her brother-in-law. My uncle Frank and Dad weren't all that chummy either.

"I'll do it," I said. "If there's anything else you need, call me."

And a few hours later, she did.

I'd just finished breaking the news to my uncle over the phone. Frank had listened quietly while I told him what I knew. He was shocked, saddened, and said that whatever service there was, he wouldn't be able to attend. He was recovering from cancer surgery and undergoing regular chemo treatments. I asked if my father had known he'd been sick. "*No*," Frank had said. He hadn't told him.

"*We haven't really talked in years*," he'd said.

The moment I ended the call, standing in our upstairs hallway after ten o'clock, the phone in my hand rang.

"Did Holden show up?" Mom asked before I'd even said hello.

"I'd have called you if he had."

Diana had poked her head out the bedroom door, and I sensed Gage, in his room with the door open, was listening too.

"He won't take my calls, and I took a taxi by the house again and he wasn't there." The worry in her voice was palpable. I was starting to worry too.

"If he's upset with you," I said, "maybe he'll answer if he sees it's me calling."

"Yes, yes, he might," Mom said forlornly, as though admitting some kind of personal failing.

"I'll try and get right back to you." I ended the call and immediately brought up Holden's number and tapped the screen. I let it ring seven times before giving up. I called Mom back and told her.

"I don't know what to do," she said.

Without even thinking about where I would start, I said, "I'll go looking for him."

"Do you want me to go with you?"

"No. Let me see what I can do. Bye, Mom."

As I slipped the phone into my pocket, Diana said, "You're going out to look for Holden." Not a question. A statement, not without a hint of judgment in it.

I nodded resignedly. "I'll give it a shot."

"Maybe you should just call the police."

I knew what she was thinking. Maybe Holden had overdosed and was in a ditch someplace. Having every Yorkton Hill cop car on the lookout wasn't a bad idea, but I wasn't quite ready to go that far.

"Let's not get ahead of ourselves."

She leaned up against the wall and crossed her arms. I knew this look. "They're dragging you under," she said.

I sighed.

"Your mother, Holden, they're two anchors taking you to the bottom."

"What would you have me do?" I asked.

Her eyes narrowed. "You're already in a bad place. You don't need this."

"Who does? And I'm fine."

I knew what she was referencing with the *bad place* comment. When WorldWide canned me, I went into a pretty deep spiral that lasted a couple of weeks. Lost my appetite, dropped ten pounds, drank a little too much. Took long, solitary walks, so long that Diana and Gage had gone hunting for me. Diana'd urged me to talk to someone but I refused. I'd come out of it, I said, and I did. I just needed some time.

"If they'd been there for *you*," she said, "maybe I'd feel differently."

And I knew what that meant too. I'd never asked my parents for money at the time, but Diana was appalled they didn't at least offer. They knew WorldWide had given me a settlement, but it was only six months' salary. We'd blown through most of that and were now going into our savings. I made excuses for my parents, telling Diana that it wasn't their responsibility to rescue us.

"They've pulled Holden's ass out of the fire—financially and otherwise—more times than I've had my hair done," Diana had countered.

My comeback for that was, Holden didn't have the wherewithal to put out the flames himself. In what was undoubtedly my weakest argument, my parents' failure to come rushing over with a check was an acknowledgment that they knew I'd find my own way forward.

"Horseshit," Diana had said.

Pretty much.

Don't misunderstand. Diana liked my parents—I'd go so far as to say she loved my dad—but this was an issue that was always there under the surface.

So here we were, in the midst of the biggest crisis the extended Chartwell family had ever faced. How was I supposed to walk away from all this now?

Diana must have realized this, too, as she let out a long breath, uncrossed her arms, and closed the distance between us. "I'm sorry," she said and hugged me. Holding on, she said, "I see what it does to you. It sucks the life out of you."

I rested my head on her shoulder. "A little."

She released me. "Go find your brother."

"I know where he is," Gage said, suddenly appearing in the hall.

Christ, how long had he been listening?

"How do you know where he is?" I asked.

Gage held up his phone. "I asked him."

While Gage had been listening to us he'd simply sent his uncle a quick message saying everyone was freaking out because they didn't know where he was. Holden had written back and said he was hanging out at one of the town's Tim Hortons near the garden center Diana and I shopped at every spring. This Tims, one of more than a dozen of the franchised coffee and doughnut places scattered across the town, was open later than most given its proximity to a nearby highway.

I could have called Mom and told her Holden had been located, but then she'd have had twenty questions about his condition. I thought it best to learn that for myself first. Gage insisted on coming with me, since clearly he was the only one Holden trusted. A couple of minutes later the two of us were in the car.

"So your uncle will take a message from you but not me or his mother," I observed.

"I don't judge him like she does," Gage said. "I'm not gonna make him go back to Sharnwood."

"And why didn't he respond to *my* calls?"

Gage shrugged. "Maybe brother relationships are complicated. I wouldn't know. I'm an only child." He offered me a grin.

"Having you was enough," I said, flashing him a grin in return. "You're pretty close to your uncle."

"And you don't like that."

"I didn't say that. You get why we worry."

"There's more to him than having a drug problem. You guys don't see the whole picture. And he's been through an awful lot of bad stuff and people should give him a break. Grandpa would have understood that."

"You just need to be careful, that's all."

"What do you mean?"

"Like say he's got a stash of illegal drugs in his place, stuff you don't even know about, and while you're there the police decide to drop by. Whatever trouble he lands in, you're going to be there right with him."

Gage went quiet, like maybe he hadn't thought about that.

The Tims was up ahead. I saw Holden's car in the lot out front, and as we pulled into a parking spot, I saw him at a table for four on the other side of the glass. There was a woman seated across from him. About forty, thin, big frizzy hair. Otherwise, not counting two people behind the counter, the place was empty. Holden and the woman each had a paper cup of what I guessed was coffee in front of them. I knew Tims outlets did not serve alcohol.

We got out of the car and went inside. Holden, facing our way, spotted us, grinned and waved us in. The woman with Holden turned to check us out.

"Hey," Holden said, getting to his feet and going right by me to give my son a hug. "How's it going, man?"

Gage slipped his arms around his uncle in return. Holden whispered some words of what I supposed were condolences into his ear, then let him go and said to the woman at the table, "Babe, this is my brother, Reece, and this here is my favorite nephew, Gage."

"I'm your *only* nephew," Gage said.

"Heard a lot about you," said the woman to Gage.

Holden clarified things. "And guys, this is my friend, Alicia. Alicia Zane."

She smiled, extended a hand. I shook first, then Gage.

"Park your butts," Holden said, retaking his seat. Gage sat next to Alicia and I settled in next to my brother. They were, in fact, drinking coffee, and on the table was a box of round minidoughnuts in assorted flavors.

"Help yourself," Holden said to Gage.

He needed no further encouragement, digging in and grabbing two, one chocolate, the other coconut.

Holden looked at me. "Want something to drink?"

"I'm good," I said.

"Can I get something?" Gage asked me.

I dug a credit card out of my wallet and handed it over. He dashed to the counter, got some kind of iced coffee with the consistency of a milkshake, returned, and gave me back my card. Holden had looked like he was ready to talk about something but wanted to wait until my son was back in his chair.

Holden said to Alicia, "Might as well tell them, right?"

"Whatever," she said.

I steeled myself. Was Alicia a girlfriend I'd never heard of? And was Holden about to announce an engagement? A pregnancy? Hadn't there been enough surprises for one day?

"Me and Alicia did time together at Sharnwood," he said, grinning, as though his rehab center had been a prison and not a treatment center. "And to be clear, Alicia's *not* one of the counselors. She's a recovering fuckup, too."

Alicia grinned.

"Oh," I said, feigning mild surprise, although Alicia had that weathered look that told me she'd traveled a lot of life's miles in less time than most of us. "Well, it's nice to meet you."

She said, "Likewise. Holden says great things about you." I didn't know whether she was just being polite, or whether it was true. "Good to have someone to talk to who understands firsthand the kind of shit you've had to deal with." She grimaced, turned to Gage next to her. "Sorry."

"Yeah," said Holden. "Watch it. My nephew's never heard that kind of fucking language."

Gage smiled awkwardly and took a sip of his drink through a straw.

"Mom's been kind of frantic," I said. "Couldn't reach you."

"Feel free to tell her I'm alive," Holden said.

"She's been worried how you're handling the news."

Holden grew solemn. "Not well. I'll admit, I went a little nuts this afternoon when she came by. Thought we should take a world cruise, get away from it all, pretend none of this ever happened. I wanted to do something *nice* for her, you know? Show her that, as awful as it is, *she* is still alive. But what does she do? She gets on the phone with Sharnwood, so I beat it. Not going back there. I got Alicia here to keep me straight."

Alicia nodded, reached over, and took Holden's hand in hers.

"And it worked," my brother said. "I know when you came by, I was, you know, dipping my beak into it, but no more. It was a blip. I'm gonna be okay. I don't have to go back to that place."

"Mom'll be relieved."

"Yeah, right," said Alicia.

We all looked at her. Here was this stranger, at least to Gage and me, weighing in with a sarcastic sneer about someone she, so far as I knew, had never met.

"What?" she said. "I'm just going on what Holden's told me."

Holden said, "In our, uh, sessions, we kind of open up about . . . everything. I've said stuff there I've never said anywhere else, and even told Alicia things that didn't come up in group. Guess I've talked about the effect Mom has had on me, how she does her best to make you think she loves you but screws you up at the same time."

It wasn't my place to defend our mother, or side with him. His relationship with Mom had always been different than mine in ways I found hard to articulate. I'd had the feeling Mom's love for Holden was, in some ways, conditional. That it was dependent on emotional capitulation, but what that capitulation entailed was a mystery to me. He was the older brother, although not by much, and maybe the experiments in mothering she'd tried on him were deemed either inadequate, or unnecessary, with me.

"I didn't mean to put my foot in it," Alicia said. "But I feel I've got a pretty good handle on the Holden-Mommy dynamic."

Gage popped another minidoughnut into his mouth, took another sip of his drink.

"It's true," Holden said. "Alicia knows me like nobody else." He winked at me. "Even you." And then a second wink, directed at Gage. I would have to ask him about that later.

"And our group session leader," Alicia reminded him. "Ben? Man, the stuff *he* knows about us."

Holden laughed. "Wonder how *he* sleeps at night."

Alicia grinned. "Bet he wakes up screaming at four in the morning."

I wanted to know more about Alicia. "So, you're from Yorkton Hill?"

She nodded. "Yeah."

"Family's still here?"

Holden stepped in. "She had an older brother, but he died pretty young."

Alicia looked surprised that he'd answered for her. "Yeah," she concurred. "Waterskiing. On Pigeon Lake, near Bobcaygeon? Went right into a channel marker. Big metal buoy thing."

I winced inwardly.

"Her family could be a fucking Greek tragedy," Holden continued. "You lost your parents, what, one after the other?"

She shook her head, as though shedding unpleasant memories. "So, okay, two years before my brother died, when I was seventeen, my mom got cancer and passed and a year later my dad was killed on the 401 around Belleville when some guy fell asleep while driving his semi and plowed into him."

"Geez," I said. "I'm sorry."

"You haven't heard the worst of it," Holden said.

Alicia looked annoyed. "Well, yeah. My aunt stepped up to look after me but she didn't get to do it for very long because she was murdered."

The table went silent. Gage stopped chewing his latest mini-doughnut for a moment before swallowing. I didn't know what to say. I actually could imagine that much tragedy befalling one person. When I was a kid, I'd had an eight-year-old friend whose parents and older sister were all killed in a plane crash. He'd been left with grandparents while his parents flew out west to bring his sister back from college.

The cards some people are dealt.

"I know, right?" Alicia said, grinning at her own tragic history, attempting to lighten the mood. "And they wonder how I ended up in rehab."

What were the right questions to ask when someone told you that? I had at least three. How? Where? And did they catch who did it?

I asked the third one.

She nodded. "Yeah. But there's none of that closure stuff they talk about. It was a long time ago. Even if you never get over it, you have to find a way to pretend you have."

The time for chitchat seemed over. And Gage was making noises with his straw, trying to suck up the last of his drink.

"We should go," I said to Gage.

It struck me that Holden was where he needed to be. Talking to someone else who'd been through some of the same shit he had. And as of today, even more, considering our father had died a violent—if self-inflicted—death.

Gage and I said our goodbyes and headed for home.

"Yikes," said Gage. "She's sure had lots of bad stuff happen to her."

"No kidding," I said. Then I asked, "Was there some kind of secret code going on between you and your uncle?"

"No. What do you mean?"

"When he was talking about secrets, he gave you a wink, like you were in on them too."

"I think he just didn't want me to eat all the doughnuts."

I let it go. Along the way, I had Gage text Diana that we'd be home shortly, that my brother was fine, and then I called Mom to report the same, all things considered. Sober, having a coffee with a friend. She was still worried, but accepted my assessment, and said she would try to get some sleep at the Marriott.

It had been one hell of a day, but by midnight Gage was in his room with the light off and Diana and I were in bed, unsure of what the next day would bring.

I couldn't say whether Holden and Alicia's group session leader woke up screaming in the night.

But a little after three, Gage did.

SEVENTEEN

Janice McCabe wasn't supposed to be working this Saturday, but there were never any guarantees. The detective division was not large—one investigator who'd retired a couple of years ago had not been replaced—and two members of the team were off. Gord Langdon was on a camping trip up in Algonquin Park, where even if there were cell service, he'd have his phone off. If their chief complained later that she'd tried to get in touch, no signal would be his excuse. No fool Gord. And Skyler Marsden was taking the week because her mother had passed away.

So if something happened that required McCabe's talents, odds were she'd get the call. And she was still waiting to hear back from the forensics people to let her know if they'd learned anything of note in the Chartwell case.

Late yesterday she'd spoken to the doctor who ran the clinic where Leah Kennard worked, but he didn't know much about her personal life and wasn't even aware she had a relationship with anyone, let alone Brent Chartwell. Even during their short in-person chat, McCabe got the impression the doctor was somewhat self-consumed and didn't have a clue what his staff members' lives were like, although he was the same doctor who had prescribed the Xanax the detective had found in Leah's medicine cabinet.

"Yes," the doctor said, "she had some issues with anxiety, but nothing particularly alarming. I wouldn't have described her as suicidal."

She also spoke to Billy, the one whose name came up in Leah's texts. She was a cousin in Winnipeg who had a two-year-old boy, and Leah liked to receive pics and video of the toddler whenever Billy thought to send some. Billy said that growing up, she and Leah had been close, and while they stayed in touch, she had few details about Leah's personal life these days. She knew both her parents had died, and that she had no siblings. Billy did know about the guy from the Toyota dealer and was relieved when Leah had told her they were through, but she had no information about Chartwell.

McCabe wanted to still believe this was a straightforward murder-suicide, something she could wrap up and put a bow on in short order. But her conversation with the dead man's wife nagged at her.

Why did Catherine Chartwell ask whether Leah Kennard had a passing resemblance to her? Was it a personal thing? Why does your husband have an affair if the person he's having it with looks a lot like you? Or was it something more serious than that?

Did Catherine Chartwell believe Kennard was mistaken for her?

Brent Chartwell could hardly have misidentified her.

So if Catherine was onto something, it would follow that Brent Chartwell had not shot Leah. There had to have been someone else in that room who'd pulled the trigger on that Beretta.

But then what? Brent is so distressed that he asks the killer for the gun so he can take his own life?

Yeah, that made a lot of sense.

And if some third party shot Brent and set it up to look like a suicide, well, he'd done a damn good job of it.

I'm overthinking this.

McCabe put on a pot of coffee, and when it was ready—she took it black—she sat at the kitchen table with her mug and a banana and read the news on her tablet. She wasn't much of a breakfast person. Caffeine and a piece of fruit were enough most days, even on a weekend, when she had time for something more substantial. Maybe, when Moira materialized, McCabe would actually prepare something. By the time her fourteen-year-old daughter made it down here, it would be closer to lunch, anyway. McCabe could whip up some scrambled eggs, warm up some pancakes. The trendy food shop she frequented sold pancakes that just had to be reheated. Were they as good as homemade? Not even close. Were they easier? Oh yeah. And if toaster pancakes were further evidence of her failures as a mother, so be it.

But she did feel obliged to do something nice for Moira. It had been a rocky week for them, what with McCabe hunting her down on Thursday night, finding her out back of a friend's house, the whiff of pot in the air. McCabe didn't have a huge problem with the stuff—there were cannabis shops all over the place now, even here in Yorkton Hill—but that didn't mean she wanted her daughter smoking it at her age. She didn't want Moira smoking *anything* at her age. Or drinking either.

God, teenagers.

If McCabe's own parents were still alive, they'd be eating this up. Payback time. Looking back, McCabe could see she'd been a handful, done things worse than Moira—taking a bus across the border to Buffalo for two nights with her boyfriend when she was sixteen probably topped the list—so Moira still had plenty of runway ahead of her to outdo her mom when it came to bad behavior. McCabe sometimes believed she became a cop because if she hadn't, she'd have been arrested by one eventually.

It would all be a lot easier if she weren't doing this alone.

Maybe, when you go into a marriage to a man who makes his living as a professional gambler with your eyes wide open, you deserve what you get. The thing was, Ned was one hell of a poker player, and McCabe had thought at the time, hey, it's kind of a sport, right? Some people are better at it than others. It wasn't like buying a lottery ticket or playing a slot machine. It took skill and patience, an understanding of mathematical probabilities. You had to know how to read people, and McCabe, as an investigator, certainly knew a thing or two about tells, about bluffing. She hadn't known, before she met Ned, that there were actually people who did this for a *living*, that it was their *job*, but she started to read up on it and learned it was a real thing.

But in order to make a real go of it, Ned had to travel. He was always heading somewhere for a poker tournament. Vegas, Reno, Atlantic City, Monaco. Sometimes he won, sometimes he lost, but he always came out ahead in the end. The ones who always lost were Janice and Moira.

Eventually, Janice realized she couldn't live like that. *Either get a real job and live with us, or live on the road and don't come back.*

Ned chose Door Number Two.

He sent home money pretty regularly, and once or twice a year he'd show up and be the Hero Dad, but when it came to day-to-day parenting, he was AWOL.

Around ten, she heard a toilet flush upstairs.

Moira shuffled into the kitchen five minutes later, still in her sleeping tee, poured herself some coffee from the pot, and sat at the table, all without saying a word.

"Morning," McCabe said with restrained cheerfulness.

Moira said, "Mmmf."

McCabe didn't have to ask what she'd been up to the night before. After Thursday night's episode, Moira was grounded for the weekend. If she'd been up late, it had been from watching TV or scrolling her phone, texting her friends about the various human rights abuses she was enduring. Maybe she'd been emailing Amnesty International, McCabe thought.

"Pancakes?"

Moira said, "The toaster ones?"

"You have to ask?"

"Two. Lots of syrup."

McCabe got up, put them in the toaster, hovered over the appliance to make sure they didn't burn, slapped them on a plate and drowned them in butter and maple syrup.

"Bon appétit," she said, putting the plate, and a fork, in front of her daughter.

While Moira ate, McCabe asked what she might like to do with her Saturday.

"I dunno."

"Was thinking we could hit the mall. The bra I'm wearing is from the Obama administration and I want to look at some new runners."

"How long am I a prisoner?"

"You're not a prisoner. You're grounded. There's a difference. Prisoners don't get to go to the mall."

"Don't prisoners get field trips?"

"You've been grounded one night, one more to go. Suck it up."

Moira had a bite of pancake. "I'm sorry I didn't let you know where I was."

"Sorry doesn't cut it. I have to know you're not going to do something stupid again." Of course she would, she was barely into her teens, but you liked to give it your best shot.

"Look," McCabe said, "you don't need or want another lecture from me but you were lucky it was me who found you and not someone else from the police who wouldn't be interested in cutting you any slack just because your mom is a colleague. It's illegal for anyone under nineteen to have or use or share pot."

"I wasn't smoking it."

"Wouldn't have made any difference."

"I need a new pair of jeans."

"There you go. We'll leave in an hour."

"Fine," she said.

McCabe's cell, sitting on the table next to her coffee, started to buzz.

"Here we go," Moira said.

McCabe picked up the phone. "Yeah."

"It's Jase."

Jason. When the reports from the forensic science center came in, they landed in Jason's inbox.

"Whatcha got for me?"

"So that Beretta had recently been fired, the slugs in the Kennard woman and Brent Chartwell came from that gun. There was gunshot residue on Chartwell's right hand, and his prints were on the gun."

“Okay.” Slam dunk. Murder-suicide.

“So Chartwell shot the woman, shot himself.”

At the mention of the name Chartwell, Moira glanced at her mother for half a second, then went back to her pancakes. She’d finished off the first and was drowning the remaining one in more syrup. She used the edge of her fork to cut it.

“That would seem to be the conclusion,” Jason said. “No powder burns on the woman, though.”

McCabe thought about that. They’d been in bed together, so close that when Chartwell shot her, one might have expected to find gunshot residue on the victim. But he could have shot her from elsewhere in the room, then got into bed and turned the gun on himself.

Slowly, McCabe said, “I can think how that might have happened. All seems pretty straightforward.”

“Not necessarily.”

McCabe sighed. “Hit me.”

“The gun was not registered to Brent Chartwell or Leah Kennard. Neither held a license to own a firearm. No luck so far tracing it. Maybe it came in from south of the border at some point. Checking records down there, but so far, big fat nothing.”

“Okay.” No surprises there. And in the grand scheme of things, maybe it didn’t matter.

“But there was something,” Jason said. “You sitting down?”

McCabe listened to him tell her the rest of what he’d learned. When he was done, she ended the call, put the phone down slowly, and stared straight ahead, as though looking for something that wasn’t there.

Moira swallowed the last of her second pancake and said, “We’re not going to the mall, are we?”

EIGHTEEN

1999

Ever since that grandiose party at Graham Wiffel's estate, Catherine had been consumed with worry over security issues. Wiffel certainly took it seriously. Had that Crane guy following him everywhere he went, even if he seemed wrong for the part, too ordinary. Someone you'd have a hard time picking out of a crowd.

What troubled Catherine most was her husband's story about that armed man in Ohio. What if that security guard hadn't been there? Brent would have surrendered his sample case, but the man might have shot him anyway. Brent continued to insist it was no big deal, that she was overreacting.

"Never tell a woman she's overreacting," Catherine had said.

What had not troubled Catherine to a great degree were Evelyn Corby's insinuations that Wiffel-Smith was up to no good, deliberately ignoring signs its painkiller was doing more harm than good. All drugs, Catherine rationalized, posed risks if not used responsibly.

Brent hoped installing a home security system would allay his wife's fears. A central monitoring center would be alerted any time, day or night, should someone break into the house once the system was engaged. Sensors on all the doors and windows. Motion detectors inside and out. A keypad just inside the front and back doors, and one up in their bedroom.

Brent showed Catherine how to set the alarm for when she was in the house alone. He went outside and waited for her to do it, then opened the front door. A deafening siren immediately began to whoop. Seconds later, their landline phone was ringing. Catherine ran to answer it while Brent entered in the code to cancel the alarm. Catherine explained they'd opened the door, forgetting the alarm had been set. Provided a password to satisfy the monitoring agent.

"You see?" Brent had said. "You're safe."

But Catherine's anxiety persisted.

One day, she noticed the same car kept driving by the house. She phoned her husband at work.

"It's been by three times now. Going real slow."

"Who's driving?"

"Just some guy. He's the only one in the car. I'm at the window now. Every time he goes by he looks at the house. What should I do? Should I call the police? Oh, he's coming back!"

"What's happening?"

"He's slowing down . . . slowing. He's stopped! He's getting out of the car!"

"Jesus," Brent said. "What's he—"

"Oh," Catherine said. "Never mind."

"What is it? What's happening?"

"He's delivering a pizza, to the Mordens." The people who lived across from them. "You can't see their house number from the street."

That night, clearing the table after dinner in the kitchen, Brent attempted to make light of what had happened. "But what if it hadn't been a pizza delivery?" Catherine asked. "What if it had been someone who wanted to break in?"

"You had the alarm on, didn't you?"

"I don't care. He could kick the door in." She paused, then said, "We should have a gun."

Brent didn't need a second to consider the suggestion. "No."

"And not just one. Two. One for me at home and one for you on the road. If you'd had one with you that night, when that man wanted what was in your briefcase, you wouldn't have needed that security guard."

Brent needed no time to think about this. "No," he said again. "And I can't take a gun with me when I'm flying."

"Can't you check it?"

"Forget it."

"We can at least talk about it."

"I don't need to. I don't want to take one with me and I don't want one in the house. What if one of the boys found it, started playing with it? You know how many people get shot in their own home by accident, or use a gun to commit suicide?"

"We'd have to be careful," Catherine conceded. "I'm not an idiot. But I *am* the one who's left alone when you're out there putting the squeeze on doctors. I'm the one who hears a bump in the night and wonders whether someone's trying to break in."

"That's what the *alarm* is for."

"What if someone snuck into the house before I set it?"

Reece wandered into the kitchen. "What are you guys fighting about?"

"Nothing," Catherine said quickly.

Brent said, "Go watch TV."

Later that week, Catherine came to a decision. She did not need her husband's permission. Her security, her need to feel safe, was her business and no one else's. And if Brent wasn't going to help her with this, she'd find someone who would.

She made a call to the Wiffel-Smith offices, identified herself by name, said she was the spouse of one of the company's top salespeople. If it's possible, she said, she would like to be put through to a man named Crane, whom she had met at Graham Wiffel's party.

"Yes," said the woman on reception, "that would be Dalton Crane. Just one moment please."

A moment later, an extension was answered. "Crane," he said.

She introduced herself. "Mr. Crane, we met, but didn't actually speak, the other evening, when Mr. Wiffel was chatting with my husband. At the party on Georgian Bay."

"I remember," he said. "And please call me Dalton."

"The reason I'm calling, and I hope this doesn't sound silly, but—"

"No, please, there are no silly questions," he said patiently.

"Mr. Wiffel has helped so many people's lives, helped them cope with pain they thought they could never deal with, and that's made him a very popular man, a public figure, and I know that can bring a lot of unexpected, negative attention. For him, and for those who work for him."

"Very true."

"Brent, my husband, he highlighted some of the risks out there for a man like Mr. Wiffel, and even Brent has had people threaten him when he was on the road." Catherine's voice grew shaky. "There was an incident where a man threatened him with a gun outside a clinic. If there hadn't been a security guard there I hate to think what might have happened."

"I remember."

"Brent's installed an alarm system in the house, and I'm grateful for that, I really am, but I don't think it's enough. I want to be able to protect myself."

"Of course," he said understandingly.

"Do you know what I'm getting at?" She was reluctant to say out loud what it was she wanted.

"I believe I do."

Catherine let out a sigh of relief. "I suppose I thought, given your role at the company, you might have some advice where all this is concerned."

"You know what I think, Mrs. Chartwell?"

She waited, almost breathless.

"We should meet to discuss this further," he said. "I hear the concern in your voice."

"That, well, that's very kind, but I don't want to impose."

"Not at all. My Wiffel-Smith safety and security responsibilities are not limited to Mr. Wiffel. My purview includes staff and their families when it is deemed necessary."

"That's comforting." And not just his words, she thought. It was how he said them, as though his concern for her welfare was genuine.

"How would tomorrow morning work? I can come by your house."

"That . . . that would be perfect. Around ten?"

"Excellent. Until tomorrow then, Mrs. Chartwell."

"Catherine. Please call me Catherine."

***

Crane showed up at ten sharp in a silver Infiniti sedan and suggested they go somewhere for a drink. A little early, he conceded, for a cocktail or anything along those lines, but maybe a coffee in a private setting? He was a member of the golf and country club about halfway between Yorkton Hill and Toronto, about a twenty-minute drive.

"Sure," she said. "We've been there a couple of times. For weddings."

The club had an outdoor patio that overlooked the eighteenth hole. They took over a small table, under the shade of a broad umbrella, and Catherine apologized for taking Crane away from his work as a uniformed staff member brought a latte for her and an espresso for him.

"This is part of my job," he said, looking at her through his thick-rimmed glasses. "Making sure Wiffel-Smith employees, and their families, feel safe and secure."

She realized, fairly quickly, that her initial impression of him had been hasty. Maybe it had been the glasses that made her think of him as a nerd back when she'd met him at the party. But he was not *un*handsome. Strong cheekbones, broad shoulders. His hair was thinning but he'd made no pathetic attempts to grow it long at the sides and do a combover. And sure, he wasn't six feet tall, but then, Tom Cruise wasn't either. What really won her over was his mix of charm and confidence. He carried himself well.

Catherine found herself wanting to know more about him. "Are you married? Children?"

He smiled. "Very briefly. Long ago. Just long enough to

have a daughter. Agatha." He smiled as he said her name. "But I rarely see her. She lives with her mother. It's all just as well. The company expects a hundred and ten percent from me. I'm afraid I'd be a very neglectful husband and father."

"How long have you been working for Mr. Wiffel?"

"Thirteen years. It's been quite a ride. The company was immensely successful when I joined, but since then the growth has been exponential." Another smile. "Everyone's done very well. Yourselves included. Mr. Wiffel holds your husband in high regard."

"He's been very good to us. Brent works so hard, he's so committed. He's a real believer in making people's lives better." She paused. "But success sometimes has its . . . I don't want to say dark side. But it can come with complications."

"My father used to say, you increase your comforts, you increase your cares. Not that he had many. Comforts, that is. He was a worker bee."

"I'm sorry?"

"A cog in the machine. Worked for a huge accounting firm. Midlevel position, a modest salary. A good father, but we weren't exactly vacationing in Paris every year. Lost him, and my mother, long ago."

Catherine cleared her throat, working up to something. "Brent intimated, at the party, that you were probably carrying a gun."

Crane took a sip of his espresso. "I like to be discreet about such things."

"Of course, I'm sorry."

"It's quite all right. Brent was correct."

"You feel you need one."

A slow nod. "I do. Things can happen very quickly. One needs to be ready."

"I want one," she said.

Crane said nothing.

"But I haven't the first idea of how to go about it. I mean, I know there are places where you can go and buy one, but then aren't there background checks and waiting periods? And I'd much rather keep this from Brent, if you can understand that. He's adamantly opposed to the idea."

"He's a wise man," Crane said. "A gun is a very dangerous thing to have around."

"I know, but—"

"But your feelings need to be considered as well." The corner of his mouth went up a notch. "And spouses are entitled to have some secrets from each other."

Catherine felt she was getting somewhere. "So how would I go about it, if I have those kinds of concerns?"

"Well," Crane said, picking up a napkin and dabbing the corner of his mouth, "why don't you leave that with me? But first, have you ever handled a firearm before?"

"No."

"Well, it would not be wise for you to acquire one without some basic instruction in that area. It's not as simple as pulling a trigger, no matter how easy it might look on TV."

"Can you recommend someone who could give me those basics?"

Crane smiled. "I believe so."

NINETEEN

Reece

At breakfast, I asked Gage if he remembered what his nightmare had been about.

"No," he said, breezing through only long enough to grab a banana. "I didn't even know I was screaming."

He'd woken Diana and me up. She'd been out of bed first, running down the hall to Gage's room. I was four steps behind her. She flipped a switch in the hallway that allowed some light to bleed into the bedroom without hitting an overhead fixture.

And it wasn't exactly *screaming*. Gage was shouting "No! No! No! No!" in his sleep.

He was thrashing about under his covers when we came into the room. Diana perched herself on the edge of the bed and gently rubbed Gage's arm as she said, "Wake up, honey, wake up. Wake up."

Gage opened his eyes, looked puzzledly at the two of us. "What?"

"You were having a nightmare," I said.

He blinked a couple of times, said "It's okay, I'm fine," put his head on the pillow, and went back to sleep. Diana and

I staggered back to our room and spent much of the rest of the night awake.

Staring at the ceiling, she said, "I guess it's normal."

I agreed. We'd all been traumatized. The shock of what had happened the day before was not going to fade from memory any time soon, and I believed it was as hard on Gage to lose a grandfather as it was on me to lose a dad.

Maybe harder.

And that got me questioning why I wasn't feeling worse about this. I was shocked, for sure. The circumstances of Dad's death had left me numb, confused, searching for answers, but his passing had yet to hit me on an emotional level.

There were times when I'd thought Gage's relationship with Dad was closer than mine. Maybe closer is the wrong word. It was different. The dynamic between a man and his grandson is not the same as between a man and his son. When I was a boy, my father was consumed with making a living. The pressures on him were different than they were in his retirement. He had more time for Gage than he had for me. And Gage wasn't expected to live up to my father's expectations, which I was sure I had not met. And grandfathers didn't have the same responsibility for guiding or disciplining a young man. That was a father's job.

Of course, Dad wasn't so thrilled about the circumstances of Gage's birth. I got Diana pregnant before we were out of college. That really made my father's day. (My mom's too.) Any hopes he'd had that I might pursue future degrees, in commerce or business if he'd had his way, were dashed. The truth was, Diana's pregnancy was something of a blessing, and not just because Gage was the result. The worlds of sales and business didn't interest me, and while I did give real estate a shot at one point, I wasn't sorry it hadn't become my career. I liked to write and found an outlet for that talent in the news business, first in radio and newspapers, and then in TV news. It was a satisfying, if not hugely lucrative, career, right up until the time I got downsized. I was never a Wiffel-Smith salesperson of the year like my father, and I was fine with that.

Diana and Gage and I had what I thought was a good, if unremarkable, life. Diana's red-light ticketing job wasn't her life's dream, but it was a paycheck. She'd once had ambitions of becoming an artist, and her Georgian Bay landscapes reminded me of works by Canada's famous Group of Seven. But that may have led some galleries to judge them as derivative, unoriginal, and few had any interest in featuring her work.

If Gage hadn't come along, she might have developed that talent, taken it in a different direction by attending a prestigious Toronto university that focused exclusively on art. But it wasn't to be. Reality had a way, sometimes, of crushing ambition.

She still got out her easel and brushes occasionally, setting up in a corner of the kitchen where the light was good, but I couldn't actually remember the last time she'd done it.

I guess what I'm saying here is, we just went along, day to day, like most people do, living our lives. And then out of the blue, you hit one of those proverbial bumps in the road that feels more like driving off a cliff.

And what of the Kennards? How was the family of Leah Kennard coping with all this? My thoughts hadn't turned to them without prodding.

It was Diana who asked, "This woman that your father . . . What do we know about her? Was she married? Did she have children? Has her family been notified? Are they local?"

I felt a sharp pang of guilt that I'd given so little consideration to the others struck by this tragedy.

"I don't know," I said. "I . . . the detective didn't have much information about her, or if she did, didn't share it with me."

"Did your mother know her?"

"I don't think so."

"Don't you think you should know more about all this?" Diana asked.

"Last night I got the impression you thought I was letting myself get sucked in. Now you want me to stick my nose into it?"

Diana put down her coffee and leaned in over the table. "Reece," she said, using my actual name, a sign she had something serious to say, "your father killed a woman. It's not our fault it happened, but it doesn't mean there might not be some blowback. Like, I don't know, maybe her family launches a lawsuit. Or the negative publicity from this affects my work, your chances at finding a new job. What if Leah Kennard had relatives who go to Gage's school?"

"None of those things are going to happen."

She nodded. "I hope you're right. All I'm saying is, your mother can be wrapped up tight. You need to pry as much information out of her as you can."

Diana sat back, ran her finger across the screen of her iPad, and said, "I rest my case."

"What?"

"It's out there."

One of the Toronto papers had a story. A short piece, quoting police about being called to a home where two people were found fatally shot. There were names, ages, a line that police did not believe there was any further threat to the neighborhood, code for a domestic.

Diana did more searching and found a one-minute news clip on CP24. I'd seen their van at the scene. And something on World-Wide's website, again not surprising, since their team had been there too. Their item had something a little extra. The reporter said the male deceased was the father of a former WorldWide news writer, although I was not named.

"Jesus," I said. "What does that have to do with anything?"

Diana said nothing. She didn't have to.

It was time to go see my mother.

I headed over to the Marriott in the BMW. I considered calling first but figured Mom would tell me not to bother, and I didn't want to have that argument. Better to show up. And if she wasn't there, I'd see if she'd gone back to the house.

The Marriott lot wasn't even half full. I found a parking spot not far from the main entrance and headed inside. Once I was in the lobby, and had checked the dining room to see whether she was there, I called her.

She picked up on the third ring.

"Yes?"

It was just one word, but she sounded rattled.

"I'm at the hotel," I said. "You here?"

"Um, yes," she said.

"I'm in the lobby. Gonna get a coffee in the dining room if you'd like to join me."

"Why are you here?"

"Gee, I don't know. Because I'm your son? And I want to help?"

I could hear background noise, which at first I thought must be a TV, but it sounded more like traffic. The distant rumble of a truck.

"I'll be there in a minute," she said.

On my way into the dining room, I happened to glance out the lobby windows to the parking lot and learned why I'd heard traffic on her end.

She was standing at the back end of a black Mercedes, talking to someone I did not recognize. A man, maybe an inch or two taller than Mom, dark suit and tie, thick-rimmed glasses, thinning hair. Early sixties, I was betting. A lawyer, maybe?

Even a mundane death presented numerous legal challenges. A will to probate, and estate to be distributed. But as Diana had pointed out, a complicated case like this? Legal headaches could abound.

Either way, why was this meeting in a parking lot? Why had she let me believe she was still in her room?

I watched for a moment. Mom was gesticulating, as if trying to make a point more emphatically, the man shaking his head. Even from my vantage point, he did not look happy to be having this conversation.

I went into the dining room, declined the waitress's offer to check out the buffet or pick something off the menu, and just asked for coffee.

Five minutes later, Mom entered the room. I pushed back my chair, got to my feet, and put my arms around her when she reached the table. She returned the hug.

I said, "You're shaking."

"I'm okay," she said, but I could see that she wasn't. "Have you ordered?"

"Coffee. Have you had breakfast?"

"I'm not hungry."

The waitress returned with my coffee and Mom ordered a tea.

I got right to it. "Who was that guy you were talking to?"

Her eyes widened. "What guy?"

"In the parking lot."

"You're spying on me now?"

"I didn't need binoculars. You were right out there in the open."

"Your father was running around on me behind my back and now you've got me under surveillance. What I do and who I see is none of your business." She looked around the room, hoping to spot the waitress. "I need a muffin."

I raised my hand, caught a waiter's attention. He hustled over. "My mother would like a muffin."

He flashed her a smile and listed their muffin offerings.

"Surprise me," she said. "Just not bran."

And off he went.

I said, as gently as I could, "Mom, I get that what's happened is still sinking in, that it doesn't seem real, but there are things we need to get into the open. If there's things going on I don't know about, this would be a good time to tell me. You could start by telling me who that man was, what you were talking about. It looked serious."

She slowly turned her head to face me and said, "An old friend."

"An old friend," I repeated. "He have a name?"

Her face suddenly lit up in alarm, and I braced myself to hear whatever it was she clearly didn't want to tell me. "Did he say carrot? I don't want a carrot muffin. He better not bring me one of those."

TWENTY

McCabe double-checked that she was parked in front of the right house. She was expecting something different.

Her recollection of Yorkton Hill Police Detective Giles Maitland, before he took his retirement, was that he was a meticulous, detail-oriented cop. His yard said otherwise. What parts of the lawn weren't overtaken by weeds didn't look as though they'd been mowed in weeks. The disintegrating webbing on the folding lawn chair by the front door didn't look safe to sit in. There was mail sticking out of the box, suggesting it hadn't been brought in for a few days.

She hoped he wasn't dead, and not just because that would be a terrible thing. She really wanted to talk to him.

McCabe went up to the front door and rang the bell. When she didn't hear a chime, she figured it wasn't operational, so she tried knocking. Rapped on the door a couple of times, waited, then rapped again.

"Hold your horses!" someone inside shouted.

Seconds later, the door opened a foot. McCabe recognized Maitland, but he had seen better days. He was heavier than the man she remembered seeing around the station. And he wasn't in a suit and tie anymore either. He was wearing gray sweatpants and a black pullover shirt and was peering at her through a pair of grimy reading glasses.

"Yeah?" he said.

She showed her badge. "Janice McCabe," she said. "I think we ran into each other occasionally back in the day."

He squinted. "I remember you. But you hadn't made detective."

"No, sir. I was still in uniform."

"What can I do for you?"

"I'd like to talk to you about a case you worked on."

"Oh yeah? What case is that?"

"May I come in?"

He opened the door wide and stepped back. McCabe noticed a foul smell she couldn't quite identify. Cabbage? Dirty socks? Spoiled milk? A blend of the three?

Maitland led her into the living room, cleared some newspapers off the couch so she could sit. Before he dropped into a recliner, he asked if he could get her something. A coffee? Soft drink?

"I'd offer you a beer but you're on the clock."

"I'm good," she said. "So, how long's it been since you retired?"

"Seven years," he said.

"Seems to suit you," she said, actually wondering to herself what she meant by that. It just seemed like the right thing to say. "I heard your wife had passed away. My condolences."

"Chandra, yeah, four years ago," Maitland said, nodding toward a picture on the mantel of the two of them. "So what's this case?"

"I've been reading up on it in just the last few hours. There may be a connection between something you investigated and an incident here in town yesterday. A murder-suicide. Maybe you saw something about it on the news?"

He shook his head. "Don't watch the news much. Still get the paper, though. Gets thinner every day."

"This was an open-unsolved back in ninety-nine. Woman in her midthirties, shot, body dumped at the side of the road north of—"

Maitland raised a finger. "When was this again?"

"Ninety-nine."

"Right, okay, go ahead."

"The case you were investigating was of a woman who'd been found in a ditch at the side of the road. Thirty-six years old, about five five, white, blondish hair. She'd been shot in the back. Like she was running away at the time."

His eyes closed briefly. "That's starting to come back to me. This was on the road that went up past the drive-in, before they went out of business, tore it down. Her clothes were in disarray, pants pulled down, blouse ripped open, as though sexually assaulted, but no evidence of rape. Yeah, I remember wondering whether it had been staged, but that was only a feeling."

"Yeah."

"There was alcohol in her system. We thought maybe she'd met someone in a bar, got in a car, things went bad."

"You've got a good memory."

Maitland sighed. "Some you don't forget. The ones you never solve, they kind of haunt you."

"You one of those detectives, when he retires, he takes all these files home with him, the open cases he had over the years, figures he can still solve them?"

"Like in a Michael Connelly novel or something?" Maitland said. He shook his head. "When I quit, I quit. I didn't want to pretend I was still on the job. Won't lie, though. Thought about it."

He closed his eyes again, thinking back. "We found her car. A little sports car. Convertible. It was parked down the road a few miles from a bar. Trying to remember which one."

"The files say it was the Village Idiot."

"Right. So we spent a lot of time interviewing men who were there that night. Checking credit card receipts. No one could remember seeing her come inside, but we thought someone might have had a run-in with her before she took a seat. We brought one guy in for questioning."

"Rufus Block?"

"Yeah, right. I'm not good remembering names, but I remember that one. Rufus Block. He frequented the Idiot—I couldn't have imagined him going anyplace else—and he had a sheet. A sexual assault conviction from a few years earlier. Not a rape, but a groping, and his excuse was that he was drunk, didn't know what he was doing. A couple of minor assaults, getting into it with other dim bulbs who'd had too much to drink. He'd been at the bar that night, left around ten. But he had a girlfriend who lived with him, said he got home around half past ten, and we couldn't break down the alibi. No physical evidence to tie him to the victim or the scene or her car. And no physical evidence putting her in his truck."

"There's something in the report about a gun."

"He owned one. We got warrants to search his truck, his home, even where he worked, which was . . . help me out here."

"The Toyota dealer," McCabe said, adding, "curiously enough."

"That's right. He was a mechanic there. Still could be, for all I know. We did find a weapon at his home, seized it, tested it, but it wasn't the gun used to kill the woman. So, there wasn't enough there to go to the Crown attorney with. And my gut was telling me at the time that it wasn't him. Why'd you twig to the Toyota dealer?"

"Had a word with someone there yesterday in relation to something else, but not the same guy."

Maitland slowly shook his head. "We had theories. Maybe her car had broken down and someone stopped, like they were going to help her but had other ideas. But the car was mechanically sound, not even a flat tire. Doesn't mean she couldn't have been standing by it, someone came along, asking if everything was okay. But here's the thing. I don't think she was killed there. I'd always thought she was killed someplace else and her body dumped there, that maybe someone moved the car too. There was some mud on her face that didn't match anything in the area where she was found."

He thought of something else. "There was a packed overnight bag in the car. Had the trunk in the front, bag was in there. No idea where she was going, though." He smiled to himself. "Can't believe how much of this I remember. Everything except the poor woman's name."

"Evelyn Corby."

Maitland snapped his fingers. "That's it. I think she worked in pharmaceutical sales. That company with the funny name."

"Wiffel-Smith."

"Bingo. Yeah."

"Anyone you were interested in that didn't make the report? You know, you get a feeling about someone but there's not enough to justify writing it down?"

"No. No husband, no boyfriend. A couple of women in her past. We interviewed a niece who was staying with her."

"Yeah, I saw her name in the file."

"And Corby had a nephew who overdosed on that drug Wiffel-Smith got in so much trouble for, eating it like buttered popcorn. Once it all came out, the company paid millions in fines, settled with thousands of families for millions more. Had their names erased from various museums and foundations. Got all those people addicted so they could buy their yachts and mansions and trips to the French Riviera and not one of them served a single day in jail."

"Maybe Wiffel himself might have, if he hadn't taken a header off the top of his corporate headquarters."

Maitland sighed. "Coward's way out, killing himself. Point is, you got enough money, you can buy your way out of anything. Even mass murder, because, let's face it, that's what it was. Anyway, nobody we talked to knew if Corby was planning to go anywhere. All there was, was a note on the kitchen table saying she'd be back in a couple of days."

"Did you ever talk to a Brent Chartwell?" she asked. "He ever come to your attention?"

"Chartwell?"

"Yeah. At the time, he'd have been early forties."

"I don't think so. Name doesn't ring any bells. Who is he?"

"He *was* a retired business consultant but back around the time Corby was murdered he also worked in pharmaceutical sales for Wiffel-Smith."

Maitland's eyes narrowed. "I'm pretty sure I never talked to him. Should I have?"

"I don't know. But yesterday Chartwell shot a woman who was not his wife, a woman by the name of Leah Kennard, in his bed then turned the gun on himself. And here's the kicker. The slugs from both of them matched the one taken from Evelyn Corby more than two decades ago."

Maitland thought about that for a moment. Finally, he said, "I guess we should have talked to him."

McCabe smiled. "No one's second-guessing."

"You're lucky they were able to make the match. Late nineties was when all that evidence started being stored on the computer. I do recall talking to her employers. Went to the corporate office, in the northwest part of Toronto, near the airport. The Wiffel guy." He nodded, remembering. "He was shook up, said she was one of his top salespeople."

"Talk to any of her colleagues?"

"Just those who were at the HQ at the time, not anyone who might have been on the road. I suppose it's possible I talked to this Chartwell guy and don't remember."

"This murder-suicide looked like something I thought I could put down in a hurry, but it opens the door to something in the past."

"Too bad Chartwell shot himself. If he's your guy, be nice to get a confession out of him. Might have wanted to get this off his chest after all this time."

"There's still his wife. She might know something. I'll have another chat with her."

TWENTY-ONE

1999

Catherine was not a great shooter. But she wasn't half bad either.

Dalton Crane belonged to a gun club that had its own indoor firing range where police officers trained, and once he had procured a firearm for Catherine, he took her there to teach her how to use it.

She enjoyed the instruction, in no small part because of the way Crane would wrap his hands around hers, teaching her the fine points of how to hold, point, and fire. In the early lessons, he used his own gun for the exercises.

"You don't just pull the trigger like you're flicking a wall switch." She could barely hear him through the heavy-duty, soundproofing headphones. "You squeeze it, very deliberately. Slowly. Okay, you try it."

At the end of the firing lane was a paper target hanging from a clip. Once she had fired off several rounds, the paper would be brought forward on a kind of mechanical clothesline and she could see how well she'd done. Her early attempts were as one might have expected.

"I fired six shots, didn't I? But there are only two holes in the paper."

"Yeah, well, those other four bullets went on vacation," Crane said.

Their third lesson, he presented her with her own gun to practice with. She was delighted, but wary.

"There's no record, is there? The police aren't going to come to my door asking to see a license?"

"No."

"Because if they do, Brent will know I have this."

"The only way your husband will learn you have this is if you leave it someplace where he can find it."

She snorted. "In that case, I'll leave it in the washing machine."

Jokes aside, Crane said she needed to keep it someplace where it was easy to get in a hurry. Burglars didn't wait while homeowners went to fetch their firearm.

"What do you suggest?"

He shrugged. "Maybe someplace you keep your own personal items."

"Lingerie drawer," she said quickly, the first thing that occurred to her.

The corner of his mouth curled up. "If I were your husband, I might be in there on occasion, perhaps offering a consult on what you could wear on our next assignation."

Catherine blinked. Now there was a word you didn't hear every day. And the way he had delivered it, there was some kind of subtext there.

This hadn't been the first time she felt there was something going on. Crane had been more attentive, more helpful than she might have expected when it came to getting a handgun. And she had been curious about how he had come to acquire it.

"Sometimes things have a way of falling into one's hands. Passed under the table, so to speak. There are instances when it's preferable to avoid a lot of paperwork, to eschew recordkeeping."

This guy, he was better than a thesaurus.

The dodgy nature of how Crane had come into possession of this weapon—a Beretta, he called it—somehow excited Catherine. Someone breaking the rules for her made her feel special, like she was operating outside societal norms.

"You'll need some extra practice," he said. "This particular gun, it's not as heavy as some, which makes it a good gun for a woman, and the trigger is a bit lighter, so it doesn't have to be squeezed as hard. It's had some modifications, like the safety has been pretty much disabled. So you don't want to pick this up and aim it at anything unless you intend to use it. It reacts very quickly. You need to learn the feel of it."

He put some emphasis on *feel*.

"We'll try it at the range, and if you find it's not quite right for you I'll see if I can find something more to your liking."

"I'm sure it will be perfect," she said. "And let's hope I never have occasion to use it. But I feel better just knowing it's available."

During their times together, she would ask him about what it was like to work for Graham Wiffel.

"Interesting. Being in his employ facilitates opportunities for travel to places I might not otherwise frequent. I think I've been to almost all fifty states and ten provinces."

"So you're not just some bodyguard for Mr. Wiffel, are you? You're more than that."

"Yes."

"Are you what they call a fixer?"

"A fixer?"

"Someone who, you know, fixes problems. Puts out fires."

Crane smiled. "I suppose I am. I fix things. Wiffel-Smith has many people who fix things. Lawyers, lobbyists, publicists."

"But if it's not a problem for one of them, that's where you come in."

"Yes. I do my best to make sure there are no waves on Mr. Wiffel's pond."

Pond, Catherine thought. She didn't like any on hers either.

She prodded him for examples of problems that needed fixing. It wasn't until they'd been to the firing range a few times before he felt more at ease talking about it.

"Some problems can be solved with a carrot. Others, a stick. Wherever possible, I prefer the carrot. For example, there was an FDA official whose approval we needed on a groundbreaking medication—not Oxy-Mirac, this was before then—and she was being particularly nitpicky. We praised her to the hilt, told her we valued her opinion so much, we would like her to work for us. Specifically in our Seattle research wing, where her family was from, and would she consider joining us at a salary twice what the federal government was paying her? She accepted our offer, and as one of her last acts at the FDA, she approved our drug."

"A carrot."

"A carrot."

"What about the stick?"

"There was a doctor in Memphis. With certain inducements, he started prescribing Oxy-Mirac for his patients dealing with pain issues. But we learned that many of the scrips he was writing were for fictitious patients. He hoarded supply, then resold the medication on the black market at a considerable profit. Mind you, even bogus scrips make Wiffel-Smith money, but we suspected he was being watched by the police, and his antics would reflect badly on us. I paid him a visit."

Catherine waited.

"I had a very serious conversation with him. I believed that, as a doctor, he would understand the negative health effects of having Drāno poured down one's throat."

Catherine felt a chill.

"I thought that prospect would prove persuasive, but our good doctor found making money on the side as addictive as some allege our Oxy-Mirac to be. The police, I became more convinced, were getting ready to pounce. The publicity from an arrest would have reinforced negative perceptions that our groundbreaking medication was attracting the attention of the illegal drug trade."

"You paid him another visit."

He weighed how much more to say. "Our doctor was an avid fisherman. Liked to get away on weekends, by himself. Had a small aluminum boat he would take out. In a little boat like that, a person can lose their balance fairly easily. And you'd be surprised how few people like to wear a lifejacket." He paused, then added. "A real tragedy. Very sad."

Catherine had a question she could not bear to utter.

He flashed a smile. "Anyway, I enjoy what I do."

For the first time, she felt frightened of this man named Crane. And something else. What was it? *Enamored.* That was it. Just the kind of word he might use.

Tamp those feelings down, she told herself. She had the gun. He'd taught her how to use it. There was no reason to see him again.

"Another lesson next week?" he asked as he pulled up in front of her house.

"Okay," she said.

That was the one she should have taken a pass on.

After, he invited her back to his place. He lived in a sprawling waterfront, tenth-floor Toronto condo. A stunning view of Lake Ontario and the airport on a cluster of small islands just off the city's shoreline.

A celebration, he said, of her progress.

"Wow," Catherine said upon entering his place. Exposed beams and ductwork, brick walls adorned with massive abstract paintings. It was basically one huge room, except for an enclosed bathroom. Kitchen area flowing into the living space, which in turn expanded into the bedroom area.

She wandered the apartment, spotted a framed photo of a girl, probably about eight or nine years old. Catherine held it up.

"Your daughter?"

"Yes."

"She's beautiful."

Crane smiled, but it struck Catherine as sad. Wandering farther, she ran her finger along the spines of some shelved books. Multiple encyclopedia sets. *Brittanica, Funk & Wagnalls, World Book*. Sets by publishers Catherine had never heard of. Some in foreign languages. All neatly arranged and in alphabetical order.

"It's like a college library," she said. "I've never seen so many reference books."

"I like to know things," Crane said, opening the stainless steel door to one of two large refrigerators. He brought out a bottle of Veuve Clicquot and went to work twisting out the cork.

"You don't have any fiction," she said, still checking out the shelves. "No novels. Not one."

He filled two champagne flutes and approached. "I don't care about things that are made up," he said.

She took her flute by the stem as he handed it to her. Tapped his glass to hers. "To my star pupil."

She took no time emptying her glass and allowed him to refill it. Crane suggested a softer seat and steered her to an L-shaped sectional. They went into the corner, Crane at one angle, Catherine at the other, their knees touching, within sight of the king-size bed not twenty feet away.

Wordlessly, Crane put his flute on the coffee table, pried Catherine's gently from her fingers and placed it next to his, then leaned in and put his mouth on hers. She responded tentatively at first, unsure how enthusiastic to seem. She had to know this was coming, and if she didn't want it to happen, why had she accepted the invitation to come up here?

Because, she told herself, some part of her wanted to step outside her life, to walk that emotional tightrope, but now that the moment had arrived, now that he was pushing her down onto the couch, she wasn't sure.

But could you say no to a man like Dalton Crane? He hadn't fully revealed himself to her, but there were plenty of hints. He was more than a fixer.

He was a killer.

Not some crazed psycho killer. A methodical, thoughtful, pragmatic killer. She wasn't sure whether that made him less, or more, scary.

And yet, the word came out, albeit in a whisper: "No."

She put a palm on his chest and pushed back. Not hard, just enough to send a message. But there was his hand, sliding up the inside of her leg.

A more forceful rejection was going to be necessary. "No," she whispered. "No, I can't. I can't do this."

The hand stopped its ascent but was not removed.

"Yes, you can," he said softly. "We're good together. We can take it slow. That's okay. Slow's good. Slow can be fun. I can be very, very slow."

"You killed that doctor," she blurted.

The hand came away. He sat back.

"I can't stop thinking about it," she said. "I don't . . . I thought this, all of this, I was liking where it was going, but . . ."

"You're afraid of me," he said.

She nodded. "A little."

A sly smile. "Do I look dangerous to you?"

Catherine blinked. "What?"

"I mean, look at me. I'm borderline nebbish. No one's going to mistake me for Clint Eastwood. You clearly have an inflated sense of my capabilities."

"It's . . . what makes you good at what you do," she said. "You blend in. You don't look . . . intimidating. That's how you catch people off guard. They think you're a pushover, and then you're making them drink drain cleaner."

He slowly shook his head. "Catherine. That doctor, he really did have an accident when he went fishing. There was an investigation. Things just happened to go our way, that's all. Sometimes it happens."

Catherine was willing to accept the lie. But there was more she had to say.

"I love my husband," she said.

"A fine man."

"I appreciate everything you've done for me, I do, but I can't . . . I want you to know I'm grateful but—"

"Let me drive you home."

"I know how it would go," she said, thinking out loud more than telling him. "It's . . . it's fun at first, but then, eventually, somehow, Brent finds out. The boys do too. And I lose everything. Not just my family, but my life."

"Catherine—"

"I *like* my life. I *like* the life Brent has made for us. We have a beautiful home. We go to Europe every other year. We can have whatever we want." She paused, then said, "I grew up in a trailer. A *trailer.* Not even a double-wide, just a sixty-foot-long trailer that was like living on a train. My father was a high school janitor. My mother took in laundry. Somehow they scraped enough money together to send me to university, where I met Brent. He took me away from that, and I will not go back. This . . . this could be fun, but it would be the beginning of the unraveling."

Crane listened.

"I'm . . . I'm flattered. And thank you for teaching me . . . I can still have the gun?"

He smiled. "Of course. Just promise me you'll be careful with it."

"Cross my heart and hope to die," she said.

TWENTY-TWO

Reece

Once Mom got over being pissed with me for asking who the man she'd been talking to in the parking lot was, she agreed to let me help her with something.

She'd heard from Detective McCabe that the autopsy on Dad had been completed, and his remains picked up by Heffernan & Sons Funeral Home. I'd called them on Mom's behalf, and they invited us to come over within the hour.

Heffernan's was Yorkton Hill's oldest funeral home, coming up on its hundredth anniversary. A family business, it had started out as Heffernan's Undertakers, and as the years went on, Undertakers was replaced with Funeral Home and the Sons were added. I wondered what it was like to be in that family, to feel that weight of expectation on you, to know that every day you would be dealing with grieving families and dead bodies and embalming fluid. But hey, as Daffy Duck used to say, *It's a living.*

Grant Heffernan, slim, good-looking, early thirties, in a black suit, white shirt, and, jarringly, a fuchsia tie, met us at the door. He led us to a small conference room with a long wooden table and heavy chairs with burgundy cushions. Mom was suitably somber through the paperwork, filling out various forms, signing her name where Grant indicated. He would have known the details of my father's death, and while discreet enough not to mention them, there was the issue of a closed casket. Despite their reputation for making their subjects presentable, even Heffernan's might struggle with my father.

Mom opted for no casket. Cremation.

"And I don't want a big service," Mom said. "Immediate family only . . . if they choose to come."

Making me wonder whether Mom was considering her own attendance.

Grant asked if we wanted to bring in some clothes for the deceased.

"Uh," I said delicately, "if there's no open casket, and my father is cremated, what is the point of . . ."

"I understand. Your father could be in simple robe or nothing at—"

"He'll wear a suit," Mom said. "Anything less is undignified."

"Of course," Grant said.

"The thing is," I said, "the suit would be in the closet of the room where—"

"After we're done here," Mom said, "we'll go to the house and get the clothes."

If that wasn't enough of a surprise, she added, "I want to see him."

Gently, Grant said, "Totally within your rights, Mrs. Chartwell. But I would caution you that—"

Her jaw was firmly set. "You are correct, it is my right, and I choose to exercise it."

Grant nodded. "Give me a few minutes."

He was back in fifteen and led us one floor down to a small, carpeted, and darkly wallpapered room. A body lay on a table before us, covered in a dark sheet from head to toe.

"Keep in mind that we have only just received the remains," he said, standing by the head, his fingers on the corner of the sheet. Mom's nod of understanding was also an instruction to proceed.

I didn't want to look. I would not have asked to come down here. But I felt that if Mom was going to do it, I had to as well.

Grant drew back the sheet, exposing my father down to his shoulders. I heard a sharp intake of breath from Mom. I could only look for a second. The room started to spin. Mom lasted four seconds longer than I did, then turned away. Grant dropped the sheet back into place.

"Thank you," Mom said.

I slipped an arm around her, felt her trembling, and led her out of the room into a hallway. Grant invited us to rejoin him upstairs when we were ready.

My stoic, resilient, rebuffer of condolences mother buried her face in my chest and began to sob.

"Oh god," she muttered into me. "Oh god oh god."

I wrapped my arms around her, not knowing what to say. I didn't think there was anything I *could* say.

Her lips pressed to my sport jacket, she said four garbled words that, as best as I could tell, were, "What have I done?"

Considering what had happened at the house only a day earlier, it felt stunningly ordinary. No police cars, no yellow tape around the property's perimeter. We parked in the driveway and got out. I had my own key out before Mom had hers, so I opened the front door. I thought it best if I went in first, in case there was some surprise awaiting us. I couldn't imagine what it would be—more bodies?—but everything looked normal.

She followed me inside and went straight to the kitchen.

"Look at this mess," she said.

Nothing had been cleaned up in here since the morning before. There were a couple of cups, some cutlery and a dish in one of the double sinks, coffee still in the pot, a small container of cream on the counter.

Mom picked up that last item, gave it a sniff, then poured its cottage-cheese-like contents into the sink and ran a tap to wash it down the drain. She opened the dishwasher and put in the cups and cutlery, then tore a paper towel off the roller to wipe down the counter.

I wondered how much of the house she would tidy before we went upstairs.

"Mom," I said, working up to something I'd been wanting to ask since the viewing at the funeral home, "what did you mean when you asked yourself what've you done?"

"I never said that," she said, getting a spray bottle of granite cleaner out from under the sink and spritzing the counter.

"Yes, you did."

Mom grabbed some paper towels and wiped the counter vigorously.

"Who was Leah Kennard?" I asked.

"I have no idea," she said, her back to me.

"I don't believe you."

She froze.

I said, "The thing is, Mom, everything's going to come out, sooner or later. Even if what happened looks cut-and-dried, that detective seems pretty determined to get to the truth."

"She was probably some fling your father had," Mom said, still not looking at me. "You come to accept certain things in a marriage."

"Where would he have met her?"

"Lately? I don't really know."

"What do you mean, lately? Did Dad know her from a long time ago?"

The question hung in the air for several seconds. Finally, Mom turned around, using the counter to support herself.

"Your father and I hadn't planned to have you and your brother so close together."

Holden and I were a year apart, but it wasn't something I'd ever given much thought to. And if there was anyone who knew about having a kid you hadn't planned on, it was Diana and me.

"If I'd ever really considered it, I'd have guessed you wanted two kids and wanted to get it done."

"I don't want Holden to know what I'm about to tell you. You have to promise me."

"Without knowing what you're going to say, I don't know whether I can do that."

"He's already on the edge."

"He's always on the edge," I reminded her.

"Your father and I tried for a long time to get pregnant. When things weren't working out, we went to a fertility clinic, but we didn't have any success there either."

"Jesus," I said. "Wait. Holden's adopted? I mean, come on, we look alike."

"No, he's not *adopted*," she said quickly. "But Leah Kennard was his mother."

I let the words sink in. "So Dad . . . this wasn't the first time he'd had a relationship with her."

Mom face flushed with anger. "No! Stop getting ahead and let me tell you."

I raised my palms in surrender and nodded for her to continue.

"We'd reached the conclusion I simply couldn't have children. So we explored other options, and one of them was surrogacy. That's what Leah Kennard was. She was our surrogate."

"But . . . Leah wouldn't really be his mother, right? I mean, don't they take, like, an egg from you and mix it with Dad's, you know, stuff, and then they just implant it and it grows in the other woman's womb?"

Mom looked at me like I had the intelligence of a toddler. "Thank Christ you didn't decide to become a doctor."

"So just tell me then."

"What you're talking about, in your incredibly uninformed way, is gestational surrogacy. We couldn't go that route. We were left with artificial insemination. Your father was the donor. There was a procedure. There was no . . . relationship."

"Not then."

"Not then. Of course, we did meet with her, to assess whether we thought she was the right one. Someone who, at least in some ways, looked like me, you know? Turns out it wasn't her that needed to win us over. We had to win *her* over. She had to like us too. You don't agree to carry a child for people, and after all that, agree to give it up, if you don't like them. Of course, the money certainly helped. Leah's family was not in a position to help her financially, she was trying to pay off school bills, and the twenty thousand we paid her probably made a huge difference in her life, at least for a time."

"But what about records? When Holden went for a passport, he would have had to get a copy of his birth certificate and—"

Mom raised hand. "There's a lot of paperwork, legal steps, prebirth agreements. The certificate with Leah's name on it is sealed, but the one Holden was able to obtain is still legitimate." She paused, then asserted, "I am his mother." The way she said it, I wasn't sure whether she was trying to persuade me or convince herself.

I said, "So the procedure with Leah worked, and nine or ten months later, Holden arrived and . . ."

"And not long after that, I found out I was pregnant," Mom said. "Your father and I weren't as careful because I didn't believe I could have a child. The doctors couldn't explain it. They called it a miracle. *You* were a miracle."

Her eyes went to the ceiling and she slowly shook her head. Finally, she fixed her gaze on me and said, "Your timing's never been that great."

TWENTY-THREE

1999

The boys had been sent up to bed.

They'd wanted to stay up and watch *The X-Files*, but that had gone horribly wrong the week before. The episode had been about an escaped convict who could alter his molecular structure to move through objects, including people, and it had totally freaked Reece out. Holden, however, had loved it, concluding that the ability to pass through walls would be a pretty handy skill. You could break into a Toys "R" Us at night without tripping any alarms and steal as many Star Wars action figures as you could carry, or maybe one of the new Nintendo Game Boys with a color screen.

Reece said that was stupid. Even if you had the power to go through a wall, the action figures and the computer game couldn't change *their* molecular structure, so you couldn't take them back through the wall with you. Holden countered, saying anything you were holding would have those same qualities. Like, the guy on the episode was able to go through a wall and still have his shoes.

"I'll try it tonight," Holden said. "Even if you lock your

bedroom door, I'll come right through it and get you after you fall asleep."

Reece began to cry. Holden was scolded by Catherine and ordered to tell his younger brother he would not come through his door or his wall or even the ceiling to get him in the night.

"Okay," Holden said. "I won't do it." And then added quietly, so only Reece could hear, "Not *tonight*."

And despite all that, when another week went by, and there was a new episode of *The X-Files*, they both wanted to watch it. Catherine said no. Both boys moaned their displeasure. Reece promised not to be scared, and Holden vowed that, even if Reece were scared, he wouldn't tease him.

The answer was still no.

Brent would have been okay with letting them watch it again, but he hadn't wanted to undermine Catherine. So both boys were sent to their respective rooms at nine. Reece's room faced the street, and Holden's bedroom window looked out over the backyard and the pond. Brent crept upstairs about fifteen minutes later, saw no light under either door, although he thought he could hear some stirring in Holden's room. Reading comics with a flashlight, Brent guessed.

Catherine had gone to their bedroom. He peered in briefly, heard her shuffling clothes in the walk-in closet, and decided to head downstairs. He considered, briefly, watching *The X-Files* on his own (he was kind of a fan) but opted to go into the kitchen and make himself a drink. He was sipping on a scotch when he thought he heard a car pulling into the driveway.

He walked through the living room to the front door; when he opened it, he saw a silver Porsche Boxster sitting there, the engine now off. He couldn't think of anyone he knew who had a car like that, but he recognized Evelyn Corby when she got out and remembered her mentioning at the party that she was driving one of those.

"Evelyn," he said, walking toward her, the scotch still in his hand.

She smiled weakly. "Brent. Forgive the unannounced drop-in."

"No, that's— Is something wrong?"

She was dressed in designer jeans and a blue jacket over a white silk blouse. Tucked under her arm was a soft, leather case large enough to carry documents.

Evelyn came up the walk, stopped in front of him, let out a long breath, as though she had run here instead of driven, and said, "I need to know if I can trust you."

"About what?"

"It's a simple question. Can I trust you?"

"Yes, of course."

He led her into the house, through the living room and into the kitchen, where he offered a drink. She looked at his glass and said, "I'll have one of those, but make it a double."

Brent handed her a tumblerful and, pointing out that his sons had just gone upstairs and might still be trying to settle down, suggested they go sit on the back deck. The sun had set, so he flipped on a couple of outdoor lights, slid back the screen of the sliding glass doors that were already pulled open, and followed her outside.

Before sitting in one of the cushioned chairs she admired the reflection of the lights in the pond.

"Your own private lake," she said.

"Yeah, well, not quite big enough to water-ski. That little rowboat's for the boys."

They sat. Evelyn laid the case across her knees and patted it with one hand.

"It's all here," she said.

"What's all there?"

"They're killing people and they know they're killing people and they don't care."

Brent sighed. "Evelyn, you know the media's on a witch hunt with Wiffel-Smith. Printing bullshit stories quoting anonymous sources and no evidence. Why don't they go after Budweiser for giving people beer bellies. When used responsibly to treat pain it—"

"Stop. Just, stop, Brent. Look who you're talking to. I know the spiel. I know the company line. You don't believe it any more than I do. I've seen the look on your face."

"What look?"

"In the meetings. The others in that room, they're brainwashed. They're in the cult. But I look at you and I can see what you're thinking. That it's all a crock. Those cooked-up studies saying if the patient's pain returns, up the dosage. Pop another pill. And if that doesn't work, pop *another* one. It's crack, this stuff. You know it, I know it. The assholes running the show know it."

"I don't know what you want from me, Evelyn. Maybe . . ." His voice trailed off and he looked out into the night, into the woods beyond the pond. "Look, maybe there are times when I have my doubts. But . . ."

"But you don't want to give up this," she said, tilting her head back toward the house. "The big house, the cars, the vacations, probably private schools for your kids. You don't want it to end. But it has to." She smiled. "I'm gonna burn this company to the ground."

"It's impossible. You can't."

"It's not impossible, and I will." She dropped her voice. "They killed my nephew. No, that's wrong. *I* killed my nephew. I did their bidding. I got him hooked, and it killed him. Did I tell you how old Miles was?"

Brent said nothing.

"Twenty-eight. Had the world by the balls. Liked to play honky-tonk piano, did a great impression of that Reverend Jim guy from that sitcom *Taxi*. Gets his shoulder banged up playing hockey. I pass on some sample packs of Oxy-Mirac. '*Motherfucker*,' he tells me one night. '*That stuff is* amazing.' No shit. Well, he's not feeling any pain now."

"Evelyn, I'm so sorry. I truly am. That's . . . it's a tragedy. It's not your fault. All you wanted was to make his pain go away."

"Not my fault? That's not what his sister says. My niece. Have I told you about her?"

Brent, feeling this is a story he can't stop her telling, said, "No."

"She's Miles's sister, but she lives with me. Over the last two years, they lost both their parents. Mom dies of heart failure first, then eighteen months later, the dad's killed in a car accident. Miles was already living on his own and would have taken his sister in with him if he had to, but Evelyn, the *wonderful* aunt, steps up, says hey, Alicia, you come live with me. One day, though, she drops in on her brother, wants to see how he's coming along, he's dead on the kitchen floor looking like six-month-old cheese."

Evelyn shook her head sadly. "You know what my niece called me? A merchant of death. Said if I hadn't given Miles that first pill, he'd still be alive. And you know what? She's right."

She patted the leather case on her knees. "It's all here."

"Jesus, what have you done."

"Before I show you, I ask you one more time, for real. Can I trust you? Because this is it. This is the whole ball game. I think they're watching me. If something happens to me, I need backup. Someone else with the courage to take them on. If it's just me, I go to the *Times* or the *Post* or whoever, maybe they think I'm some kind of nut at first, but if there's two of us, then we've—"

"For the love of— Evelyn, you want me to be a goddamn whistleblower? I can't— I couldn't."

"So you're okay with it?"

"I'm not saying that. For fuck's sake, Wiffel-Smith is the General Motors of the drug world. Whatever you've got in that case, I don't care what it is, it'd be like going after Godzilla with a peashooter."

"You think?" She unzipped the case, brought out several papers, and handed them to Brent. He shifted his chair slightly so that he could get some light on the documents.

"What . . . am I looking at?"

"Memos from the desk of Graham Wiffel. Copies, by the way." She gave him a sly grin.

Brent started reading. "How did you get all this?" he asked, his voice filled with a terrified sense of wonder.

She smiled.

"You'd be surprised what people will toss into the trash, thinking no one will ever see it. But overnight custodians, with the right financial incentive, will happily pass it all on to you the next day. Sometimes, Wiffel tears things up, but as long as it's not shredded, it's not that hard to piece together. A little Scotch tape and you've got yourself a smoking gun."

She pointed at the papers in his lap, made a *go ahead* gesture. "Read. Fake testimonials. Bribes. Bogus studies. All to make more and more money. This is straight from Wiffel himself. Plans on how to maximize profits at the expense of human misery. They *want* people addicted. They don't give a flying fuck about improving anyone's quality of life."

Brent picked up a page and started reading. At the top, a red EYES ONLY stamp. It was a ten-point "action plan" from the president himself to counter growing negative publicity about their product and still increase sales. Proposals included secret payouts to major personalities and media outlets for positive stories. A video team would produce testimonials from patients crediting Wiffel-Smith with changing their lives for the better, and the actors who would play these patients could be sourced from various talent agencies. People alleged to have overdosed on Oxy-Mirac would be investigated and evidence "found" that they had a history of drug abuse. Details of how to conduct smear campaigns were included.

Brent looked up. "Oh my god. It's dynamite. I mean, *literally* dynamite."

"No shit," Evelyn said.

Brent read on, still shaking his head. "They're soulless," he said. "They've got the moral rectitude of an alligator. Christ."

"You already knew all this. We all knew it. Not what's in those memos, but the general drift. You knew it but wouldn't admit it to yourself."

He set the papers down, looked at Evelyn. "Maybe."

"What are your boys' names?"

"What?"

"Your sons. What are their names?"

"Holden and Reece."

"How would you explain it to them? What it is you do? You think what you've been doing would make them proud? Are you the man they would want you to be? One day, it'll all come out. If it's not through me, through somebody else. This kind of depravity will implode from its own meanness. You have to ask yourself, do you want to get ahead of it? Or hang in till the bitter end, when your shares in the company aren't worth wiping your ass with?"

He said nothing.

"I can't do this alone. I want someone along for the ride. And it's going to be a fucking bumpy one too. Crane?"

"Yeah?"

"He makes a New York rat look like a chipmunk. He's dangerous. Soon as he gets an inkling about what I've got, I'm toast. That's why I have to move on this. Skipping local media. *New York Times*, baby. Walk in like Daniel Ellsberg did at the *Post* with the *Pentagon Papers*. I want to be able to tell them I've got someone who can back me up." She paused, then grinned. "That'd be you."

She pointed to the papers in his hand. "Those are your copies. Mine are in the car. I'm heading for the border, then straight on to New York. Eight, ten hours if I don't get pulled over for speeding. I'll be there by daybreak."

"And if don't back you up on this?"

"Don't break my heart, Brent. Do it for your boys. Make 'em proud."

Brent stood, paced the deck. "I'll be throwing everything away."

"You'll reinvent yourself. You're a salesman, and a good one.

Sell something else. Consult. Invent something. I don't care if I end up bagging groceries. I can't do this any longer."

Brent stopped, stood a little straighter, nodded. "Okay," he said. "Okay. I'll do it."

"No, you won't."

They both turned. It was Catherine, on the other side of the screen. She slid it open slowly with one hand, her other hanging down at her side, out of view.

She stepped outside. "You can't do that, Brent."

"Honey, hey. You remember Evelyn, from the party at—"

"I remember."

Evelyn stood, nodded respectfully. "Hello, Catherine. Don't know how much you heard but what I'm asking of Brent—what I am asking of *you*—is to do the right thing."

"The right thing."

She nodded. "For your consciences, for yourselves, for your boys, and—"

"Don't talk about my boys. Don't talk to me about the right thing. What do you stand to lose? A job?" She scoffed. "How about a husband? Children? A *family*. A wonderful *life*. You want us to throw that away? Because you have some little pangs of conscience?"

"Catherine, just—"

She cut off her husband. "He won't help you."

Catherine showed what she'd been hiding in her other hand. A gun. She pointed it at Evelyn Corby, who froze, a stunned look on her face.

Brent said, "Christ, Catherine, where the hell did you get—"

"I *told* you," she said. "I tried so *hard* to tell you but you wouldn't listen. I haven't felt safe. And I've never felt more threatened than right now."

"Put that down," her husband said. "Catherine, we can work this out."

Evelyn's eyes were darting from side to side, looking for an escape. Struggling to keep her voice calm, she said, "Read those papers. They've done terrible things. *Evil* things. Your husband isn't an evil person, and I know you're not. The evidence is right there. It's overwhelming. All I'm asking is—"

Catherine raised her arm, trained the gun more squarely on her target.

Evelyn bolted.

She couldn't head back into the house. Catherine was in her path. She jumped the two steps that led down to the yard from the deck and started running in the direction of the pond, legs and arms pumping.

Catherine went after her, rushing past Brent in pursuit.

Raised her weapon and fired.

A few feet short of the pond's edge, Evelyn went down, her arms stretched out ahead of her. Her head touched the muddy ground where the pond met the yard.

"No!" Brent cried, racing after his wife, now kneeling next to Evelyn's lifeless form.

"You stupid bitch!" Brent shouted. "You goddamn stupid fucking bitch!"

Catherine was fixated on the red blossoming stain on the back of Evelyn's jacket. When Brent tried to wrestle the gun from her hand, Catherine resisted.

"Give me that! Give it to me!" he said.

Catherine broke free long enough to bring her arm back and throw the gun into the air. It sailed over the pond and landed with a splash.

"You want it, go get it," she said, struggling to her feet.

Brent stood there, mouth agape, looking down in shock at Evelyn's lifeless form.

Catherine happened to glance back at the house and noticed, in the second-floor window of Holden's bedroom, the dark silhouette of a child, watching.

TWENTY-FOUR

Reece

There are bombshells, and then there are *bombshells*.

Holden was, at least genetically speaking, my half brother.

"You can't keep this from him," I said to my mother, standing in her house. "He deserves to know."

"Not knowing hasn't been a problem for him up to now, so I don't see any reason to change things."

I felt myself coming to a boil. Keeping this from Holden was not only a betrayal to him, but me as well. I'd believed Holden was a full brother, and not that it would make any difference in how I felt about him, but didn't I deserve to know the truth? If I were Holden, wouldn't I be entitled to know how I'd come into the world?

"God, what a piece of work you are," I said.

Mom slapped me across the face. "How dare you."

My cheek was hot, but the slap wasn't enough to quell my anger.

"No, how dare *you*," I said. "Keeping secret who we *are*. What we are to each *other*. You'd no right to do that."

"Don't talk to me about rights," she snapped.

"Look how it's paid off for you, having our family live a lie all these years. That detective will figure it all out, and she'll want to know why you weren't more forthcoming with her. Once she knows what Leah did for you and Dad and talks to Holden—"

"There's no reason for her to talk to Holden!"

"There will be. Once she puts it together."

"She won't," Mom protested. "She didn't strike me as all that bright."

That made me laugh. Mom wishing other people were stupid wouldn't make it so.

"I have to find your father a suit," she said, turning and heading for the stairs, clearly eager to put an end to our conversation.

I'd almost forgotten that was why we were here. To get some clothes to take back to the funeral home. I was taken aback by how briskly Mom headed upstairs. She'd evidently gotten over her reluctance to not only be in this house, but go into rooms one might think she'd never want to enter again.

She walked right past the king-size bed without looking at it, which was just as well. Dad and Leah were long gone, of course, but the room was still a crime scene. The bed, the linens, it would all have to go. The bloodied carpet ripped up. The walls scoured and repainted or wallpapered. The framed painting above the bed, with traces of brain matter on it, disposed of.

Mom walked past it all so blithely that for a moment I thought it might be because she'd already seen it. I put the idea out of my head as quickly as it had come to me.

"This should do," she said, coming out of the walk-in closet, in one hand a hanger bearing a dark blue suit, and in the other, a folded white shirt and blue-striped tie. With both hands full, she managed to open a dresser drawer, pull out a pair of socks, then head for the door, conducting the entire exercise in less time than I could get a Big Mac and fries at the McDonald's drive-through window.

I went into the closet, saw a pair of dress shoes, grabbed them, and met her in the hall. She looked at what I'd brought her and frowned. "Not brown," she said.

I went back for a black pair and by the time I returned she was down in the front hall, ready to hand me the clothes.

"You can take these over," she said.

"You're not coming?"

She shook her head. "No. I'm . . . going to stay here. I'll move my things into the guest room. Would you help me with that?"

I nodded.

"And when you have a moment, could you get my things from the hotel?" She went into her purse, brought out a plastic room key. "It's all packed."

"Okay."

"This is my house. I'm not leaving. I won't let your father's foolishness force me out." *Foolishness* struck me as something of an understatement. "If I let tragedy dictate where I live I'd have left here long ago."

I didn't know whether to pursue that one or not. I already had another question ready to go and launched it.

"Did you know?" I asked. She looked at me, seeking clarification. "About Dad, and Leah."

"I need to sit down."

She went into the living room and settled onto the couch while I took a chair opposite her. She took a breath, put her hands in her lap, and laced her fingers. "He thought he was so good at keeping it a secret, at least for a while. Had an extra phone and everything."

"How long had it been going on?"

"A year, maybe two. I confronted him about it a couple of months ago. Not that I was as upset as you might think. Things have been strained for a long time."

"Was Dad seeing her back in the beginning? Before Holden came along?"

"No. Like I said, it was all very clinical, getting her pregnant. When I got him to admit he was seeing her, he told me how it happened. He spotted her one day. On the street, in a store, somewhere, I don't know. She looked distraught, and he went up to her, asked if she was okay, then realized who she was. Her life was something of a mess, she'd been living with a man who was abusive, and I guess he set out to rescue her."

"So it didn't start out as an affair?"

"I don't think so. He felt indebted to this woman who carried his child, who gave birth to our Holden, who was clearly struggling. To give your father the benefit of the doubt, I think his original intention was to help. He gave her money. A hundred here, a hundred there, sometimes a thousand. Their friendship turned into something more. She kicked out her boyfriend. But I never thought . . . I never thought your father would meet with her here." She seethed briefly. "I could put up with almost anything, but to do it here . . . I didn't know he hated me *that* much."

"Dad didn't hate you."

She gave me a wry smile that hinted at my naivete.

I had another question, but before I could pose it, we heard a car pulling into the driveway. I got up from the chair and went to the window, pulled back a drape.

"Detective McCabe," I said.

"God, no," said Mom. She didn't sound angry. More defeated.

"Maybe she spotted my car, wants to talk to me."

"I'm not here," she said, got off the couch, and started heading for the door to the basement.

McCabe was opening the door to her car.

"Mom," I said.

She paused, glanced at me.

"Who was the man in the parking lot?" I asked.

"I have no idea what you're—"

"Cut the bullshit, Mom. Who was he? Why'd you look so upset?"

McCabe was halfway to the front door.

"I want to know. Were *you* having an affair with *him*?"

She looked completely exasperated. "For Christ's sake, you have no idea what's going on." With that she disappeared down the stairs. I went to the door before McCabe could ring the bell.

"Mr. Chartwell," she said. "How are you doing?"

I shrugged.

"I need to speak with your mother. Is she here?"

Fuck it.

"Yes," I said.

TWENTY-FIVE

1999

"Catherine," Brent said, no longer screaming, but struggling to regain his composure. "Catherine, look at me."

His wife was still kneeling over the body of Evelyn Corby. The rose of blood on her back was expanding. Catherine turned her head and said to her husband, "You fool."

"Have you lost your mind? Do you realize what you've—"

"I've saved us, that's what I've done," she said, standing. "You would have *helped* her? Helped her *ruin* us?"

"I'd have talked her out of it. Made her forget the whole thing."

"No. No. I *heard* you. You're *weak*."

"Where did you get that gun?"

She shook her head, ignoring the question. "Crane."

"What?"

"We have to call Crane. He fixes things."

"Catherine, we have to call the *police*. We'll . . . we'll tell them it was self-defense, that she attacked you or something. We just . . . we just need to come up with a story."

"That I was defending myself by shooting her in the back as she ran away?" Catherine asked him. "Crane," she said again.

"I don't know how to get in touch with him."

"I have his number."

That stopped Brent cold. Before he could say anything, Catherine said, "Do you want to get into that now, or do you want to solve this problem?"

Brent wasn't sure which way to go. "How's he supposed to make this go away?"

"It's what he does. He solves problems."

"How could you possibly know that?"

"He told me."

Brent looked at Catherine as though she were someone he was meeting for the first time. He glanced back at the dead woman, then focused again on his wife.

"You're fucking him," he said.

Her eyes danced. "Would you even believe me if I said no?"

Before he could respond she started leading him toward the house. As they crossed the yard, she said, "I'll find the number, you call him, and then I have to talk to Holden."

Brent grabbed her arm and made her stop. "Why?"

Her eyebrows tilted in the direction of the upstairs window. "He saw."

Brent had no words.

She shook off his arm. Once they were in the kitchen, she found her purse, brought out her wallet, and found a yellow Post-it note tucked inside. On it was written a phone number with no name attached. She handed it to her husband.

"Tell him exactly what happened. He'll know what to do."

Catherine left him standing there, stunned, as she headed upstairs. She went straight to Holden's room, found the door closed, and rapped softly on it.

There was no sound from inside. She quietly turned the knob, entered the room, and closed the door behind her. Holden was under the covers, the blanket pulled up far enough to cover the lower half of his head.

"I know you're awake," his mother said, sitting down on the edge of the bed.

Holden didn't move.

"Stop pretending. I saw you at the window."

Holden pushed down the covers with his arm and rolled over to look at his mother.

"What did you see?" she asked him.

"Nothing," he whispered.

"Don't lie to me."

Holden was silent. "It's okay," she said soothingly. "It's okay to tell me what you saw."

"The lady was running."

"And what else?"

"And you were running after her, and then I heard something, and then she fell down."

"Okay," she said, worry creeping into her voice. "That's what you saw. What is it you think actually happened?"

"You shot that lady."

Catherine nodded slowly. "Did you tell your brother what you saw?"

His head moved back and forth on the pillow.

"Are you sure?"

A nod.

Catherine was inclined to believe him. Reece was a sound sleeper. One night, when the smoke alarms went off by accident, everyone woke up and leapt out of bed, except for Reece.

"You must never tell him what you saw."

"Okay."

"And not just your brother. If anyone were to find out what happened here tonight, it would destroy this family. You wouldn't have a home anymore. You'd lose your father, you'd lose me, you and your brother would be sent to live with different families."

Holden, tears forming in his eyes, said nothing.

"That woman was a very bad person. She came to hurt us. She was going to hurt me and your father and Reece and you. So she had to be stopped. Whatever you think you saw me do, it was done to save this family."

Holden managed a nod.

Catherine felt she needed to drive her point home one more time. Up the stakes.

"You can't ever tell anyone about this. They wouldn't understand. It's very complicated."

"Okay."

"And if you ever did tell anyone . . . and this might be the worst thing of all . . . you know what would happen?"

"No."

"I wouldn't love you anymore. You wouldn't want that, would you?"

"No."

"Okay, then. Now give us a kiss."

Crane was there in forty-five minutes.

He stood over the body, hands gloved, looking down, thinking. He was up to speed. Evelyn's plan, Catherine shooting her with the gun Crane had provided.

Mixed feelings, to be sure. A fuckup, giving Catherine that gun, while at the same time, if she hadn't used it, Evelyn might be across the border by now, pedal to the metal all the way to *The New York Times*. Crane had given the documents a cursory glance. A nuclear weapon, no doubt about it.

"I need a tarp, a large blanket, something that will make it easier to move her," he said.

Brent stood there, frozen, still trying to get his head around it all.

"Did you hear me?" Crane said. "A tarp?"

Brent came out of his trance. "I-I might have something in the garage. I rake the leaves onto it so I can drag them—"

"Go. And find yourself a pair of gloves first."

Brent ran off, leaving behind Crane and Catherine, who was still glancing up occasionally at Holden's window.

Catherine said, "It just . . . happened. I had no choice."

"The gun."

"What about it?"

"Give it to me."

"I don't have it."

He looked at her, blinked. "Where might it be, Catherine?"

She pointed.

"In the pond," Crane said, sounding defeated. "You threw it in the fucking pond."

"Brent was trying to take it from me and I just—"

"Shut up." With only the deck light and the stars to help him, he looked out over the pond, assessing its size. "How deep?"

"In the middle? Maybe five, six feet."

"What's the bottom like?"

"Muddy," she said, glancing back to that upstairs window again.

He paused a moment, coming to a decision. "The police would have to already know a lot before they'd think to drag the pond. If they've gotten to that point, you're probably already in their crosshairs. So we can't let it get to that point. Why are you looking at that window?"

"I'm not."

"Oh shit," he said quietly, figuring it out on his own. He closed the distance between them, grabbed her wrist firmly and drew her in, face-to-face. She tried to shake him off but he was locked on.

"Tell me."

"He's just a boy."

"Your son?"

She nodded.

"Which one?"

"Please . . ."

"Which one?"

"Holden."

"You've talked to him?"

"He doesn't know what he saw. He's a kid. You don't have to worry about him. I made it very clear."

Crane stared at the window.

"He's not there now. He went to bed. It was dark. Crane, please."

He was breathing in and out, slowly, hand still clamped around her wrist. "What did you tell him?"

"I put the fear of God into him. That if he ever told, we'd lose everything. He and Reece would be taken away from us. I told him . . ." And at this point, she choked on her words. "I told him I wouldn't love him anymore."

Crane's face seemed to crack. He relaxed his grip.

"I had to . . ." Catherine said, turning away. "He had to know this was serious . . ." Her head was down, her shoulders hunched, as though closing in on herself. "I would never really . . . I never would have said that to Reece . . ."

Brent was returning, a black plastic tarp rolled up under his arm. With gloved hands, he handed it to Crane, who unfurled it onto the grass.

"Shoulders," he said to Brent.

Brent got hold of Evelyn's upper body, planting both his shoes—an expensive pair of Florsheims—into the water at the edge of the pond. Crane took the feet. They moved her body onto the center of the tarp, which was more than big enough to roll up her body and tuck in both ends.

Carrying her like a carpet, they went around the side of the house, through the gate, then set the body down at the back end of Crane's car. He popped the trunk, and together they stuffed Evelyn in there. He walked over to Evelyn's Porsche, tried the door, and found it unlocked. He glanced inside, then turned to Brent and said, "A purse?"

"On the deck."

Brent disappeared around the back of the house, returned with a handbag and the leather case Evelyn had brought. "She had the documents in this."

Crane had already taken the copies Evelyn had given Brent. He rooted around in the purse until he had found a set of keys for the Porsche.

"Tell me you can drive a stick," he said to Brent.

He didn't understand the point of the question at first, then said, "Yes."

"You'll follow me. But first . . ."

Crane opened the front trunk of the Porsche. "You said she had another set of docs."

"Right."

Crane hauled out an overnight bag, placed it on the driveway, unzipped it, rooted through, finding only clothes, a makeup bag, a hair dryer, and shoes. There was a shallow pouch on the outside of the bag. In there, a manila envelope. He opened it, peered inside, nodded to himself, and set it on the driveway while he closed up the bag, returned it to the car, and shut the trunk. He put the envelope in his car, then tossed the Porsche keys to Brent. He fumbled them and they hit the ground.

"God help me," Crane said under his breath as Brent scooped up the keys. "I'll lead the way," Crane said, opening the door to his own car. To Catherine, he said, "You stay, look for anything—*anything*—that says she was here. Anything she touched."

Catherine nodded and watched as the two cars—Crane's first, and then Evelyn's, with Brent behind the wheel—backed out onto the street and drove off.

Catherine stayed up until Brent returned.

Almost three hours later, Crane's car came down the street, stopped in front of the house long enough for Brent to get out, then did a three-point turn and disappeared. Brent came up the drive like someone who'd just run a marathon.

Catherine had the door open before he got there. He walked past her without saying a word or looking at her. He went to the kitchen, poured himself a scotch, downed it, poured himself another.

"Brent," she said.

He ignored her.

"Brent, talk to me."

He didn't acknowledge her as he headed for the stairs and up to their room. He stripped down, walked into the bathroom naked, and turned on the shower. He stayed in there ten minutes, hands on the tiled wall, head bowed, letting the water rain on his back. Finally, he came out, toweled off, put on a pair of boxers, Catherine watching him the whole time.

"It had to be done," she said.

He went back to the kitchen, opened a lower cupboard door where they kept garbage bags, grabbed one and returned to the bedroom, where he bagged everything he'd been wearing. He knotted the top of the bag, pulled on a bathrobe, then went back outside, where two metal garbage cans were already at the curb. He lifted the lid of one, stuffed the bag inside, then came back into the house.

"Brent . . ." Catherine, who had followed him downstairs, began.

He stopped, eyed her, and said, "Evelyn won't be the last. Someone else will come forward. Maybe not this week, or this month, or even this year. But it will all come out eventually."

Catherine eyed him warily.

"Don't worry. It won't be from me. But I'm quitting. I'll wait a few days, wait for things to die down. Don't want it to look suspicious, me walking out the same week one of the company's star employees is found murdered. And then I'm selling all our stock while it's still worth something. We'll be okay until I find something new."

He had one last thing to say.

"For the sake of the boys, I'll stay with you. But we're done."

And he went to bed.

TWENTY-SIX

As it got to be eleven on Saturday morning, Alicia rolled out of Holden's bed and planted her feet on the floor.

"Coooffeeee," she said, reaching for a pack of cigarettes on the bedside table and lighting one up.

"Ermmm," Holden said, his face in the pillow.

Alicia glanced back at him, at the rumpled bedclothes, at the dresser so littered with personal items including headache remedies, tissues (still in the dispenser as well as used), crumpled receipts and parking tickets, dirty glasses and empty beer bottles that there was hardly a spot to put anything else, and said, "Did you not hear me? I need coffee."

Holden rolled over and stood. Wearing only his boxers, he trudged from the bedroom to the kitchen and could be heard running water from the tap, banging around cups and plates and other items that had been left in the sink.

"You want toast or anything?" he called out.

Alicia was propped up in bed, waving her cigarette in the air. "*This* is my breakfast. I just need the coffee."

"You think I deliver or something?"

"You delivered not half bad last night, for a man your age," she said, thinking it might not be a bad idea to spend another night here, though that was up in the air. Very *much* up in the air.

"Getting some cereal," he announced.

"I'll alert the media."

She could hear cereal being poured into a bowl. Seconds later, Holden reappeared, spoon in one hand, bowl in the other, shoveling cereal into his face, milk dribbling down from the corner of his mouth.

"Coffee will be a minute," he said, chewing.

He sat on her side of the bed, his butt up against her legs. "Thanks for everything."

"Hey," she said. "No problem."

"I've been going through some serious fucked-up-edness."

"No kidding."

"I flushed everything when I thought the cops were here for me. And now I'm thinking, it was for the best. I wanna stay clean. Not counting, you know, the odd drink here and there."

"The odd one, sure," she said, blowing smoke in his face.

"I mean it. Don't want another day like yesterday. I can barely remember it. Like I had a blackout or something. It's all fuzzy."

"You did kind of go overboard. Not saying I blame you. You can't bottle up your feelings. Don't let anyone tell you you're not allowed to feel the way you do."

Holden spooned some more cereal into his mouth. Another drop of milk ran down his chin.

"Look at you," Alicia said. "You should be in a high chair." There was a ding from the kitchen. "Get me a coffee."

"I have a more urgent matter to deal with," he said, leaving the unfinished bowl of cereal on a bedside table and heading down the hall to the bathroom.

Alicia got out of bed, wearing black panties and a black tee, went to the kitchen, tossed the end of her cigarette into the sink, rinsed out a dirty cup, and poured herself coffee from the pot. She opened the fridge, saw a container of milk, gave it a sniff, deemed it on the edge of acceptable, and poured some into her mug.

She blew on it, had a sip. She went back to the fridge and was looking for anything edible, when there was a knock at the door.

"Holden!" she called. "Someone's here!"

From behind the closed bathroom door, he called out, "Busy!"

She went to the front door, opened it an inch to see who was there. "Oh, hey," she said. "Gage."

Gage looked taken aback. "Oh, sorry, I didn't know—"

"No, it's okay. Your uncle's in the bathroom. Ordering a pizza for all I know."

"Oh, okay," he said, crestfallen. "I can come back."

As he turned to leave, Alicia opened the door wider and grabbed him by the collar. "Get in here."

He spun around and entered, but upon noticing Alicia's skimpy attire, averted his eyes.

"I'll put some pants on so you don't die of a heart attack," she said, heading back to the bedroom and leaving him alone in the living room/kitchen area. Before Alicia could return, there was the sound of a toilet flushing, and then Holden was strolling down the hall.

"Hey, my man," he said, as he pulled the boy into his arms and hugged him the way he had at the coffee shop the night before. It lasted a good ten seconds. "How're you doing?"

Gage shrugged. "I don't know."

Holden gave him another hug, nearly as long as the first. "Everything's good, right?"

Gage said nothing.

Holden nodded understandingly. "I get it, I get it, but I think everything's going to work out. It's normal to feel all sad and fucked-up. I know I do." He pointed to himself. "My dad, your grandpa, was a good guy. My heart's broken."

"I had bad nightmares last night."

"Me and you both," Holden said, laying a hand on his shoulder.

"There was something I was supposed to give you but never did."

"In your dream?"

"No, like, for real."

"Was it important?"

Gage shrugged. "I don't think it really matters anymore."

"You want some coffee or something?"

Gage took in the grimy carafe sitting in the coffee maker. "I'm okay."

"I got cereal too. Where'd I leave that bowl?"

Alicia, now in jeans, strolled into the kitchen, bowl in hand. "Where do you think?"

Holden took it, scowled at the soggy flakes in the bottom.

"You guys, like, a thing?" Gage asked, prompting Holden and Alicia to exchange glances. "I thought you were just, you know, like when people are in Alcoholics Anonymous, supporting each other."

"I don't know," Holden said, looking at her. "We a thing?"

She shrugged. "This morning we are. I'm sure Ben would disapprove."

"Ben?" Gage said, although he thought the name had come up before.

"Our counselor at Sharnwood," Holden said. "Rehab's not supposed to be for hookups."

Gage took a seat at the cluttered kitchen table. "So will you get in trouble?"

Alicia laughed. "No. There's no rehab HR that's gonna come after us. It's more like a workplace romance. Sitting in a circle pouring your guts out, you kind of start bonding with people who've been through stuff as bad as what you've been through."

"Yeah," Holden chimed in. "Getting it off your chest, you know. Like how your parents screw you up."

"My parents haven't screwed me up," Gage said.

Holden grinned. "You just don't know it yet. You need some distance. You look back and think, okay, when was the moment when things really started to go south? For me, I know the exact second. For other people, it's lots of little stuff that builds up over time." He gave Gage a knowing look. "You know what I'm talking about."

Gage nodded slowly.

"I kept it in for a long time," Holden continued. "Finally opened up to you. But then I end up in therapy with a bunch of fellow fuckups—"

"Thanks," Alicia said.

"—and meet her and she's like the best listener ever. Better than Ben, God's honest truth. I can tell her stuff I could never tell the group."

Alicia shrugged. "I should have one of those newspaper advice columns."

"We had shared experience, you know? I mean, mine was

very different from hers, but we'd both been through stuff that scarred us."

Gage, thinking back to the night before, said to Alicia, "You said your aunt got killed?"

"Yup."

"How did *you* deal with something like that?" Gage asked, like he was looking for tips.

"Well, I got high. I don't recommend that. But hey, if that hadn't been my strategy, I never would have met your uncle."

"What happened to your aunt, if it's okay to ask?"

Alicia thought before she answered. "She was a bank teller, you know? In Oshawa? And one day, these three guys came busting in wearing ski masks, and one of them, he tells her to open the till and give him everything in there, and she did just like he asked her, and after she handed over the money, the bastard shot her."

"Oh my god," Gage said. "And they caught him?"

She nodded. "Him and the other guys. Someone walking by the bank saw what was going down, called the police, and they were waiting for them when they came out. There was a big shootout and all three guys were killed by the cops. One of the cops got hit in the shoulder but he was okay."

"That's wild," he said. "When was this?"

"Ninety-nine. Before you were even born."

Gage was shaking his head in wonder. "What was her name?"

"Huh?"

"Your aunt. What was her name?"

"Mary. Mary Zane. I was living with her. She was looking out for me after I lost the rest of my family. And once she was gone, I was on my own. I already had a job, but it didn't pay much, and I sure couldn't afford to stay in her place, which was really fantastic. She was making so much money and—"

"I didn't think tellers made that much," Holden said.

"Huh?" Alicia said. "Right, you're right. I'm just saying, compared to what *I* was making, what she was getting paid seemed like a fortune. And when she died, I got nothing. She had this older brother in Montana she hadn't been in touch with in years but he was the closest relative and all her money and the house sale, it all went to him. He didn't give me a dime."

Gage had nothing to say to all that.

"Listen," Holden said to his nephew, "you hang in there. If you need to talk, you call me. We good?"

Gage could tell he was being dismissed. He got up from the table, accepted one last hug from his uncle, then half of one from Alicia, and left.

Outside, he put one foot on his skateboard and started for home. It was a few miles, but he always made good time on his board. Along the way, he kept thinking about Alicia's aunt getting blown away in a bank robbery. No wonder she was so messed up, he thought. Something like that would screw with your head big-time.

He heard a text as he rolled along, figuring it was his parents wondering, as always, where he was. He took out his phone, saw the message before he actually read who'd sent it.

How u doing?

Who wanted to know? He came to an abrupt stop, one foot on the pavement, one on the board, and took a closer look.

Moira.

He'd last seen her Thursday night—or was it Friday morning—just before her mom crashed a party being hosted by a mutual friend whose parents were away. Passing around a joint, chilling out before a long weekend because there was no school Friday. Gage had slipped away seconds earlier, departing down a different path so he didn't run into the mother.

Was Moira's question general in nature, or did she know something?

He typed back: Kinda shitty.

Heard.

How?

Come by and find out. I'm grounded.

That sounded like a plan.

TWENTY-SEVEN

Reece

"Mom!" I shouted, standing at the top of the stairs that led to the basement. "Detective McCabe is here."

No response. She'd either found a way to crawl out a basement window or was pretending not to hear me.

"Mom," I called out again.

She appeared at the bottom of the stairs, glaring up at me, probably wondering how it slipped my mind that thirty seconds earlier she'd told me to tell the detective she was not there.

I was tired of playing games with her.

"She's coming," I said to McCabe, who was standing just inside the front door.

Mom shifted past me as she reached the top step, slapped a fake smile on her face, and said, "Detective."

"Mrs. Chartwell. I had a few more questions."

She sighed audibly. "What more could you possibly need to know?"

Quite a bit, I thought.

"Perhaps we could sit," McCabe said, inviting herself into the living room. She hadn't asked me to leave, so I chose to stay.

She led off with: "I wondered, since we last spoke, whether you might have remembered anything about Leah Kennard."

I exchanged a quick glance with my mother.

"No," she said, looking first at McCabe, then fixing her eyes on me, as though daring me to contradict her.

I was definitely thinking about it. But in that moment, I wasn't sure what would be gained by ratting Mom out. In the end, what difference did it make whether Mom knew Leah? Dad had shot her, then himself. Did the other details matter?

"Let me run another name past you."

Mom raised her chin somewhat defiantly, like she could handle whatever was coming. "Go ahead," she said.

"Evelyn Corby."

That chin quivered. Did McCabe see what I saw at that moment? It lasted no more than a second, but Mom had just experienced some kind of earthquake. And just as quickly, she restored her look of resolve.

"Could you repeat that, please?"

"Evelyn Corby."

"Evelyn Corby, Evelyn Corby," Mom said. She shook her head slowly. "I don't . . . it does sound somewhat familiar, but it's not a name I've heard in a long time."

"When do you think you might have heard it?"

"I'd have to think."

McCabe waited, gave her ten seconds, then said, "Anything?"

"Maybe you could give me a hint."

"Wiffel-Smith."

"That's the company my husband once worked for," Mom said. "But he left them around nineteen ninety-nine. Did this Corby woman have something to do with Wiffel-Smith?"

"She was an employee, in sales, doing the same kind of work I believe your husband did for them."

"Oh."

"Did your husband ever mention her? Did her name ever come up in conversation?"

Mom looked as though a memory had clicked in. "Now that you mention it . . . I remember around that time someone Brent had worked with was killed. Murdered, I think."

McCabe nodded. "Yes."

"I knew I'd heard that name somewhere. I'm sure Brent must have mentioned it. Something like that happens at work, it's a shock for everyone. But I don't recall the details."

"Evelyn Corby's body was found alongside a road, just down the embankment a ways. Shot in the back. Her car was found a few miles away outside a bar."

"Terrible," Mom said.

"It appeared she was killed elsewhere, her body moved and dumped."

Mom shook her head, made a *tsk* sound with her tongue.

"Her killer made it look as though there'd been a sexual component to the murder, but the evidence didn't bear that out."

Mom shrugged. "It's all horrible, but I still don't understand why you're telling me about it."

"It's what they call an open-unsolved case. Police try their best to close it, but when the leads dry up, there's not much they can do but hope for a development someday that will give them another kick at the can."

"I see."

"And that's what's happened."

"What's happened?" Mom asked.

"There's been a development."

McCabe had me on the edge of my seat. Mom was, too, but she looked more uneasy than intrigued.

"After we did a ballistics check on the slugs that were recovered here yesterday we fed them into our database. Just a routine thing we do. And something interesting came back."

"What?" I asked.

"We got a match. The gun that killed your husband and Leah Kennard is the same gun that was used to kill Evelyn Corby."

Mom had the face of a statue.

"You understand what I'm saying?" McCabe asked.

Mom opened her mouth to say something, but no words came out. After a couple of seconds, she managed two:

"That's impossible."

Then, a few more: "It's . . . I don't . . . it's impossible. That's all. It's as simple as that. It's impossible."

"The evidence suggests otherwise."

"But that gun—" Mom stopped herself, shook her head slowly.

I stepped in. "Is there any way these tests you do, they could be wrong?"

"No," said McCabe.

"But are you suggesting my father killed this Evelyn Corby? I mean, I have to agree with my mother. There's no way. My father wasn't capable of something like that."

"It would appear he was yesterday," McCabe countered.

I had no comeback for that.

Mom whispered, "Maybe it *isn't* impossible."

"Mom," I said imploringly. "Come on. Shooting some woman and leaving her body at the side of the road? That's not Dad.

I don't believe that. I *won't* believe that." To McCabe, I said, "Just because that same gun was used in both cases doesn't mean my father pulled the trigger."

"That's true."

"Dad didn't even like guns," I said. "Didn't want them in the house. I still can't believe he had one. It doesn't add up."

Now I was thinking back, way back. To a vague recollection of my parents having an argument. They were in the kitchen and I was in the adjoining TV room.

"I remember," I said, slowly, "a fight—maybe not a fight, but a discussion—where you and Dad were talking about getting a gun because of Dad's job, in case some crazy addict thought he had samples at home. In case we were a target."

"Then your father *was* thinking about it," McCabe said.

I hesitated. "It might have been the other way around."

The detective turned to my mother. "Is that how you remember it?"

Mom blinked. "I have no memory of a conversation like that."

"No, wait," I said, things becoming clearer. "Because I can sort of recall, I was watching *Beavis and Butt-Head*, but I had the volume turned way down because you hated that show, and that's how I was able to hear what—"

"You're wrong," Mom snapped. "We never discussed it. You imagined it."

She turned on McCabe. "Even if I were to say to you, right now, gosh, maybe Brent *did* kill that woman years ago, it wouldn't be proof, would it?"

"No."

"After all this time, there's really nothing that can be proved, one way or another. You might have a suspicion, you might *think* you have an idea of what happened, but you're never going to know for certain."

"True," McCabe said.

"Then I don't know why we're having this conversation," Mom said abruptly. "As you can see," and she pointed to the suit and other items we had collected from the upstairs closet, "we have to make a trip to the funeral home."

The detective nodded, got to her feet, and showed herself out.

"Mom," I said, "what in god's name was that all about?"

She ignored me, got up, walked through the kitchen, opened the sliding glass door, and stepped out onto the deck. Stood there a moment, then went down the two steps to the yard and walked toward the pond.

She stopped ten feet short of the edge, not far from the old, rotting rowboat that wouldn't have stayed afloat five seconds on that smooth, murky water. She stared out over the pond and waited, as if she expected the Loch Ness monster to raise its head and say hello.

TWENTY-EIGHT

Gage found Moira sitting on a front porch step, like she'd been waiting for him. He hopped off his skateboard, tucked it under his arm, and walked up to her. They had some of the same classes together, had made out a couple of times, and had been hanging out two nights earlier. Not together, exactly. They'd both just wound up at the same place at the same time with the same people.

"Sorry about your gramps," she said.

"So it's on the news."

Moira shrugged. "I don't know. Maybe."

"How'd you know?"

"I heard my mom talking. I heard your name."

"Why would *she* be talking about me?"

"She got some forensic report or something."

"Wait, what?"

"You don't know my mom's, like, a cop? A detective?"

Gage said nothing for several seconds. "Since when?"

"Whaddya mean, since when? It's not like she became a cop on Tuesday. She's been doing this for years. You must be the only one who doesn't know. Why do you think everyone was freaked out when she tracked me down?"

But Gage had missed that, leaving moments earlier. "When was your mom talking about me? What did she say?"

"Okay, I don't think she was actually talking about you, she said your last name, but she was talking to some guy about another Chartwell, and I figured that was your grandfather or something. Right?"

Gage let out a breath, nodded. "Yeah. He died."

"And not, like, from a heart attack or something."

"No. Is your mom here now?"

Moira shook her head. "She had to work. Because of the call she got. And I'm just hanging around, because I'm on lockdown and she's supposed to come back and if I'm not here I won't just be grounded for this weekend but probably till I go to college or something. She went nuts because she could smell weed, gave me the whole lecture about how even if I'm not smoking it, if some other cops came by I'd be in as much trouble as everybody else. Like, at least till I'm nineteen."

"So your mom doesn't know you were the one who bought the stuff."

Moira grinned. "Yeah, and I'd kinda like you to keep that on the down-low."

"How'd you get it?"

There were cannabis stores everywhere these days, but the owners were usually pretty strict about checking for proof of age.

"Guy I know, goes to Humber. He sold me some. You wanna sit down?"

She edged her butt over a couple of inches so Gage could plunk down next to her.

"You look deep in thought."

"I guess," he said.

"Were you close?"

"To my grandpa?"

"No, Batman. Yeah, your grandpa."

"Yeah. He was great."

"I don't have any grandparents. I mean, I did, I must have, right, or I wouldn't be here, but they were all dead before I was born."

"You mean, your mom's parents and your dad's parents?"

She nodded, bit her lip. "Even if my dad's were alive, probably wouldn't see them because he's not in our lives. He's a gambler."

"What, like, scratch and win tickets?"

That made Moira laugh. "Geez, farm boy, is that what you think gambling is?"

"I know there's casinos and stuff too."

"He's a professional gambler. It's his job."

"Fuck off."

"It's true. He goes all over the world, playing poker and stuff. Real high stakes, like in a James Bond movie. Does okay most of the time."

"I never heard of that. That's weird."

"That's my dad."

"Well, everybody's got shit they're dealing with I guess," Gage said. "I was just talking to someone whose aunt got killed in a bank robbery. She was a teller and even though she handed over the money the robbers shot her. And then the cops killed them when they came out of the bank."

"That'd make a good podcast," Moira said.

"Huh?"

"You don't listen to them? There's hundreds. True crime. I love them. I guess it's in my blood or something. Maybe they already did one." She got out her phone. "What's the name of the dead lady?"

Gage tried to recall what Alicia had told him. Her aunt's last name—Zane—that she'd been killed in 1999, in Oshawa.

Moira added more key words, like *bank* and *holdup* and *takedown*.

Finally, she said, "There's no podcast, and there's no story about it either. Not one thing."

"Maybe it's too old. Stories didn't go online back then."

"I can find other stories from around that time, but not your friend's."

"It doesn't matter," Gage said. "I don't even know why I brought it up."

"Because everybody's got shit they're dealing with. That's what you said."

"Oh yeah, right."

They sat for another minute, saying nothing. Moira nudged him playfully with her elbow. When he didn't return the nudge, she gave him a stronger poke.

"Come on, talk to me."

Gage seemed to be trying to work up the nerve to say something. He wet his lips, getting ready.

Finally, he said, "Can I ask you a question?"

"Is it a math question? I'm not good with those."

"I'm being serious."

"Fine, yes, you can ask me a question."

"If you knew that someone in your family had done a really bad thing, would you tell or would you keep it a secret?"

"What kind of a bad thing?"

"Just . . . really bad."

"I don't know. Like, I guess it would depend on how close I was to that person. And when you say tell, do you mean, like, the police? Or other people *in* that family? Like if you saw your sister's husband having sex with someone else, would you tell her? Because for sure, I would tell. She'd have a right to know. Except I don't have a sister. But just pretending. Like that?"

"Not really. Something worse."

"In my book, cheating would be pretty bad, but okay. Would this be something that you actually saw this person do?"

Gage thought about that, then shook his head. "Not exactly."

"Because if it's just a rumor, then I would say no, until you really knew for sure, and then, maybe. But you're not giving me enough details."

Gage offered none. He got to his feet. "I have to go."

"No rush," she said.

"No, I can't stay. Thanks for talking to me."

He started to walk away, but she grabbed his arm and stopped him. Gage, startled, stood there as she got to her feet, wrapped her arms around him, and squeezed.

"You'll do the right thing," she said.

He was inclined to break her grip, but it felt good, and he decided to let her hold him for another thirty seconds. But he knew, any longer than that, and he'd lose it.

TWENTY-NINE

"Off to the coal mine," Alicia said, slipping on a light jacket not long after Gage had left Holden's house.

"Huh?" said Holden.

"My *job*? You remember I have a *job*?"

"Oh, right, the thing at the thing."

"Yeah, the thing at the thing," she said. "My weekend gig at FreshCo?" One of Yorkton Hill's discount grocery stores. Alicia worked Saturday and Sunday afternoon shifts as a cashier. The store was shifting to self-checkout, but a lot of the older customers refused to use it so they kept one or two checkout lanes open on weekends, when they were busiest.

Holden asked. "When're you done?"

"Seven. I don't know if I'm coming back here or going home. Might depend on whether you can figure out how to wash your sheets."

"I've been studying."

"I'll text you."

Thinking of something else, he asked, "How'd you think Gage was?"

"I don't know. Okay, I guess."

Holden shook his head worriedly. "He's a good kid."

"Sure."

"Hope he gets through this okay. Big traumatic stuff that happens to you when you're young, it can stay with you."

Alicia smiled. "You being the textbook case."

"He was quiet."

"Maybe he's just a quiet kid. Look, I gotta go."

"Want me to drive you?"

"Don't worry about it."

She was out the door. She already had her phone out, having ordered an Uber to take her to work. Her ride was five minutes out, if the app was to be believed. A gray Honda Civic, with a plate that began BBA.

What Gage was, she thought to herself, was not quiet, but a little too inquisitive. Asking her how her aunt died. How she was murdered, whether they caught the guys who did it. For the sake of consistency, she gave him the same story she'd given Holden, that she was killed in a bank holdup that went horribly wrong. Even gave Gage the same name she'd given Holden. Mary Zane, though her aunt's name had been Evelyn Corby.

Alicia hoped she'd told Gage enough to satisfy his curiosity, because if he went online, searching for more details, he wasn't going to find much. At least Holden hadn't done that. He accepted her story as told. But Gage struck her as sharper than Holden.

There was her ride. A gray Civic. It slowed to a stop outside Holden's house. She opened the back door on the passenger side and hopped in.

"How you doin' today?" the driver, a young Hispanic man, asked.

"Fine," Alicia said, in a tone that did not encourage further conversation.

She wondered whether she would go back to Holden's place after work, even if he did do laundry. She could use a break. It was hard pretending. Okay, she wasn't totally putting on an act. She did like the guy. He was a sad case, for sure, but then again, wasn't she? A pair like them, it only made sense they would meet in rehab. Alicia didn't like to think of it as a contest, but she believed she was doing better than Holden at getting her life back on track. She hadn't used in a long time. Some booze, a little weed now and then, but she was off all the other stuff. And she believed she could keep it that way, because things were different now.

Alicia had a purpose.

For the first time in more than twenty-five years, she had a chance to get even.

At first, she thought it had been a hell of a coincidence that she and Holden ended up in the same group, a bunch of recovering addicts trying to come to terms with why their lives were so fucked-up. But then she thought it wasn't so crazy that they would end up crossing paths. They were both products of tragedy, both had turned to drugs or alcohol to deal with the pain, and both had ended up in treatment. Both lived in the same town.

But still, fate had played a role.

At Sharnwood, they were going around the circle, each coming forward with their stories. One guy, he'd been in a car accident that was his fault. His girlfriend had died. Drank to forget. There was a woman who'd lost her four-year-old to cancer. Couldn't get past it. Not everyone had as sorry a tale to tell. "I just like it," said one guy about why he drank. Another, addicted to crack, couldn't explain the need, except to say, "It gets me through the day."

When they got to Alicia, she wasn't sure how much she wanted to talk about it. But she disclosed that her parents both died when she was in her teens. From there she went to live with her aunt, and not long after that, her brother died. And the real capper? Her aunt was murdered.

"Holy shit," said several in the circle.

Including Holden, who said, "Oh man, that one kind of gets to me, but in a different way."

Rather than push Alicia to provide more details, Ben, the group leader, asked Holden to explain what he meant by *different*.

Holden didn't speak for several seconds. "I've never really talked about this," he said. "Not for years. In the beginning, I wanted to, but was scared to, because . . ." His voice started to break. He sniffed a couple of times. "Sorry."

Ben said, "Take your time."

"I couldn't talk about it because . . . I wanted to be loved. And if I told, I wouldn't be anymore."

All eyes on Holden.

"So as the years went on, I tried to forget about it, forget it ever happened, and I guess that's why I'm so fucked-up. I've pushed all this shit so far down, it's taken all the energy I've got to keep it there."

Ben went back to his earlier question. "What did you mean by *different*?"

Holden took another moment, then said, "Alicia's life got messed up because of a murder, and mine got messed up because I was keeping quiet about one." He paused. "I don't think I can really say more than that."

"Nothing leaves this room," Ben said.

Holden cast his eye around the circle. "Yeah, well, I don't know. Everybody here seems okay, but I don't think I want to get too specific? I can say this much. I was just a kid, and the person who did it, it was . . . it was somebody really close."

"When did this happen?" Ben asked.

"Like I said, I was just a kid. It was nineteen ninety-nine."

This was the first time Alicia thought, *What?*

"I saw something I shouldn't have seen. I was in bed and I heard a shot."

Shot, Alicia thought.

"I got out of bed and went to the window, because it sounded like the shot was in our backyard. The houses were kind of spaced out, so if anybody else heard it, they probably didn't think much about it. So I looked out and I saw her body on the ground."

Her, Alicia thought.

"Oh my god," Ben said.

"I could see her, she was face down and she wasn't moving."

Face down, Alicia thought. *Like she'd been shot in the back.*

One of the other men in the group had a question. "Is this, like, still unsolved? Was anybody ever arrested for what happened?"

Holden shook his head.

Unsolved, Alicia thought.

There were more questions, but Holden held up his palms,

said he couldn't really say much more, except to add, "You figure, there are some people who will love you no matter what. You could kill the president, and they'd say, yeah, you probably shouldn't have done that, but hey, we still love you. When you find out they really *could* stop loving you, that's not something you forget."

The group took a break.

When they came back, Ben went back to Alicia.

"I feel we cut you off back there, when you were telling us about your aunt, and we kind of veered off to hear what Holden had to say. But I want to get back to you. Tell us about your aunt. What happened to her?"

During the break, Alicia kept thinking, *Is it possible?*

The few details Holden had provided matched up. The murder he'd witnessed had been of a woman. Most likely shot in the back. It had happened the same year. It had never been solved.

How many unsolved murders did Yorkton Hill have from that year? Assuming, of course, the incident Holden had talked about was local. He hadn't been very clear on that.

Alicia needed to know more. And she didn't want to tip her hand.

So when Ben asked whether she wanted to continue her story, she said, "I'm good."

"You sure?" he asked.

"Maybe next time," she said.

After the session, she sidled up to Holden at the coffee stand.

"Hey," she said.

"Hey," he said.

"What you were saying, that sounded pretty heavy."

"Yeah, well, right back atcha," he said. "Losing your aunt, that's awful."

"I couldn't say anything else. It hurts to talk about."

"No shit."

"You wanna sit down?"

He said sure. There was a common area at Sharnwood where residents and staff could hang. Alicia and Holden found two cushy chairs across from each other and sat down with their paper cups of coffee.

"I shoulda gotten a cookie," Holden said.

"Hold this," she said, handing him her coffee as she ran back to the table. She returned with two chocolate chip cookies for him and two for her.

"You a first-timer?" she asked.

"I wish. Been here so much I should have my mail sent here."

She laughed. "First for me. Costs a lot, but I qualified for some special program that would cover it, at least this once."

"My parents keep throwing money at these people, thinking one time it'll work." He shrugged. "Maybe one of these times they'll get lucky and I'll come out as this big success story." He laughed. "As if."

More small talk. Where they were from, schools they'd attended. Finally, Alicia asked, "Maybe you don't want to talk about it, but man, what you've been holding in all this time, that's nuts. So who is it who wouldn't love you anymore if you talked?"

Holden looked down, shook his head.

"I'm sorry," Alicia said, reaching out and putting her hand on his knee. "I've got no business asking." A pause, and then, "It's just, sometimes it helps to talk about these things."

"You didn't tell your whole story either," he said.

She took her hand off his knee. "You're right. Point taken. Okay, so this is what happened."

Alicia had always been imaginative. Back in high school, she'd taken a creative writing class. She'd loved to write short stories. Ideas just flew into her head. There was a time when she thought that was what she'd like to be: a writer. But after the death of her parents and her brother, and then her aunt, she'd lost any enthusiasm she might have had in that direction. Anything she might want to write about was too painful.

Didn't mean she couldn't spin a good tale when she had to. She was a good liar. After all, isn't that what writers are?

"A bank robbery," she said. "My aunt—Mary was her name—was shot and killed in a bank robbery."

"God, that's awful," Holden said. "And you were living with her at the time?"

She nodded. "I was out on my own after that."

Alicia was ready with more details. She could embellish if necessary. But Holden didn't ask.

"Okay, over to you," she said.

Holden ate his first cookie.

"I don't know . . ."

Alicia didn't push. Waited.

Holden took in some air, let out a very long breath. "Oh boy."

"Take your time."

"It was my mom."

Didn't see that coming, Alicia thought.

"Your mom? You saw your *mom* kill someone?"

Holden put his index finger to his lips and looked around in case anyone was listening. "Yeah," he said.

"Why? What happened? Who did she kill?"

Holden was close to hyperventilating.

"It's okay, it's okay. Take it slow," she said.

"I swear, I've never talked about this."

"Maybe you *need* to. After all this time."

He took a few more breaths to calm himself and said, "This woman."

"What woman?"

Whoa, Alicia thought. *Don't push too hard. Let him take his time.*

"I didn't know for a while. But you start putting the pieces together over time, right? It was this woman my dad worked with. They both worked for the same company."

"What company was that?"

"Did you see all that stuff in the news a few years ago? About this drug company that was knowingly getting people addicted to painkillers?"

She felt her heart starting to beat more quickly. "Maybe . . ."

"Wiffel-Smith," Holden said.

In her head, Alicia heard: *DING DING DING DING DING!*

"Yeah, I think so," she said.

She could barely breathe.

"She was going to expose the company or something like that, and my mother didn't want that to happen."

"Wow. That's wild. Did you ever find out the woman's name?"

Like she even needed it at this point.

Holden shrugged. "I knew it once but I'm not sure I remember it. A lot of this stuff, I find I try to block it out. But I can't."

She nodded sympathetically. "What's your mother's name?"

"Catherine."

"Catherine," she repeated. "I don't know how you begin to deal with something like that."

"She said if I ever told, that it would destroy the family and she wouldn't love me anymore."

"Harsh." Alicia had a sip of her coffee, ate her cookie. "That's really fucking harsh. But you're not worried about that now? I mean, is she still alive, your mom?"

"Oh yeah."

Alicia nodded. "Huh. You're not worried she'll deliver on her threat now?"

"Well, first of all, she doesn't have to know I've told you. And second, I don't know if I give a fuck anymore. If she could say something like that, did she even love me in the first place?"

"There you go."

"Look, maybe I was messed up from the start, and it wouldn't have mattered what happened that night. But what if I could have been normal, and she took away my chance? And the more I think about it, the more I wonder, what do I care whether she loves me or not? Some days, I think, if she died, I wouldn't shed a tear. Not only that, I'd feel like I'd been released, you know? Like I'd have my freedom. That I wouldn't have to worry about it one more fucking day."

"I hear you," she said. "I do." She reached out and touched his face gently with the tips of her fingers. "You're a good person. You didn't deserve this. You don't deserve to have this held over you. I'm honestly really the first person you've ever told?"

He hesitated before answering. "I kinda told one other person. Not as much as I told you now, but nibbling around the edges."

"Who's that?"

"My nephew," he said. "Gage."

"Gage."

Holden nodded.

"When we get out, when they've cured us," and at that, she grinned and rolled her eyes, "and they send us back out into the world, I'd like to keep in touch."

"Yeah, that'd be nice."

"We could hang out."

"Sure." He took her hand and squeezed it. "Let's."

As Alicia smiled, she was already thinking about what she would do with this new information. How she could get her revenge on one Catherine Chartwell.

She could go to the police with what she knew.

But where was the fun in that?

THIRTY

Dalton Crane was unsettled. Someone had talked. There were only so many people it could be. And at first, Crane was pretty sure who it was.

Catherine Chartwell, standing in that hotel parking lot, had told him she'd received, in the last few weeks, several calls to her cell phone from a blocked ID.

They'd been short and to the point, these calls. As best as Catherine could recall—not easy, because she was dumbstruck when she received them—they went something like this:

"*You think you got away with it, but the chickens are coming home to roost.*"

"*You're gonna pay for what you did, you miserable cunt.*"

"*You better keep looking over your shoulder because we're coming for you.*"

Catherine told Crane she hadn't said a word when she received the first call. She was too stunned, and besides, the caller didn't stay on the line. On the second call, Catherine demanded to know who she was—the caller's voice was definitely female—and what she wanted.

But again, the call ended.

The third call went pretty much the same way. Catherine pleading with her tormentor, asking what she wanted, why she was doing this to her. But her anonymous caller had nothing more to say.

What was there to do, really? Maybe the threats would fall off. The caller would have her fun and move on. After all, if she really had something, some proof, why wasn't she going to the police with it? Plenty of nutcases out there made threats, but they never followed through. The news was full of them. Politicians, other public figures, got death threats all the time but almost nothing ever came of them.

Catherine couldn't call the police. She couldn't talk to Brent about it. It would dredge up so much old baggage. Was her caller someone who really knew something, or was she only guessing? Trying to rattle her? Well, with everything that had happened over the past few days, she was *rattled* all right.

"I should think it's fairly obvious," Crane said.

"Really?"

"Leah Kennard made those calls. Your husband confessed to her what the two of you had done and—"

"The *three* of us," Catherine reminded him.

Crane sighed. "Brent told her everything. But unbeknownst to him, she started harassing you. Who knows what her plan was, exactly. What she hoped to achieve. Maybe she was looking for leverage, blackmail. A way to force you out so she could have Brent for herself. And then Brent found out what she had done, how she could expose both of you, and he killed her. And then himself."

Catherine said, "No."

"And why not?"

"I've had another call since it happened."

It had come Friday night, when she was getting ready for bed at the hotel. Short and sweet.

"You were lucky. Next time we'll get it right."

"Oh," Crane said.

Catherine's theory as she explained it to Crane: The killings were payback. Her caller had entered their home, found Brent and Leah, assumed Leah was Catherine, and shot them. Staged it to look like a murder-suicide.

"At a glance, she looked like me. And even if she hadn't, whoever shot her would have just assumed it was me."

"Staging a suicide is not as easy at it sounds," Crane said, sounding as though he spoke from experience. "Even if we accept that it's what it appears to be, there's still someone out there who knows, or is pretending to know, what happened to Corby. Perhaps your husband confided in someone other than Leah, or he told her and she told someone else."

"I just . . . I just don't think he would have told."

"Maybe he loved her. Wanted to confess all."

Catherine looked pained. "I still don't think he'd have said anything."

"And it wasn't you."

She shook her head vehemently. "Of course not."

"That leaves one person."

Catherine paled. "It wasn't him."

"Perhaps you should ask him."

"I did. I asked him if he'd kept his promise and he said he had."

A slow nod. "And tell me about young Holden. What kind of a man has he grown up to be?"

Catherine looked away. "He's had his troubles."

"Troubles. Perhaps you could elaborate."

"He's had a rough time. In and out of rehab and—"

Crane's eyebrows went up like two rockets. "So, a drug addict? They have a reputation for always telling the truth."

Catherine pointed a finger. "Stay away from him."

Crane's lips pursed with regret, as though thinking of something he should have done on that night long ago.

"And even if it's him," Catherine said, "and I'm not saying it is, what's done is done."

Crane was thinking differently. Maybe it was time to correct his earlier mistake. If Holden had told one person, he could tell another.

"We can ask him again whom he might have told, or we can hope your caller gets in touch again. And when she does, we dangle some bait."

"Bait?"

"If we can't figure out how to get to her, we have to make her come to us. If and when she calls, and I'm betting she will, before she hangs up, you say 'I'll pay.' Simple as that. If she doesn't hang up, you've set the hook. Tell her to name her price."

"What if she asks for, I don't know, a million dollars?"

"You agree."

He nodded.

"I don't know . . . I don't know if I can pull together a million. And she'll want it in cash, won't she? I mean, we had investments, but now there'll be an estate to settle. It could take time before I can get to the money. And there'll be questions if I start converting that kind of money to cash and—"

Crane waved a hand to silence her. "Don't worry about that. Arrange a time and place to make a drop. Then call me."

"But if I can't pull together the money in time—"

Crane, wearying, closed his eyes for a moment. Catherine finally clued in.

"Oh," she said.

And here he thought he was done with this kind of work.

The last fifteen years or so had been pretty mundane for Crane. He'd stayed with Wiffel-Smith almost to the end. Evelyn Corby would have been pleased with how things eventually turned out. Her *Pentagon Papers* weren't necessary. Wiffel's addiction to profits was its undoing. The lawsuits mounted. Federal investigations on both sides of the border were launched. Charges filed. Like hanging out in the bunker with Hitler, Crane continued to work for Graham Wiffel right up until the day he went up to the roof of the corporate headquarters and jumped off.

At least, that was how it looked.

Stoking Wiffel's fears that his office might be bugged, Crane had invited him to the roof to bring him up to speed on his latest adventures in fixing and intimidation. Crane knew the authorities were closing in on Wiffel, and when they did, would he reveal the things Crane had done at his behest?

That wasn't a chance worth taking.

It couldn't have been simpler. Crane got Wiffel close to the edge and tossed him off. And on his way back down, he'd left a short note on the man's desk.

Forgive me.

Crane did a good enough job replicating his boss's handwriting that the veracity of the note was never questioned.

In his experience, fear was a great motivator. You generally didn't have to kill people. You just had to scare them. Make them understand there were consequences to not going along. But sometimes, fear wasn't enough. And when it was your own future on the line, options were limited.

This was looking like one of those times. Crane's fate was very much tied to Catherine's.

When and if she got another call, Catherine would see if she could set the hook, then have Crane reel in the culprit.

She got back to him sooner than he'd expected. But it wasn't about the money drop.

THIRTY-ONE

Alicia had been discharged from Sharnwood first. When Holden got out a week later, she was the first person he phoned.

"How's it going?" he'd asked her.

"So far, so good. Got a lead on a job but it's just weekends so I got time Monday to Friday if you want to hang or anything."

"Let me check with my secretary," he said, paused, then said, "My schedule appears to be wide open." He did have a line, he said, on doing some drywall work, but it would be intermittent.

The thing was, Alicia did kind of like him. He was funny, self-deprecating, not full of himself. Did an impression of Ben that was spot-on. And he wasn't totally wrapped up in himself. He went on one time about frogs, how he used to find them in the pond behind his house, but now you hardly saw them anymore, same with toads, and how if a species vanished, it could throw off the entire ecosystem.

Like she cared about whether toads disappeared from the face of the earth.

But yeah, he was a generally nice, if severely messed-up,

guy. So she felt a little badly, lying to him about who her aunt really was.

She'd actually considered coming clean, admitting that based on what he'd revealed, it was as good as certain that his mother had murdered her aunt. But that could go very wrong. He'd probably freak out. And why wouldn't he? He'd have set his mom up to be arrested. All Alicia had to do was make one phone call and the police would be at Catherine's door before dinner.

But there was a slight chance that Holden would want to make amends somehow. Be an ally in getting justice for her aunt, even if it meant betraying his mother.

Too risky, Alicia figured.

That was when she started thinking about doing it herself. If you wanted something done right, as the saying goes. Kill the bitch and be done with it. But did she have it in her? She believed she did, but the larger question was whether she could get away with it. She wanted justice for her aunt Evelyn, but she didn't want to spend the next twenty years in a penitentiary either.

And then she hit on another plan. Something far more poetic. Persuade Holden to get justice for *himself.*

She would work on him slowly.

The local Tims became a regular spot for them. Coffee, a couple of Boston creams. Talk for hours.

"It's just so unfair," she said.

"What?"

"What your mom put you through. You've had to carry her guilt."

She'd struck on something that had occurred to him many times over the years. "Go on," he said.

"She gets away with murder, she's in the clear, gets to go on and live her life, not a care in the world. But you, you're the one holding that big secret, letting it eat away at you. Year after year. Like a cancer. And it just keeps growing and growing inside of you. It's metastasizing."

That seemed like enough for their first meeting. Plant the seed. Over their next coffee, she'd ramp it up a bit.

"How could any mother do that to a kid?" Alicia said, as though thinking out loud, shaking her head. "Tell them they wouldn't love them anymore."

"I don't know," Holden said.

"I'll bet you Jeffrey Dahmer's mother still loved him. The guy that ate people?"

"Was his mother still alive when he did that?"

"Okay, I don't know," Alicia said. "It's a for instance. Like the BTK killer, or Lee Harvey Oswald, or even Hannibal Lecter. If their mothers were alive, I'll bet they still loved them, even though they did bad things."

"Lecter's not a real person."

Alicia rolled her eyes. "You're missing my point."

"But they were the ones that did the bad things. They killed and ate people but at least they weren't ratting out their mothers. She said if I ever told, the family would get torn apart. She'd go to jail, my dad would go to jail, they'd split me and Reece up and put us in different foster homes or something like that."

Alicia shrugged. "And she put all that on *you*. Like you were the one responsible for keeping the family together when the real person at fault was *her* for killing somebody. You don't see that? How she manipulated you? Dumped her guilt onto you? Jesus."

She sprung for another round of coffees, figuring they'd get kicked out if they didn't keep buying something. But she got herself a decaf. Didn't want to be up half the night.

"You need to be free," she said. "Liberated."

"How would I do that?"

She shrugged. Thought, save that one for next time they got together.

That turned out to be a movie. Some big noisy thing where massive robots were fighting monstrous sea creatures. Totally dumb, but fun. When they came out, Holden said, "I liked the part where the robot punched the monster," and Alicia couldn't stop laughing because there'd only been two straight hours of that.

She said, "Take me to your place and fuck my brains out."

Holden nodded. "I can do that."

The closer she drew him to her, she figured, the better chance she had of getting him to do what she wanted. And again, she did kind of like him. But if he hadn't had the potential to be her instrument, would she have stayed with him?

Not a chance, Charlie.

When she saw his place, her resolve hardened. She wanted Holden to kill his mother not just for her. He needed to do it for himself. How could his family let him live here? Okay, sure, they'd dropped a bundle on his treatment, but couldn't they spend a few extra bucks and maybe send in a cleaning lady once a week?

Fuck it, she'd do it herself. Manipulating Holden—*God, was she no better than his mother?*—meant putting in the time here, and she couldn't live in this mess. When she wasn't on the stuff, she was something of a neat freak. Holden, on the other hand, was oblivious to the mess around him, straight or high.

She put in an afternoon once, when he was doing his drywalling gig, tackling the mess in the kitchen. Took care of the dirty dishes in the sink, scrubbed the countertops, then went into the fridge, a black hole of expiration dates. She still had some energy left, so she started on his bedroom, hanging up clothes that didn't need to be laundered, vacuuming, rearranging the top shelf of his closet so stuff wouldn't fall out on somebody's head.

Moved a shoebox that felt too heavy to just have shoes in it. Brought the box down, put it on the bed, took off the lid.

"What the," she said.

A gun.

Worried that it might be loaded, that she might discharge it by accident, she made no attempt to pick it up. But she wasn't going to put it back either. When Holden returned, she brought him into the bedroom and pointed.

"Explain *that*," she said. "And don't get all why-you-messing-with-my-stuff. The box nearly fell on my head."

"You kind of already know," he said, but there was still a story to tell.

Holden and Reece had loved that pond in their backyard. Donning tall rubber boots, they'd try to catch tadpoles with little nets. When they got to be frogs, it was even more challenging. Those dudes could jump. One time, their dad bought them two remote control boats so they could have races. That fun ended when the boats crashed into each other and sank to the mucky bottom.

Brent did them better with the real thing. A small, wooden rowboat and two paddles. They'd pretend to be pirates, and when they reached land, otherwise known as their backyard, they'd imagine it to be an island where buried treasure might be found. Brent later bought them fishing poles, but the novelty of dropping a line in the water wore off soon because the pond had no fish.

Brent tried to rectify that. A couple of weeks after *the incident* (as Holden had come to think of it) he went on a four-day fishing trip with some Wiffel-Smith colleagues. It was designed as a bonding exercise, and Brent was happy to take part. More and more, he accepted opportunities that put distance between himself and Catherine. He returned with several perch that he'd kept alive in a covered bucket. He dumped them into the pond, hoping the boys might later catch them. The perch didn't survive their relocation, unfortunately, and floated to the surface in no time.

Holden, however, had faith.

A few days later, when Holden was home alone—Reece was at an after-school soccer practice, Brent at work, Catherine in downtown Toronto checking out the shops in high-end Yorkville—he took the boat out on his own. That was against the rules. A parent was always supposed to be home when the boys played in the boat.

Holden didn't care.

He was already channeling his mother's threat into antisocial behavior. Downing the last few drops of his parents' drinks when they weren't looking. Sniffing glue he used for his model kits. Pitching a rock through the odd window.

This particular day, he decided to give the pond one last chance to offer up a real, live fish. He attached part of a Kraft cheese slice to the hook of his fishing pole. Did fish like cheese? Who knew? But mice supposedly did, so why not give it a go?

He reached the center of the pond and brought in the paddle. (There was only one by this time.) The boat might drift, but there was no wind that day, and there certainly weren't currents. Holden picked up the pole and cast out, slowly reeling the line back in, then casting out again. He did this over and over again. Frequently, the hook would catch something in the mucky bottom. A twig or branch that had fallen from an overhanging tree. A long weed that hung on to the hook like a strand of spaghetti.

"Shit," Holden said aloud, because when you were all alone on the pond you could say whatever you pleased.

He'd long since lost that piece of cheese on the hook and had no more. He'd eaten the rest of the slice. Anyway, it didn't seem to be working. Fish, if there were any in this small body of water, clearly didn't care for cheese.

He decided to cast out one last time with an unbaited hook, and damned if he didn't land something. Reeling in, he thought, if this was a fish, it was a heavy one. But it wasn't putting up much of a fight. It was like dead weight. He brought his catch in close to the boat, gripped the line and lifted it out of the water.

"Fuck," he said, once again demonstrating that out on the pond you could say anything and get away with it.

The hook, miraculously, had snagged the trigger guard of a gun. And not just any gun, Holden knew immediately.

Still dangling the gun, he lowered it gently to the bottom of the boat. Gently worked the hook from the trigger guard, careful not to touch the trigger itself. Delicately, he wrapped his hand around the grip.

Was it still loaded? He wasn't about to stare down the barrel for a look-see. Nor was he going to fire it to find out. He was smart enough to know there might be bullets in it, so he would have to be very careful.

He considered what to do with his find.

The sensible course of action would be to present it to his parents. They'd want to dispose of it, and they would know how to do it. He could recall, in the days after the incident, his father out in the boat, trying to see to the bottom of the pond, poking about with a paddle.

Holden and Reece had been inside, having breakfast, and a curious Reece went outside to the pond's edge and asked his father what he was looking for. Back in the kitchen, Catherine had given Holden a sharp look. He was not to say a word.

Brent told Reece that he had lost a credit card. Thought it had slipped out of his wallet the last time he'd been out there. Reece found that answer puzzling, given that their father never took the boat out. It was just for the boys.

"Go finish your breakfast," Brent had said.

And then his father, in frustration, swung one of the two paddles down onto the side of the boat, snapping it in two, the broad end falling into the water. He tossed the splintered end still in his hand into the bottom of the boat.

So yeah, Holden's parents would want to know what he'd found. But Holden wasn't sure he wanted to tell them.

He had to move quickly, before anyone got home. He paddled back to the pond's edge, pulled the boat a few feet up onto the yard, gingerly took the gun into the house and up to his room, placing it on his bed. In the hall linen closet he found an old hand towel, one his mother would never notice was missing. After rinsing the gun off and taking a hair dryer to it, he wrapped it up. He emptied a shoebox filled with Toronto Blue Jays and

Toronto Maple Leafs trading cards and put the gun in it. He dumped the cards back on top, covering any trace of the towel, and put the box on the top shelf of his closet.

And there it stayed.

For years.

Occasionally, when no one was home, he would take down the box, bring out the gun, hold it, feel it in his hand, still not knowing whether it was loaded, whether it would even work. When he got older and it was time for him to live on his own, the box was the first thing he packed. Eventually, he took it to a friend who knew a lot about guns.

"Where'd you find this?" his friend asked.

"Just around. Is it any good?"

"Yeah, but it needs cleaning up. I think it can be salvaged. Leave it with me."

Holden came back a week later.

"You're lucky you didn't kill yourself with this thing," his friend said. "It was loaded and it's got a kind of sensitive trigger. It's a wonder you didn't blow your head off. I cleaned it up, oiled it, checked it out all over, test-fired it. It's now shipshape."

"Is it loaded *now*?"

"Hell no."

As Holden came to the end of his tale, gazing at the gun in the same shoebox where it had been stored for years—the trading cards long since gone—Alicia said, "That's one batshit story."

"Yeah."

"I mean, this is *it*. This is the gun your mom used to shoot that woman."

She shook her head in wonder.

The possibilities, she thought. In this box, right here, was more than just evidence the police could use to convict his mother. It was fucking *karma*. Meant to be.

To get even, with *this* gun. It was a thing of beauty.

Now, weeks later, one day after Holden's father and mistress were found dead, scanning groceries over the barcode reader and listening to those incessant beeps at FreshCo, Alicia was thinking it hadn't worked out quite the way she'd planned.

The wrong woman was dead.

But that didn't have to mean the fun was over.

THIRTY-TWO

Reece

I left my mother's house feeling enraged. No, more than that. Stunned and horrified. Baffled and betrayed. But more than anything else, plain old outraged.

She'd lied to us. Lied to me and lied to Holden. Was that too harsh? At the very least, she lied by omission. She allowed us to *live* a lie.

Holden was my half brother. His biological mother was Leah Kennard.

We'd both lost a father, but Holden had lost his true mother, as well.

And he didn't know.

After I dropped off my father's suit at the funeral home, I wanted to drive straight to Holden's and tell him, but there was part of me that knew, despite my anger, that Mom was the one who would have to deliver that news. I would compel her to do it if I had to. Would this revelation damage Holden? Was there a risk this would send him into a downward spiral that could find him back in rehab? Very possibly. But we were so far past the point of covering things up. People were dead. This shit was real.

And while I believed I needed to hold off telling him the truth about his parentage, I didn't see any reason why I couldn't head to his place and ask him if he'd ever heard of Evelyn Corby and whether he had any memory of Dad owning a gun. Despite Mom's denials, I was sure I recalled Dad and her having a discussion about getting one. Maybe Holden had heard something I hadn't. I didn't see a way not to tell him that the same gun Dad had used to kill Leah, and then himself, had been used in the murder of someone Dad would surely have known. Did he believe Dad might have killed her?

God, what a mess.

On the way to Holden's, I phoned Diana, told her where I was headed, and gave her as tight a version of everything I'd learned as I could, like I was writing a newscast, starting with the ballistics revelation.

She said, "A situation where someone might shoot his lover and then himself, as awful as that is, it's something I can almost get my head around. But that your dad would kill some woman and leave her body—no, I can't believe it. I *don't* believe it."

I wanted to share her conviction. "Mom was totally blindsided. I'd never seen her look that stunned. But there's more."

Diana said, "Hit me." She sounded numb.

"Holden is my half brother. Leah Kennard was a surrogate. Dad supplied the sperm—in a lab or whatever—and she got pregnant, and she had Holden. They hired her."

Nothing on the other end of the line.

"You there?"

"I'm here." Like I said, numb.

"Mom couldn't get pregnant, they went the surrogacy route, and then miracle of miracles, a year later I came along."

Any other time, Diana would have had some kind of crack about me being a miracle, but my news had put her off her game. She did have a question, though: "And your dad was having an affair with the surrogate, with Leah, all these years?"

"I don't think so. Mom made it sound like it was the last couple. I feel like my parents had been going through the motions for a long time. Looking back, it started when I was a kid, maybe ten or eleven. Something happened. One day we were a more or less happy family, and the next everyone was walking on eggshells. Hang on, I'm at the funeral home."

I tossed the phone onto the passenger seat and kept the car running while I grabbed the suit off the back seat hanger, ran it in, and handed it to the first person I saw. I was back in the car in under a minute and picked up the phone.

"Still there?"

"Still here. You going to Holden's now?"

"Yeah."

"You can't tell him the stuff about who his real mother is. That's got to come from your mom, whether she wants to do it or not. It's not just about finding out who his mother is. It's finding out who she *isn't*."

Diana had a way of putting things. Before I could respond to that, she said, "Swing by. You need me there when you see Holden."

I didn't have to think about that. "Five minutes," I said.

Holden's car was in the driveway. As I pulled up in front of the house, I had to admit part of me was hoping he wouldn't be home. I was all fired up about coming here, and now that I was, I was worried about whether I was going to be laying too much on him.

Diana, sensing my apprehension, said, "We'll take it slow."

He must have spotted us through the window, because he was already coming out the front door to greet us. He approached Diana first as she got out the passenger side.

"Hey, sis." His pet name for Diana since we'd gotten married. He threw his arms around her, catching her off guard at how pleased he seemed to see her.

"Hey," Diana said.

Holden came around the car and gave me a hug as well. "'Sup?" He had a smile on his face that looked genuine enough.

I glanced across the hood of the BMW at Diana, who gave me a look that seemed to say, *Let's do this.*

"Listen," I said gently, "there've been some developments and I wanted to bounce a couple things off you... Going way back, you ever remember Mom and Dad talking about getting a gun?"

The smile evaporated. "What?"

"Okay, I'm just gonna lay it all out here," I said. "The police say—"

Diana raised a cautious hand. "Holden, Reece found out some troubling things today and you're entitled to know about them." She paused, then said, "The gun your father used yesterday . . . was used years ago to shoot someone your dad would have known."

"The hell are you talking about?" He looked at me. "How come *she* gets to know stuff first?"

"I told her," I said, not liking the tone he was taking with my wife. "I was at Mom's when the detective came by."

"I've never even met this detective," Holden said, as if that somehow discounted anything she might have told us.

"The thing is," I said, controlling my voice, "maybe Dad had this gun all these years and we never knew about it. Look, I'm surprised, because I remember Dad hating guns, but how else do you explain what—"

Holden made a sudden, sweeping gesture, first crossing his wrists and then extending this arms, putting a stop to all this. "I don't want to hear it."

And then he did something I wasn't expecting. He put his palms on my shoulders and pushed. Hard. I stumbled back, catching myself just before I might have lost my balance and hit the ground.

"*Holden!*" Diana said.

He looked her way, then back at me. He stook a step back and said, "I just . . . just can't handle any more of this. Go, okay? Just go."

"I'm not going until you tell me—"

"Reece," Diana said. She waved her phone at me. She'd had a text, but of course I couldn't make it out from the other side of the car. "It's Gage."

He was waiting for us on the front step. His text to his mother had been simple enough:

Where is everybody?

Diana had written back, asking if he was okay. The three dots danced for a few seconds, but then stopped, like he had something he wanted to say but couldn't get the words out.

"You okay?" Diana asked as we both got out of the car.

"I kind of freaked when there was no one here," he said. "Where were you?"

I said, "There's been a lot going on." I told him the gun his grandfather had used was linked to the unsolved murder of someone who'd worked for Wiffel-Smith. A woman named Evelyn Corby.

"That's crazy," he said. "There's no way. If they think Grandpa had anything to do with that, they're nuts."

I didn't want to remind him what his grandfather had done the day before.

"We want to think that too," Diana said. "Look, I'm with you. I don't believe he could do that."

Gage sat on the front step, looked down, and said, "There's something I should tell you."

I was so not in the mood for more surprises. But I said, "About?"

"It has to do with Grandpa."

"Something about yesterday?"

"No. A while back."

We waited.

He raised his head, looked at his mother, then me. "I stole something."

Diana, calmly, asked, "Where was this? What did you steal?"

"Just don't freak out. Let me tell the whole story."

I nodded. "We're listening."

"It was like, a year, year and a half, something like that. But I was with my friends, at the store, and they kind of dared me to steal something. So I grabbed this bag of chips and tried to sneak out with it but got caught."

"Go on," Diana said.

"The manager, he called the cops, and they came, and they took me to the station, and I was really scared, and they told me to call my parents, but I didn't. I called Grandpa instead."

"Why would you—"

"Mom, just let me tell it. I was . . . I was afraid to call you guys because I knew you'd be mad and I couldn't face that so Grandpa came down and he said he was my father and they bought it and he sat in with the cops and I can hardly remember what anybody said because I was so scared they'd send me to jail or something. But Grandpa saved me, said he would take me back to the store and make me apologize and that's what we did."

"He never said a word about it to me," I said.

"That was the deal. He promised he wouldn't, but he said it was my one chance. If I did anything like that again he wouldn't bail me out or cover it up for me. But what he did, it was like the nicest thing he ever did for me, up to then."

I couldn't be angry. This wasn't something that had happened recently. I couldn't see the point of a lecture at this late date. And while I would have preferred that he'd called his mother or me, I understood why he'd called his grandfather. In the same situation, I might have done the same.

"I thought you should know," Gage said. "I'm sorry I didn't tell you sooner."

He was crying. Diana sat next to him, put his head on her shoulder.

"Why tell us now?" I asked.

Gage sniffed, hunted in his pocket for a tissue, and wiped his eyes and nose. "Because you need to know Grandpa was a good person. You need to know he would never mean to hurt anybody, not now, not in the past. And maybe he did some wrong things, like having an affair or whatever, but I don't think he was happy, and you'd have to be blind not to see it."

"I hear you," I said. "I do. But—"

"I know what you're going to say," Gage said. "It's all bullshit. He was the best person I've ever known and you should be ashamed for thinking any different."

He got up and went into the house.

THIRTY-THREE

Crane answered his phone. "Yes."

"It's the same bloody gun!"

"Catherine, calmly please."

She ignored him. "The gun they found *yesterday*, it's the one I threw in the pond!"

Crane thought about that for a moment, wondering how that must have been determined. A ballistics test. They would have compared the bullets recovered from the previous day's scene to the one recovered from Evelyn Corby's body.

"It's impossible," she said. "Brent tried to find it. He raked the bottom of the pond. It had to have sunk into the muck."'

"And yet," Crane said, "here we are."

"That detective, she thinks Brent killed that woman."

Crane gave that a moment's thought. "Let her."

"What?"

"Let. Her."

"I don't understand."

"It's better than the alternative. I don't know the nature of this detective's questions, but if she seems to be zeroing in, you might lead her in a more advantageous direction. That you hate to think it, but perhaps it's possible Brent killed that woman. After all, he's gone and established a pattern. Dead men don't generally have the opportunity to defend themselves. Has she been in touch?"

"The detective?"

"No. Your mystery caller."

"Oh, no. No, she hasn't."

This was not good. They couldn't sit around waiting for the phone to ring. They needed to be proactive.

"Has this detective spoken to your son?"

"Many times," Catherine said. "Reece was here with me when she started asking about that gun, if Brent had it years ago, if he knew that woman."

"Not that son. Your other son."

Catherine went quiet.

"Has she talked to *him*?" Crane asked, pressing.

"I don't think so. There's . . . there really isn't any reason for her to."

"You're being naive. With this development, she'll want to talk to everyone."

"He was a *child*! There'd be no *reason* for her to talk to him!"

"But if she does—"

"He's kept it a secret this long."

"But *has* he?"

"You don't have to worry about him."

"Of course. A mother should know."

"He won't— Hang on, I'm getting another call."

Alicia was on a break. There was a staff room at the back of the grocery store where employees had their lunch or sat and scrolled their phones or read a book or just sat on the old, vinyl couch and closed their eyes for a few minutes, taking a nap.

She could use one. Working the checkout, scanning groceries, bagging them, dealing with people who were dumber than shoes, might look easy but standing there, hour after hour, was murder on your back and your feet. She'd been ready to throttle the last customer before she put up the "Sorry Closed Use Next Checkout" sign on the conveyor belt. He'd waited until the last item had been scanned and bagged before he started searching all his pockets for his wallet to bring out some cash, like it hadn't occurred to him until that moment that he was going to have to pay for all this shit.

When Alicia came into the break room, one of the young kids who stocked shelves was sitting at the lunch table, playing a game on his phone. Everyone called him Corky, although Alicia thought the *C* would be better replaced with a *D*.

"Hey," Alicia said.

The boy didn't so much as grunt, transfixed as he was by what was happening on the screen. Alicia went over to the coffee machine, poured herself a cup, then sat down opposite him.

"I think Wilkins was looking for you," she said. The store manager.

The boy glanced up. "Huh?"

"You piss him off somehow?"

He paused the game and pushed back his chair. "That asshole," he said as he shuffled out of the room. He'd be gone a few minutes, she hoped, trying to track down the boss, whom Alicia knew wasn't even in today.

Long enough to make a phone call.

She didn't really have a plan as she brought out the burner phone from her purse. Nothing more than keeping Catherine Chartwell off-balance.

Holden's account of her visit to his place on Friday made it clear she was pretty shaken up. Who wouldn't be, after learning your husband was found dead in bed with his whore. Holden had gone a little manic, too, so relieved his mother was alive that he tried to talk her into a cruise.

All of which confounded Alicia. Hadn't he *wanted* her dead in the first place? Hadn't Alicia persuaded him he'd never be free until the witch was toast? They'd come so close, and when things took a turn, he couldn't have been happier. All that guilt, lifted.

And she'd done such a good job of getting him to that place. Bit by bit, little by little. Planting the seeds.

Talking him into doing a line here and there. Softening up the old brain, making him susceptible to her suggestions.

And finally the kicker: "I mean, you've got the gun right there."

Wouldn't it be fitting? That Catherine Chartwell be shot with the same gun she'd used to kill Alicia's aunt? Balance in the universe, that's what it was.

Holden would be her instrument. That *had* been the plan. Get *him* to do her bidding. It wasn't like she was too chickenshit to do it herself, to kill this woman she'd never actually met, never actually seen, but there was something poetic about having her son take her out.

One day, she had pocketed the gun without Holden's knowledge, found a guy who could supply the right ammunition. Brought the gun and bullets home, loaded it just the way the guy had showed her. “Be very, very careful,” he’d advised her. “That thing’s got a light trigger.”

That night, when she and Holden were in bed, she said, “Got a surprise for you.” He thought it was going to be some kind of sex toy when she opened the drawer of the bedside table. But what she brought out was his gun.

“What’s that doing there?” Holden asked.

“Not much good to you up in your closet,” she said. “I want you to feel safe. Don’t you want to feel safe? It’s a crazy world out there.”

“I . . . guess.”

“And even if you keep it someplace where you can get your hands on it right away, it’s pretty useless if it’s not loaded.”

He sat up in bed. “What did you do?”

She brought out the box of ammunition, which had also been in the drawer. “You are good to go.”

“It’s loaded?”

Alicia smiled and nodded. She set it back in the drawer and closed it slowly. “There when you need it.”

“Nobody’s gonna break in here.”

“You never know.”

He looked unconvinced. “Makes me nervous.”

“Come on. You’ve kept that gun in your place for years. And you were a *kid*. You kept it with your baseball cards. *That* was irresponsible. This is different.”

Alicia won him over. The loaded gun stayed in the drawer. She was getting there. Now to get him to use it.

One evening, a breakthrough.

She’d got him wound up about how differently his life might have gone if his mother hadn’t screwed him up. He had all this natural talent. He could have become a comedian, maybe, he was such a good mimic. Or an environmentalist, a champion of causes. But that fear of losing his mother's love, it gnawed away at him, made him feel worthless. He paced the living room, shaking his head, agreeing with her, saying he'd always had this dream of being a mountain climber.

Alicia thought, *Seriously?*

But he lacked the ambition, he said. Not just to climb mountains, but to accomplish anything of note. Alicia had come to the conclusion that Holden was, at his very core, an underachiever, and that his mother didn't have all that much to do with it, but that didn't mean she wasn't happy to feed his need to blame her.

As he ranted, she went into the bedroom, returned with the gun, and put it in his hand.

"If she were here right now, what would you do?"

He looked at the gun, as if appreciating its real power—its potential to change his life—for the first time. He raised the gun, pointed at the door, as if someone were standing on the other side of it.

"I'd shoot her in the fucking head," he said.

The following morning, he'd expressed regret for his behavior. Took the gun from the drawer, put it back in the shoebox, and placed it back on the closet shelf, as though afraid of what he might do with it if it were too close at hand.

She was starting to doubt whether he had it in him to get the job done. Sometimes, if you wanted something done right, you had to do it yourself.

And then yesterday happened.

Talk about your clusterfuck.

Okay, so maybe things didn't go off the way she'd hoped.

That didn't mean you let up the pressure. You didn't give the enemy time to recover. You kept the heat on.

With Corky out of the room now, Alicia entered a number on her phone.

One ring. Two rings. Three rings. Four.

Was she not going to accept her call? Maybe the cops were there. Or she was in the—

"Hello?"

Catherine sounded frazzled. *Let's turn that screw down a little tighter.*

Alicia said, "Think you're in the clear? Not a chance. We missed you yesterday but—"

"I'll pay!"

Alicia said, "What?"

"I have money. Name your price. I'll pay you to leave me alone."

"You think this is about *money*?"

"It's always about money," Catherine said. "If it's enough."

Alicia reflected on where she was, sitting in the break room of a discount Yorkton Hill FreshCo, wearing her "Hi! I'm Alicia!" button, waiting for that pimply-faced dweeb to come back in here and play games on his dumb phone, and wondered whether a change in strategy was in order.

After all, she couldn't do anything to change what happened to Aunt Evelyn now. But she'd be a fool to throw away a chance to make things better for herself.

"Throw out a number," Catherine said.

Alicia threw out a number.

THIRTY-FOUR

Janice McCabe felt a talk with the other Chartwell son, Holden, was long overdue. She'd spoken to Reece at length, and he'd been present when she'd interviewed his mother again at the house. Maybe Holden would know more about his father's affair with Leah Kennard, and possibly the death of Evelyn Corby, although that was more of a long shot, given that it had happened so long ago.

On the way to his house, a call came through on her cell, which was mounted on a bracket attached to the dash. On the screen: MOIRA.

"Hey, honey," she said.

"I'm ready," her daughter said.

"Ready?"

"To hit the mall."

"I've got one more stop to make."

"So now I'm in, like, solitary confinement? You've been gone all day. I'm going to call Greenpeace or something."

"They save whales. You're thinking of Amnesty International."

"Whatever."

Moira ended the call.

There was a car in the driveway of Holden Chartwell's house. She pulled over to the curb, got out, went up to the front door and knocked.

Ten seconds later, the door swung open, and McCabe did a double take.

Holy shit, she thought. *I know this face*.

"Yeah?" said Holden. A little wide-eyed, on edge, she thought as she identified herself, showing her badge.

"I've spoken to your mother and your brother, but before I wrap up my investigation of what happened yesterday—and condolences on your loss—I'd like to ask you a few questions."

"I don't know anything," he said, not opening the door any wider.

She smiled. "Sometimes people know more than they realize. Just a few questions."

He hesitated a moment before admitting her into the house. "I guess," he said.

As she stepped inside, thinking Holden had the decorating and tidying skills of a college freshman, McCabe said, "You live here alone?"

"Yeah. Uh, look, I don't know what to tell you about my dad. It's pretty obvious what happened, right? My dad left a note?"

"Yes."

"And it was Dad's handwriting, right?"

"Your brother seemed to think so."

"So what else is there to say?"

"You must have been shocked when you found out."

"Shocked? Sure, yeah, I'm *shocked*. We're all *shocked*."

He went to the cupboard, grabbed a glass, ran some water into it from the tap, and took a drink.

"How's your mother doing?" she asked, not mentioning that she'd just come from talking to her.

"Haven't seen her today. She came by yesterday and she was pretty torn up about it. I mean, not just that Dad was dead, but, you know, the circumstances and all."

"You know the name Evelyn Corby?"

She tossed it out, no buildup. Wondering how he'd react.

He blinked.

"Uh, who?"

"You'd have been a kid at the time, but did you ever hear the name? Hear your parents discussing her?"

"Sorry, Evelyn who?"

"Corby."

"No," he said quickly.

She waited a beat, then asked, "You're not curious?"

"Curious?"

"About who she is? Why I'm asking?"

"Not . . . really. But okay, who is she?"

"She was a Wiffel-Smith colleague of your father's who was murdered back in nineteen ninety-nine."

"Oh. Okay."

"The gun your father used yesterday was the same one that killed Evelyn Corby."

"That's . . . that's weird. That doesn't make any sense to me."

"You don't look surprised."

"There've been so many surprises the last couple of days I guess I'm getting used to them." He drank some water, wiped his mouth with the back of his hand.

"Was there ever a time, growing up, when things seemed particularly tense around your house? Your parents were going through a difficult time?"

Holden appeared to think. "Not really. I mean, there was the whole Wiffel-Smith scandal, but that happened after Dad left, so it didn't hit him that hard."

"Anything else?"

He shrugged, managed a small grin. "There was me. I was a huge pain in the ass for my parents since I was in my teens."

McCabe nodded, decided to switch gears, ask what she'd wanted to from the moment she'd laid eyes on him.

"Who's Tom?"

"Tom?"

"Ever go by that name? Is Thomas a middle name?"

"Nope."

"No one's ever referred to you as Tom?"

"How many times do I have to say it?"

"How about Leah Kennard? You know that name?"

"I hadn't heard of her until yesterday."

"Your father never spoke of her? Maybe you met her at some point?"

Holden shook his head. "I don't even know what she looks like."

"Let me help you with that."

McCabe went into her purse and brought out the driver's license she had taken from the wallet in Leah Kennard's handbag. "Not a great shot, but this is her."

He took it between his thumb and index finger, studied it, handed it back. "Nope."

"Then how would you explain this?" From her purse she

brought out the small photo album she had taken from the drawer in Kennard's bedroom, handed it to Holden.

He opened it to the first page, where Kennard had written, in calligraphy, "My Boy Tom." What followed were pictures of Holden from different periods in his life, often in shots where the other people who might have been in them had been cut out.

"What is this?" he said, leafing through the pages. He looked back at McCabe. "This is *me*."

"I know."

"I don't— I don't understand." His puzzlement and distress were genuine. "Why would she have these? Why's everybody else cut out?"

"You tell me."

"How would *I* know? Some of these go back years. Here's one where I had a *beard*. I shaved that thing off like ten years ago. What the fuck?"

"There has to be a reason."

"Well, I have no idea what it is!" He tossed the book onto the kitchen table, shook his head, paced.

He dug his phone from his pocket and entered a number.

"Who're you calling?" McCabe asked.

"The only person who might be able to explain this," he said.

McCabe said, "Speaker."

Holden looked at the detective, took a second to consider her request, then tapped the button on the screen that would allow her to hear a conversation.

"Hello?" a woman said.

McCabe recognized the voice as Catherine Chartwell's.

"Who the fuck was Leah Kennard?" Holden shouted, the words flying out of his mouth.

"We *know* who she was," Catherine said with forced calmness. "Some fling your father was having."

"Why'd she have pictures of me?"

"What?"

"Hundreds of them! In an album! They—"

"Holden, *Holden*, slow down! What are you talking about?"

"She calls me *Tom*!"

Silence at the other end.

"Why's she call me Tom?" he asked.

There was another short silence before Catherine said, "We'll have to talk about this. But not now. I'm in the middle of—"

"There's shots of my graduation! That Montreal trip. And there's notes scribbled on them, like *I miss you* and *my boy* and . . . What's going on?"

McCabe listened.

"I don't want to do this on the phone," Catherine said. "There are things I need to tell you, that I've wanted to tell you for a long time, and—"

"*My boy!* What does that *mean*?"

"Holden, calm down."

"Who *are* you?" he asked.

"What?"

Slowly, deliberately, Holden said again, "Who *are* you?"

"I'm your *mother*, Holden."

"*Are* you?" he asked, the two words hanging out there like bombs floating through the air, ready to detonate.

Several seconds went by before Catherine said, "We've all gone through a terrible thing, Holden. It's hit you hard. You need to go back to Sharnwood. I'll set it up. I'll call them now."

"I'm not high, Mom. In fact, I don't think I've ever been more sober. Things are starting to get clearer. Clearer than they've been in a long time. Is this why it was so easy?"

"What on earth are you talking about?"

"If someone's not your real son, not your real flesh and blood, does that make it easier to tell them you'd stop loving them?"

A moment of silence at the other end. Then:

"Holden, you might think you're clearheaded right now, but you're not. Trust me. I'm your *mother.* I *love* you. I've always loved you and *will* always love you. And if I ever said something that suggested otherwise I didn't mean it and I'm sorry. From the bottom of my heart, I am sorry. Believe me."

Holden seemed to be shrinking into himself. He dropped slowly into a chair, shoulders hunched, head down, the phone still in his hand, McCabe watching the whole time.

"Holden?"

"So Dad was seeing her for years?" he asked. "Never broke it off? She had a baby—she had me—and you faked birth records or something?"

"It's not like that. I'll explain it all. I will. I promise. You sound . . . you sound far away. Holden? Are you on speaker?"

Holden exchanged glances with McCabe.

"Holden! Is someone there with you?"

"I have to go," he said, ending the call, letting the phone slip from his hand to the floor. He put his head in his hands and began to weep.

THIRTY-FIVE

Reece

Diana followed Gage into the house, but I stayed on the front step a moment, gathering my thoughts, wondering what to do next. What I really wanted to do was tell Diana and Gage to each pack a bag, load up the car, and just drive. Head to Montreal or keep on going to the east coast. Diana had family in Halifax. I wanted to put some distance between ourselves and Yorkton Hill and all that had happened here.

In short, I wanted to run away.

I didn't get to consider the idea for long. My phone rang.

Mom.

I picked up. "Yeah."

"You told him," she said accusingly.

"Told who what?"

"Holden. He knows. You were going to let me tell him. How could you *do* that?"

"Mom, I swear, I didn't—"

"He had a photo album. Pictures of him, but calling him Tom. Where'd you find that? Why would you give him—"

"*Mom!*" I shouted. "I didn't tell him."

A moment's quiet. Then Mom said, "That policewoman. It had to be her. Oh god. That means she knows too."

I thought back to something she'd said seconds earlier. "Who's *Tom*?"

"Tom is Holden."

Christ, I thought, feeling almost lightheaded. What new bombshell was she about to drop?

Mom explained. "Back when we got Leah to be our surrogate, she said if Holden had been her child, she'd have named him Thomas. She wanted *us* to name him Thomas, but the name had no special meaning to your father or me. I think it was Leah's dad's name, but Holden was named after your father's favorite uncle."

"How could he have found some photo album?"

Mom was thinking. "He had the phone on speaker. She must have been there. She must have found the album in Leah's house."

"McCabe?"

"God, what must he have told her?"

I didn't know that Holden had anything of note to tell McCabe. It struck me Holden was the one who'd been in the dark, who'd been deprived of information, so what could he possibly tell McCabe that the rest of us, or at least my mother, didn't already know?

"I need to talk to him, explain," she said. "It wasn't an affair. Not back then. We *hired* her. But I can't, not right now. I need you to go talk to Holden. Explain things."

What could she have to do that was more pressing than helping my brother deal with a revelation that was nothing short of an emotional earthquake?

"What?" I asked. "Is there another arts council luncheon?"

"Go to hell," she said.

I felt that as sharply as when she'd actually slapped my face.

"Look, Mom, I don't know what kind of mess you're in, I don't know what might have happened years ago, between you and Dad, with this Corby woman, with Leah Kennard, with all this shit. I hardly know who you are right now."

"That's hateful."

"I don't mean it to be. But I can't help you if you're not honest with me."

"You don't understand."

"So help me understand."

"Your father didn't kill himself."

It was my turn for a moment of silence. "I don't think so, Mom."

"He didn't. I'm sure of it."

"What are you saying? There was someone else in the house? Someone else came in and shot Leah and shot Dad and made it look like suicide?"

"That's right."

Three words went unsaid in my mind: *Was it you?* I was ready at this point to consider just about anything. After all, if you were looking for someone with a motive, Mom fit the bill. Finding her husband in bed with another woman? What was the saying? *A story as old as time?*

But what I said was, "I saw the note. Dad wrote it. It was his handwriting."

"He could have been forced."

"By who?"

"We're going to find out, and then everything will be fine," Mom said.

We? Was she enlisting me in this?

"I don't know how to help you with this," I said.

"Oh, honey, not you," she said, ending the call.

If not me, who? And then something occurred to me. She was talking about the man I'd seen her talking to in the hotel parking lot.

THIRTY-SIX

Alicia had said, "Five hundred thousand dollars."

What the hell, right? If she had said a hundred thousand, and Catherine had said yes right away, then she'd kick herself for not asking for more.

"That's ridiculous," Catherine said, although she didn't sound as taken aback as Alicia expected. "I can pull some cash together even though it's Saturday, but not that much. I could give you a down payment. And then, when the banks open on Monday, we could talk again."

How much cash did someone like Catherine keep lying around the house? Alicia wondered. She said, "If you can pull together a hundred thousand today, we can make this work."

There was a long pause at the other end, followed by, "Okay."

Whoa, Alicia thought. She had that much money in the house? And how could the Chartwells let Holden live in that shithole with that kind of cash at hand? What was wrong with these people?

But what she said was, "Great."

Now she had to figure out how to do the handoff. Definitely

not in person. Couldn't let Catherine find out who she was. She'd have her drop the money someplace Alicia could retrieve it. Like in the movies when the ransom money is left in a trash can and the kidnappers pick it up later. But this time, the criminal roles were reversed. Catherine was the bad guy. And her crime was worse than kidnapping. She wasn't going to be calling the police. No one would be staking out the drop-off point.

And hey, who said this had to be the last payment? Soak the bitch for even more money before making her pay the ultimate price.

"I'll call back with the details," Alicia said, ending the call.

Think, think, think.

Corky had returned. "He's not even here today," he said.

"What?"

"Asshole Wilkins. He's off. You said he was looking for me."

"Yeah," Alicia said. "But I didn't say he was looking for you *today*. I just said he'd been looking for you."

"What did he want?"

"I don't know."

Corky, annoyed, sat back down, got out his phone, and resumed his video game. Alicia glanced at the clock on the wall. Her break would be over in two minutes.

Her regular cell phone rang. She took it from her pocket, glanced at the screen.

HOLDEN.

She didn't have time to talk to him now.

She went back out into the store, returned to her station, removed the "Sorry Closed Use Next Checkout" sign. She turned, looked out the window and across the street, where a small hardware store and a laundromat flanked an alleyway.

Halfway down it sat a dumpster, up against the wall. Alicia knew trash pickup was not until Monday, so anything left in that bin wasn't at risk of disappearing right away. If she told Catherine to leave it there at quarter to seven, it wouldn't sit there long.

An elderly man was already emptying his cart onto the belt. Alicia gave him a smile and said, "Just one second." She turned away, got out her burner—she almost used her regular phone by mistake—and called Catherine.

"You know the Home Hardware and the Coin-Op Laundry, across from the FreshCo, on Cornwall?"

"I . . . uh, yes, I think so."

"There's an alley between them, a dumpster in there. Put it there at quarter to seven. And not in a garbage bag! Something that stands out."

Catherine recalled a recent trip to a high-end Toronto mall. She'd bought a purse.

"It'll be in a Longchamp bag," Catherine said.

Alicia couldn't believe Catherine would leave a designer purse in a dumpster. "You're throwing out a purse?" Alicia couldn't afford a Longchamp, but she knew the brand.

"The bag the purse came in," Catherine clarified.

"Oh, right."

"And—"

Alicia ended the call. The woman had been told all she needed to know. The dumpster, quarter to seven.

Now Alicia just had to get to the end of her shift. How was she supposed to concentrate? Good thing you didn't need an engineering degree to wave items over a barcode reader. A few hours from now she could quit this shit job. Once she had that money in her hands, her first call Monday morning would be to Mr. Wilkins. Take this job and shove it. No, she wouldn't even call him. She just wouldn't show up.

She heard a text arrive on her other phone. Holden, again.

Really need to talk to you.

"There was no price on the shelf for this one," the elderly man said, holding up a can of beef stew for her to examine.

Alicia looked up from her phone. "Huh?"

"There's no price."

"I'll scan it."

"If it costs too much I don't want it."

"Hang on."

Beep!

"Four fifty."

The man pondered this information, grimaced. "I'll take it."

She sent it on down the belt to be bagged in a moment, picked up her phone again, and typed:

At work. Later.

She scanned the rest of the man's items, stuffed them into the two reusable bags he'd brought, and even though it was still a few hours before Catherine would make the drop-off, she kept stealing glances of the dumpster, making sure it was still there.

"It's all set," Catherine told Crane over the phone.

"You do what I said?"

He'd instructed her to find a small box, fill it with paper, heavy enough to feel like cash. Old magazines, a catalog. Once filled, wrap the box in plain paper and secure it with several rounds of duct tape.

"Don't want her opening it on-site," he said. "Ideally, she takes it home with her, opens it there."

"I did all that."

She told him where she had been told to leave the bag, a dumpster in an alley.

"I can find it," he said.

"I heard beeps."

"What?"

"The last time she called me, I could hear beeps. Like when you go to the grocery store and they scan your items. Lots of beeps."

Crane thought about that. "There's a grocery store across the street?"

"Yes."

"You sound on edge. Can you do this?"

"Yes. It's the least of my worries. Call me after you've talked to her?"

Her false naivete made him smile. Acting like she didn't know what was going to happen. Like she was worried someone was listening in, that this would be proof she had no idea what was going to happen. Deniability.

"Of course," he said. "We'll have a little chat."

Alicia missed it when it happened.

When it got to be fifteen minutes to seven, she was dealing with a woman whose credit card was declined. All the checkouts were busy and there were four people with loaded baskets behind this woman. When the first card failed, she tried a second, and when that one was declined as well, she opened up her wallet for cash and found she only had eight dollars. There was more than fifty bucks' worth of groceries on the register.

"I don't know why this is happening," she said. "Can we try this one again?"

Alicia indulged her, but she could see how this was going to go. This woman would ask if she could just take the groceries now, run to an ATM, and come right back with the cash.

Fat chance, Sally.

Although, for the briefest of moments, Alicia considered treating her. She was coming into a small fortune. Why not share the wealth?

And then, just as quickly, she came to her senses.

The woman abandoned her groceries at the bagging end and stormed out. Corky was called to gather up the items and reshelve them. The people still in line were rolling their eyes and shaking their heads. Alicia finally snuck a peek across the street, but there was nobody lifting the dumpster lid, no one in the alley at all.

Fingers crossed, Catherine kept her promise.

When it was seven, Alicia took one last look around the store, thinking she would never have to come here again. She cashed out, hit the break room—Holden texted her again and she ignored it—and took off her grocery store smock, grabbed her purse, and was out of there.

Don't be too obvious, she thought. Don't come tearing out of the store like it's on fire, run across the street so quickly she'd have to dodge traffic. No, she came out the front door slowly, hung a right, walked down to the corner, waited for the light to change and crossed the street, then backtracked, pausing to look in the window of a dress shop along the way, then when she reached the alley slipped in when she was confident no one was looking her way.

She went straight to the dumpster, lifted the lid.

Phew. The stench. Maybe she should have picked a different spot. But there was the paper Longchamp bag sitting atop a pile of green garbage bags, within easy reach, thank god. The last thing Alicia wanted was to jump in there.

She slipped her fingers into the handle of the bag, lifted it out, let the lid slam shut. It had a nice heft to it, this bag. She'd wondered what that much money would feel like. She looked inside, saw a box, about the size printer paper would come in, mummified in duct tape. She'd hoped to get a glimpse of the cash right away, but she'd have to wait until she got home. Annoying, but then again, Catherine was smart to have the cash wrapped up tight.

Alicia tucked the box under her arm, tossed the bag it had come in, and headed for home. Yet another text dinged on her phone, probably Holden. Whatever his current crisis was, it could wait.

Her apartment was in a low-rise not far from her work. A fifteen-minute walk most days, except in winter when the sidewalks were icy or hadn't been cleared of snow. She used her key to get into the lobby, went to the elevator, and took it up to the fourth floor.

Once in her small apartment, Alicia put the box on the kitchen table, brought out a pair of scissors and a sharp knife from a drawer, and started hacking her way into it, cutting through tape that ran along the top flaps.

Her heart hammering away with expectation, she opened the box.

It was filled to the top with old copies of *National Geographic*, *Time*, *The New Yorker*, and car magazines. She started lifting them out of the box, tossing them onto the table, hoping that maybe beneath them she might find some actual cash.

"That cunt!" she said out loud. "That fucking cunt!"

Enraged, she grabbed one magazine and flung it across the room, where it hit the wall and landed on the couch.

She got out her phone, the one she used exclusively to make her calls to Catherine, but just as she was about to enter the number, there was a loud knock at her door.

THIRTY-SEVEN

Reece

I went into the house, called out, "Diana!"

"Up here!" she called back, sounding like she was up in our bedroom, or Gage's. I met her at the bottom of the stairs as she was coming down.

Before I could tell her about my mother's call, that Holden had somehow learned about his parentage, most likely from McCabe, Diana said, "Gage isn't here."

"I was out front all this time. I didn't see him."

"Then I guess he went out the back way."

"Did you call him?"

She held her phone up so I could see she had tried to text him. "He's not answering."

I wasn't yet convinced this was a crisis. Gage had come, said what he had to say to us about his faith in his grandfather, and then taken off.

"Has something happened?" she asked.

"Mom called. Frantic. And maybe a little paranoid."

"Start with frantic."

"She says Holden knows. About Leah being his biological mother."

"So she told him."

"No. She accused me of doing it. But then we figured it must have been the police."

"Do we know how he is?" she asked.

I shook my head. "I can only imagine. How would you handle it, suddenly learning something like that?"

She had no answer.

I took a breath and then hit her with the next thing. "Mom says Dad didn't kill himself."

Diana wasn't sure how to take that at first. "She thinks . . . he's alive? Has she lost touch with reality?"

"No. And maybe. She's saying he was murdered, and maybe that *is* evidence that she's lost touch with reality."

Diana used the banister to support herself. "I can see it."

"That he was murdered?"

"No, not that. But look, if he's committed suicide, she's going to feel like it's on her somehow. That she wasn't worth sticking around for. Or she didn't see it coming. She didn't get help for him. But if someone came in and shot him, it's not her fault, right?"

"Unless the reason someone shot him is on Mom too."

I had that fleeting thought again about packing everyone into the car and heading for the hills. But Mom's request, that I go check on my brother, explain things, was wearing on me. When I told Diana, she wasn't thrilled with the idea.

"He wasn't exactly receptive when we were over there earlier."

I hadn't forgotten.

She added, "Right now, I'm more worried about Gage."

"Let's start with him," I said, turning to head for the front door.

That was when something caught my eye. On the mat where we leave our shoes if they're wet, was Gage's skateboard.

"He can't have gone far," Diana said.

Gage didn't go anywhere without the skateboard. The thing was practically welded to his shoes when he wasn't home.

"You think he went for a walk?" I asked.

Diana gave me a look. "Have you *met* Gage?"

She was right. Gage would no more go for a walk than I would take the Space Shuttle to go into town. Gage did have an Uber app on his phone, but we'd almost never known him to use it. It was intended for emergencies. And given that most of his friends were his age, none of them even had driver's licenses yet.

The only person Gage knew who had wheels that I could think of was Holden. Diana came to the same idea about the same time I did.

"You think they're together?" she asked.

"I don't know why they would be."

"You said they seemed to have some kind of connection."

I thought back to the previous night, when Gage and I had found Holden and his friend, Alicia, at the coffee place. How they'd exchanged glances, like sharing a private joke or something.

"I think they've spent more time together than they've let on," I said.

If they had, it would make sense that Gage kept it a secret. He knew we had reservations about him hanging out with his uncle, for obvious reasons. But Gage was fourteen, and you really couldn't control who your kid hung out with at that age no matter how hard you tried. And to his credit, Gage saw the best in his uncle.

I had my phone out and called my brother.

It rang several times before it went to voicemail. "Hey, it's me," I said. "Give me a call when you have a sec. We're looking for Gage, wondered if he'd been in touch."

I put the phone away.

"I can't believe I'm saying this," Diana said, "but maybe we should do your mother a solid and head over to Holden's again."

As I nodded my agreement and started heading for the door, she put a hand on my arm to stop me.

"What?" I asked.

"Could she be right?" She maintained her grip, sensing that I was ready to pull away, leaning toward the door.

"Could who be right about what?"

"Your mother. Could she be right, thinking that it wasn't a murder-suicide? That your father didn't kill himself? That he didn't shoot Leah Kennard?"

"Come on, Diana. My mother's not being rational right now."

"Maybe not, but I think Gage is."

I stopped my lean, and she let her hand fall from my arm. "What do you mean?" I asked.

"When Gage told that story, about stealing the chips, your father going to the police station, rescuing him, he was offering that up as proof that your dad was at his core a decent man. That was proof enough for him that Brent couldn't have shot Leah, or that other woman he used to work with."

"I know, but—"

"I have a story like that too," Diana said.

I said nothing for a moment, holding my breath. I didn't

know whether I was ready for another revelation. Finally, I said, half-joking, "Are you a shoplifter, too?"

"No," she said. "It was bigger than that."

I waited.

"I wrecked his Barracuda."

"I'm sorry, you what?"

My father's beloved 1972 Plymouth Barracuda? He'd bought it a year or two before Gage was born. A recapturing-his-youth moment. There were times I believed he loved that car as much as he loved any of us.

"Gage was four months old," Diana said. "I didn't even have a job yet. We were fresh out of school. I had that old Volvo that had been my mom's, and she gave it to me because we were pretty desperate at the time. It was a tank, that car. Your dad was still doing his consulting work then, working from home, and as much as your parents were not thrilled with our situation, he adored Gage and invited us to drop by after I'd done the groceries. And so we did."

I listened. This was all new to me. I remembered, around that time, I was working at a small community newspaper, making a miserable wage. We were just getting by. Tough times.

"Your mom was in the city—I don't know what she was doing—so it was just your father. We came in, your dad gave Gage a bottle, played with him. Gage was so happy he didn't want to leave and when I got him back in his car seat he was crying and I was frazzled and as I was backing out of the driveway I hit a car parked on the opposite side of the street. It was your dad's Barracuda. He'd had it out earlier and hadn't put it back in the garage."

"Oh god," I said.

"I got out, saw what I'd done. I'd totally bashed in the driver's door. The mirror'd fallen off, the glass was shattered. I burst into tears. Your father heard the crash, came running out. And he did the most amazing thing."

I waited.

"He laughed. He looked at what I'd done and he laughed. Just kind of lost it. And then he put his arms around me because I was pretty hysterical by that point and he said it was just a car. Metal and plastic and paint and it could all be fixed. I offered to pay, but it was an empty gesture because it was going to cost thousands and we had like three hundred dollars in the bank. And the Volvo, of course, didn't have a scratch on it." She smiled at the recollection. "You could drive that car into battle."

"You've never told me any of this."

"Your father swore me to secrecy. I wasn't to tell you, or your mother. He said he'd send it to the body shop, but tell Catherine he was getting it tuned up at some mechanic's. It would all be like it never happened. He said to me, 'you take care of your little boy, you take care of my son, and I'll take care of this.'"

I didn't know what to say.

"I always loved your father," Diana said. "Your mother, okay, she's an acquired taste. But Gage is right. Your father was a good man. Gage believes that. So do I." She squeezed my arm. "You need to too."

"I hear what you're saying. I do. But if you and Gage believe, in your gut, that Dad wasn't capable of this, then who shot him and Leah?"

Diana didn't have an answer for that.

We left for Holden's.

THIRTY-EIGHT

Alicia went to her apartment door but did not open it.

"Who is it?"

"Catherine Chartwell sent me."

She put her eye to the peephole, saw a man standing there. Hard to get a good look at someone that way, but he was not that imposing a figure. Balding, glasses, no more than five six, probably late fifties.

Alicia felt a wave of fear coupled with anger. The fear was easy enough to explain. She'd been followed, found out. She hadn't spotted anyone following her, and now she was kicking herself. And the anger? That box filled with magazines instead of cash was more than enough to raise her hackles.

"She fucked me over," Alicia said through the door.

"I'm here to make that right," the man said.

"Unless you've got the cash on you, forget it."

"Did you really think she'd leave that kind of money in a dumpster? All it would take is one homeless guy to find it before you got there. Makes more sense to deliver it in person."

Alicia wasn't so sure. "I'm not buying it."

"Very well," he said and went quiet.

Alicia looked through the peephole again. He was gone.

Shit.

What if he *had* come with the cash? Was she going to let him walk away? No, it was a trick. Don't take the bait. Let him go.

What should she do? Call Catherine, tell her all bets were off, she was calling the police, telling them everything? Scare the shit out of her, tell her if she didn't come up with the money, right now, then—

Maybe that *was* why the guy'd been at her door. Catherine knew she had no choice but to pay up and had sent this shmuck to settle things.

Alicia unlocked it, slipped off the chain, and—

The door burst open, knocking her off her feet and sending her onto the floor on her ass. The man was in the room in less than a second, the door closed a second after that.

He loomed over her, looked down, and said, "We should talk."

"Yeah, sure," she said, moving crablike on her back, farther into the room.

"Get up."

Alicia got to her feet. With his foot, Crane pulled a chair away from the table in the kitchen nook and nodded, inviting her to take a seat. She sat. He glanced at the now empty box, the periodicals and catalogs scattered across the table. Yellow-spined copies of *National Geographic*, a thick catalog from *Restoration Hardware*. Something about that one caught Crane's eye.

He lifted out the catalog, saw stamped right there on the cover for all to see, Catherine's name and address.

Crane closed his eyes for a moment and sighed.

Alicia, mustering some false bravado, said, "You better have the money on you, or get it here, ASAP."

Crane eyed her as a cat might look at a mouse. "First, I need the answers to some questions."

"Like what? If I want it in twenties or hundreds?"

Crane gave her a sly smile. "Your actions insinuate that Mrs. Chartwell has something to hide."

"Yeah, well, her wanting to pay me off is kind of a clue, isn't it?"

"What is it you think she's done?"

"I don't think. I know." She grinned. "I know it like I know you're a four-eyed fuck face."

"Convince me."

"Maybe I should call the cops and convince them."

Crane smiled. "Go ahead."

She made no move to get out her phone.

Another smile. "In a little too deep, aren't you?" He gave her a long, contemplative look, narrowed his eyes and asked, "How much did he tell you?"

Her eyes danced. "Who? About what?"

He used his foot again to pull the chair opposite her out and sat. "How do you know Holden? And spare me the obfuscation. It tries my patience."

Her mouth was dry. "I need some water."

He raised a hand toward the sink. She got up, found a glass, ran some water into it from the tap, and sat back down. She took a long sip and said, "Rehab."

"Go on."

"In the group, Holden said stuff about covering up for someone, that it fucked him up. Something that happened a long time ago."

Crane ran his tongue over his upper teeth. "So he gave the whole group the details?"

She shook her head. "No. But he said enough that I got curious. The timing, some of what he said, it lined up with what happened to my aunt."

Crane nodded very slowly. "And your aunt. Evelyn Corby?"

She was unable to hide her surprise. "Yes."

"Holden told you his mother had killed her."

Another head shake. "Not exactly. I told him I had an aunt that got murdered but changed the name and circumstances. But we still had kind of a bond, and then he told me what happened. Pretty much all of it." She tried to puff herself up. "And if she doesn't want me telling anyone, she needs to come up with the money she promised. She *owes* me. She ruined my life."

Crane said nothing.

"Holden saw it all. Saw his mom shoot her. Saw his dad and I'm guessing you take her away. So Brent had it coming, too, if you ask me."

"The gun," Crane said.

"Huh?"

"Did Holden tell you anything about the gun?"

"He found it, in the pond. Fishing. Kept it, cleaned it up, got it to work."

"It worked, but you killed the wrong person."

"Whoa, whoa," she said, raising her palms.

"What, you *meant* to kill that other woman?" Crane gave her a dismissive shake of the head. "That must have been a shock, finding out it wasn't Catherine. You'd never seen her before, had you? Made an assumption. Here's what I'd like to know. How'd you get Brent to blow his brains out? You drug him?

Knock him out or something? Whatever you did, my hat's off to you. Cops bought it."

"Listen—"

"Did using the same gun make it special? Give it a kind of cosmic resonance?"

"Look," she said, "forget the money. I don't care anymore. Tell her she'll never hear from me again. I'm done. I made my point. I wanted to rattle her."

"Consider her rattled." He was thinking. "You must have a burner you've been harassing her with?"

She nodded. Crane held out his hand. She pointed to her purse, which she'd left over on the couch. "May I?" she asked.

Crane nodded.

She walked over, pulled the phone from the bag, set it on the table. Crane pocketed it carefully, making sure his fingertips did not touch the tabletop.

"Fine, keep it. I don't need it anymore."

"Who else did Holden tell at rehab?"

"No one. Just me. I mean, I'm pretty sure. I had to pry it out of him. He never talked about it in the group, not the details, and I don't think he told his doctor. I mean, if he had, the doctor would have had to report it, right? It's not like he's a priest."

"So *no one* else?"

Alicia hesitated.

"Tell me."

"It's nothing to worry about."

Crane stared at her, moved his lower jaw from side to side, saying nothing. He reached into his jacket and slowly withdrew a gun. It had something attached to it that was designed,

Alicia thought, to dampen the noise when it was fired. Crane placed the gun on the table.

"Let me ask you again. Who else did Holden tell?"

Alicia's eyes were on the gun. "I tell you, and we're good, right?"

"Yes."

"Far as I know," she said, "only Gage."

"Gage?"

She nodded. "His nephew. They're close. But Gage wouldn't tell a soul."

"How old is this Gage?"

"Thirteen, fourteen." She chuckled nervously, eyes still on the gun. "Any other questions? Just ask. You put that away and I'll tell you anything you want to know."

He nodded, picked up the gun, and shot her in the forehead. She toppled from the chair onto the floor.

Crane stood, gathered all the scattered magazines that still bore Catherine's name and home address and put them back into the box. Talk about stupid. He would take the box with him when he left.

He put in a quick call to Catherine.

"Yes?" she said anxiously when she picked up.

"It's done."

"Who was she?" Catherine asked breathlessly.

"A friend of your son's," he said. "Evelyn Corby's niece."

"Oh god."

He could sense the wheels turning in Catherine's head.

"It was her," Catherine said. "She did it."

"So it would seem."

Silence from Catherine's end. After a moment, he asked, "Are you home?"

"Yes."

"Stay there. We have a few things to go over."

"Yes . . . okay."

Crane ended the call. Best to have her stay put. Easier to find her there later after he'd dealt with the other two.

THIRTY-NINE

Yesterday

It had been a chance encounter. Two years earlier.

Brent Chartwell had been taking his classic Barracuda for a spin. The last time he'd taken it for a drive, the front wheel alignment had felt off, the car dragging to the right when he briefly relaxed his grip on the steering wheel, even when the road was dead flat. He wanted to see whether he'd been imagining it. If the alignment was indeed off, it would cause uneven wear on the front tires, and he didn't want that.

Damned if it wasn't still doing it, so he drove straight on to a mechanic he'd trusted in the past with his baby. He didn't have an appointment, and if Harry couldn't take him right away, he'd leave the car there and take an Uber home.

When he went into the small office, there was a woman at the counter in the middle of a conversation with Harry.

"But can't it be, like, patched or something?" she asked. "I have to get an entire new muffler?"

"Be like trying to hold a piece of wet toast together with jam," Harry said. "It's shot. It's all gotta be replaced or you're gonna go down the street sounding like a Sherman tank."

"How much is *that* going to cost?"

Harry told her.

The woman bit her lip and shook her head slowly. "Do they have to be new parts? Do you have any older parts that would work for now?"

"Look," Harry said, his voice not without sympathy, "I'll give you a break on the labor, but there's nothing I can do on the parts. You wanna think about it?"

She nodded, and as she turned to leave, quickly wiping a single tear from her cheek, Brent got a good look at her.

I know her, he thought, but he couldn't place from where.

Instead of asking Harry about his wheel alignment, he followed the woman to her car, an older-model Toyota. She was about to get inside when Brent said, "Excuse me."

She stopped, looked at him blankly, said, "What?"

"I'm sorry, you just, when I saw you, I thought, I know you from someplace but I can't quite—"

"Oh my god," she said, looking at him. "You're Brent Chartwell."

He smiled. "Yes, that's right. So we *have* met somewhere, and now you have me at a disadvantage because I can't—"

"Leah," she said. "Leah Kennard."

It took him a moment. Then it was his turn to say, "Oh for heaven's sake."

And then he closed the distance between them and gave her a quick hug. "I knew it was you. I mean, I didn't know it was *you*, but I knew—"

She laughed, though her cheek was still wet from that tear. "I get it! How have you been? How's— How's the *family*?"

What a loaded word, coming from her. This woman who made it possible for Catherine and him to start one.

"We're good, we're fine. And I guess . . . I don't know whether anyone ever told you, but after all we went through, wouldn't you know it, but Catherine became pregnant."

"You're not serious."

"I am, it's true. So, two boys. Both grown up now, of course. Holden—your contribution, to put it mildly—and his younger brother, Reece."

"So you didn't name him Tom," she said, a sad smile.

"No."

"I understand, that's okay. I just had to ask. And I have to apologize for that scene in there. This car, it's all I can do to keep it together, and what they want to repair it, I just can't—"

"Do you have time for a drink or something?"

That was how it started. Innocently enough. Coffee, a shared muffin, catching up. Who could have predicted how it would change his life, how it would change *both* their lives. And now here he was two years later, and he had come to care deeply about her, this woman who was the mother of his older son. Not only did he care for her emotionally, he had been, to some extent, caring for her financially.

Leah had been through some tough times, Brent soon learned. She was in the process of getting out of a difficult relationship. She'd lost one job, found another, then lost it, and was currently out of work, although not long after their first meeting she would get a job working reception in a medical clinic.

After that first coffee, he went back to the car repair shop and paid for her new muffler. "Least I can do," he'd told her. "It's nothing compared to bringing a life into the world for us."

"I was compensated for that," she said, insisting she would

pay him back for the muffler. He said she could make it up to him if she let him take her to lunch.

One thing, as they say, led to another. Within two weeks, the relationship had become intimate. They would meet at her house, never his. There were no risks having sex at her place, given that she lived alone, although there had been a run-in with her former boyfriend when he'd come by, trying to patch things up.

She had so many questions about Holden. What he was like as a child, what his interests were, how he did in school. She wanted pictures. Brent still had plenty from when you took in a roll of film to be developed and got back an envelope stuffed with prints. "We have hundreds of pics we've never bothered to put in an album," he told her. "I can slip a few out of there. Catherine will never notice they're missing."

Unbeknownst to Brent, Leah would take those pictures and edit them with a pair of scissors, cutting out other family members, leaving just Holden. She displayed them in a small album that she kept next to her bed.

They had been having their secret rendezvous for the better part of a year when Brent told Leah that Catherine had figured out what was going on.

"Oh no," Leah said.

"It's okay," Brent told her. "Honestly, it makes my life easier. I mean, I'll still keep the other phone, just for our exchanges, but the truth is, Catherine and I live pretty much separate lives these days. We long ago reached a kind of, I don't know, accommodation. A way to carry on. She has her interests, I have mine. We live under the same roof, we keep tabs on each other, we probably still care about each other at some level, but it's not . . . I don't know how to describe it."

"Why haven't you ever divorced, or gotten a separation?"

"I guess we're bound together by our pasts," he said, offering little more by way of an explanation, and Leah didn't push.

"What about now?" Leah asked. "I mean, what sort of future do we have? Do things just keep going on the way they've been going?"

Brent had no answer for that. He knew Leah wanted more of a commitment. She'd reached a time in her life where she craved stability, and an affair with a married man didn't offer that.

Was leaving Catherine even an option? The very thought filled him with dread. Not so much the emotional toll it would take, although that would be considerable, but it was all the other issues. The house, their assets. Trying to explain it to their grown sons.

Given how much this issue was on Leah's mind, he shouldn't have been surprised when she rang his doorbell this Friday morning.

"Leah," he said when he saw her standing on the front stoop. "What are you doing here?"

"I wanted to talk," she said. "I remembered you saying today was Catherine's arts group lunch or whatever. Don't worry, I parked down the street."

"You've caught me by surprise." Leah had never been to his home. He was unsure how to handle her presence here.

"Are you going to let me just stand out here?" she asked.

Leaving her on the doorstep where neighbors might see her was not an option. Brent opened the door wide, admitting her, then closed it.

She stepped inside, scanned the spacious living room, the art on the walls, the high-end furniture. "You have a lovely home."

The observation embarrassed him. He might have lived many years in anguish, but his creature comforts far outstripped hers.

She shook her head. "This won't take long."

He motioned for her to settle into a living room chair but she held her spot near the door.

"What is it?" he asked. "What's wrong?"

But he knew.

"I can't do this any longer," she said. "I can't be . . . that woman. The one on the side, the one whose bills you pay, the one who's sitting around waiting, wondering if this is the day you'll decide to come over, but never spend the night. I have to be able to look myself in the mirror. I didn't have much before I met you, but I had my self-respect. I need that back."

"Leah, Leah, come on. It's not like that. I care about—"

"I need more than *care*. I can't survive on *care*." Her eyes were welling up. "You say you *care* about me, but I *love* you. And that can't work one way. If it's one way, then I'm out."

Brent perched himself on the stairs, looking down at his feet, thinking.

"Say something," Leah said. "Or don't. It doesn't matter. If you have nothing to say then I'll just—"

"I'll leave her," he said, raising his head and looking at Leah.

"What?"

"I'll do it. I'll end it." He managed a broken smile. "I'll leave her."

Leah had her hand over her mouth, afraid to be happy. She managed to say, "Don't say it if you don't mean it. Don't tease me. Don't give me false hope."

He stood, took her in his arms, put his mouth to her ear, and whispered, "I mean it. I love you. I want to be happy again."

And then his mouth was on hers, and within minutes, they were upstairs in the master bedroom, the first time they had ever made love here, and maybe, Brent thought, it would be the last, because when Catherine came home he would tell her. He would tell her he was leaving her, that he would move out, that he would give her the house, that he would give her whatever she wanted because all he needed was his freedom. And he'd assure her the dark secret that had somehow bound them together long past their marriage's expiry date would never come to light.

Maybe, just maybe, she'd been longing to start over too.

That could be a naive hope, but in this moment, he was a little starry-eyed, not seeing how difficult the path ahead would likely be.

But fuck it, damn the torpedoes.

It was not a furious bout of lovemaking. They were, after all, not kids anymore. But it was tender and heartfelt and it marked what they believed was a new beginning.

And then Brent heard something downstairs.

He sat up in bed, held his breath, listened.

"Christ," he said. "The front door. Catherine's back."

She wasn't.

FORTY

Moments before Gage had left his house, his cell had rung. He'd already had the phone in his hand and, seeing who it was, answered before it rang a second time. He didn't want his parents asking who he was talking to.

"Hey," Gage said.

"Hey, kid, look," said Holden, "where are you right now?"

"Home."

"What're you doing?"

"Just, you know, *parents*."

"What's that mean?"

"The usual shit. Nothing to worry about."

"Can I pick you up?"

"What for?"

"I'll explain when I get you."

"Okay."

"But not out front. I don't know how your dad would feel about us hanging out right now. Kind of had a bad scene with him and your mom a while ago."

"I can go out the back way, meet you one street over."

"Deal."

He slipped out of the house undetected and without his skateboard and two minutes later, Holden's old Honda CR-V appeared on the street one over from Gage's place. Holden left the motor running as Gage jumped in on the passenger side, the door creaking on rusty hinges.

"Sorry to drag you away," Holden said, taking his foot off the brake and hitting the gas. "Sorry about everything, really."

"What's going on?"

"I've been trying to get hold of Alicia, you know? Been calling and texting and she should be off work by now but she keeps putting me off. I really need to talk to her, and if I can't talk to *somebody*, I'm gonna start doing something I shouldn't, and right now, I'm ready to get so high that I'd be looking down from space, you know? More than ever, right now, I need a clear head, to be able to deal with all this. And you and me, we got a good rapport, right?"

"Right."

"I've told you stuff I never told anyone else except Alicia, and you've been good about keeping the lid on it. Maybe I shouldn't've, but I've always believed you need to know the truth about this family."

Glumly, Gage said, "I wish I'd never known."

"Shit, I get that. Sorry to dump on you."

"So where are we going?"

"My mom's," he said.

"Why?"

Holden gripped the wheel a little tighter. "A whole bunch of things got real clear today, like the clouds opening up and the sun shining in?" He shook his head slowly, as though still putting the pieces together. "I'm the lesser brother."

"Huh?"

"I'm not whole like your dad. Not to my mom. Explains a lot."

"I'm not getting any of this."

Holden took one hand off the wheel and waved it around. "It's okay. I'll get her to explain it, you can get it firsthand."

"You're gonna confront her?"

"Yeah."

Gage shook his head vehemently. "No way, not again."

"It's different this time," Holden said.

"Let me out."

"No, come on, man, I *need* you."

"I want to go home."

"Okay, okay, look. I'll swing by Alicia's, see if she's there, and if I can talk her into coming with me, you're off the hook."

"I'm off the hook no matter what."

Holden sighed. "Fine, I'll see if Alicia's there, drop you off back at your house, regardless."

"Thanks."

They were silent as Holden made a couple of turns, bailing on the route to his mother's place and instead heading to Alicia's.

Quietly, Holden asked, "You okay?"

"No."

"It's all going to work out."

Gage shrugged.

"My dad," Holden said, "did some dumb stuff in his life, but at his heart, he was a good guy. Cared more about others than he did about himself. Had a conscience. That's why he quit Big

Pharma. He was even willing, for my sake and Reece's, to stay in a marriage he didn't want to be in. That says something, right?"

"Yeah," Gage said. "I know."

"Just up here," he said, looking ahead, nodding. "She's in that building on the right."

He parked on the street and tried texting Alicia one last time. When he didn't get a reply, he said, "If she doesn't want to talk to me, she can tell me why to my face. Come on."

They got out of the Honda and entered the lobby of the low-rise apartment. Holden had a key, so he didn't have to buzz to get Alicia to let him in. They took the elevator up, headed down the hall, and stood together outside the door to her place.

Holden rapped on it with the knuckle of his middle finger. "Hey, Aleesh?" he said, putting his mouth to the doorjamb. "It's me."

The knock went unanswered.

He knocked again, louder this time. "If I did something to piss you off, just tell me." He waited another moment, then turned to Gage and shrugged.

"What's this?" Gage asked.

He was staring at the crack between the bottom of the door and the floor. Holden took a step back so that the hallway lights would better illuminate what Gage had spotted.

"That oil?" Gage asked.

A thick, dark liquid was seeping out from the room. Like something in there had spilled and this was the farthest point it had trickled to.

Holden said nothing as he knelt down and tentatively touched his finger to it, then examined what was on the tip.

"Oh, Jesus," he said.

Gage swallowed hard. That dab of liquid on the end of Holden's finger was deep red.

Holden tried the door, found it locked, inserted a key, and slowly pushed the door open.

"Oh shit oh shit oh shit," he said under his breath.

Gage, behind him, peered around his shoulder, and seeing Alicia on the floor, took two steps back, pressing himself up against the opposite hallway wall. His mouth hung open, and his hand was frozen halfway to it, as though he couldn't decide whether he was going to need it to stifle a scream or keep it away so he could puke.

Holden stepped slowly into the apartment, careful not to get blood on his shoes. He didn't need to be a coroner to know it was too late to help her. He could see the vacant stare in her open eyes, the hole in her forehead, the blood that ran from the wound to the floor and out the door.

But that didn't stop him, once he had reached her, from getting down on his knees, huddling over her, running his hand softly over her hair and starting to whimper.

"Holden," Gage whispered, barely able to get the word out.

Holden's back began to heave as he cried. "No no," he said softly. "No no no no no . . ."

"We gotta split," Gage said, glancing up the hallway in one direction and then the other.

At the far end, the ding of an elevator.

"Shit," Gage said under his breath. He couldn't be seen standing here, with the door open, the body visible. He quickly stepped into the room, taking the same care his uncle had to avoid stepping in blood, then closed the door behind him.

Holden looked up, his eyes wet. "Look what they did to her . . ."

Gage didn't have time for that. He had to find a toilet, and fast. He was unfamiliar with the layout of Alicia's place, but it was far from palatial and it only took a second for Gage to find the bathroom.

He flipped up the toilet lid, leaned over and vomited. Once, then again. Finished, he slowly sank to the floor. He pulled the handle to flush it, then collapsed against the tiled wall, butt on the floor, his legs extended out toward the toilet.

Gage sat there, breathing in and out in quick, shallow gulps. He didn't want to move, didn't want to go back out there, see that dead woman.

He jumped when his phone started ringing. He took it from his pocket, saw it was his mother trying to reach him. He muted the phone but it kept vibrating, and he'd barely recovered from that when he jumped again. Holden was standing in the doorway, and for half a second, Gage thought Alicia's killer could still be in the apartment.

"Just me, man."

Gage took a breath. "Who did that? Who did that to her?"

Holden raised his hands in a *beats me* gesture. "I don't know, kid."

"Maybe there's like some crazy serial killer living in this building?"

Holden shook his head. "It— it looked like a hit."

"A what?"

"I mean, like, one shot to the head. That's no serial killer."

"You mean like a hit man?"

"I don't know!" Holden shouted, then looked panicked, as though someone in a neighboring apartment might hear him. He dropped his voice low and said, "I don't know what kind of shit she could be into that would get her killed. I mean, okay, like, she probably knows a few dealers—so do I—but I can't think why any of them would want to hurt her. She wasn't even using."

Something suddenly occurred to him. "You touch anything?"

Gage thought, *You kidding?* He'd had his hands all over the toilet, his puke was everywhere. There was enough Gage Chartwell DNA in this bathroom to make a new him.

"I was sick," he said.

Holden extended a hand to help Gage to his feet. "Shit, I'm sorry, man, I'm sorry you had to see this. But we have to be smart now. Clean up in here. Get a bunch of toilet paper and wipe down everything you touched and any barf that missed the target and flush it away."

Gage nodded and went to work, pulling yards of toilet paper from the roll, balling it up and wiping the handle, the rim of the bowl and the floor. He threw the wad into the toilet, got some more paper and did it again and flushed. He rejoined Holden in the kitchen area.

"Don't think I touched much," Holden said.

"The door," Gage reminded him.

"On the way out."

Holden was examining the room from where he stood, careful not to move even his feet without thinking first. He noticed some shreds of duct tape on the floor and a knife and scissors on the table, as though someone had used them to open a package. But there was no empty package to be seen.

Gage spotted something over on the couch. He walked over, examined it without picking it up, then asked, "Was she into cars?"

Holden turned. "What?"

"Did Alicia like old cars?"

He shrugged. "No idea. Who cares? Hey, don't touch that—"

Too late. Gage had already picked up a magazine off the couch. He held it up for Holden to see.

It was an issue of *Collectible Automobile*, a magazine for classic car enthusiasts. On the cover was a picture of the green Mustang Steve McQueen had driven in the movie *Bullitt*.

Gage pointed to a sticker on the cover's bottom right-hand corner.

"It's addressed to Grandpa," Gage said. "It was mailed to Brent Chartwell."

FORTY-ONE

Reece

Diana was still trying to raise either Gage or Holden as we got closer to my brother's house.

"Still nothing," she said. "Why the hell won't Gage respond?"

The answer seemed obvious. He didn't want to talk to us. He was still too upset about his grandfather to discuss his feelings at length. Maybe he was angry with us for even considering the possibility my father had killed Leah Kennard or that other woman years ago. I envied Gage's faith in his grandfather. Diana's too. I desperately wanted to be able to share it, but I had little faith in anything at that moment. Maybe that was what writing news copy did to you. It made you a slave to facts, and the facts weren't in my father's favor.

Everything was unraveling. I had a strong sense of foreboding, that the events of the last couple of days were moving quickly toward some kind of resolution, one that would bring no sense of closure, but open even more wounds.

I kept those thoughts to myself. Diana was already on edge.

"You texting or calling?" I asked.

"Both," she snapped, annoyed I would even have to ask. "And I've left him two voicemails."

"No car," I said, referring to Holden's Honda. His house was just up ahead, and there was no car in the driveway. There was one car parked on the street, a black Mercedes sedan, but it was four or five houses past Holden's.

"Where to now?" I asked, having brought the car to a stop out front, engine on, my foot on the brake.

Diana impulsively opened the door and said, "I'll see if he's home."

"The car's not here so—"

"Maybe he sold it for drugs. Or crashed it someplace and came back."

It was a cruel, uncharitable thing to say, but also within the realm of the possible, so I didn't chastise her for it. I put the car in park, killed the engine, and caught up with her as she reached the front door and started knocking.

"Holden!" she shouted. "It's Diana!"

We stood there a moment, waiting to sense some motion within the house but heard nothing.

"Let's go," I said. "Let's take a drive by—"

"Hang on," Diana said, grabbing my sleeve. "I heard something."

"I didn't hear—"

"*Shhh!*"

She had her ear to the door. "I heard someone bumping into something."

I took a turn listening, turning my head and getting it within an inch of the door. "I don't hear anything."

"I'm telling you I heard something. He might not want to talk to *us* but I want to talk to *him*."

She tried the door and found it unlocked. She opened it about a foot and called out my brother's name again, but there was still no response.

"Hey," she said. "Check it out."

The wood in the doorjamb was splintered around the lock, as though the door had been forced open, maybe kicked in and reclosed.

I shook my head, not sure what to make of it. Had someone broken in? Or maybe Holden misplaced his keys at one point and had to bust his way in?

Whatever the answer, it was concerning, and more than enough reason to enter. Diana had been here before, although not in some time, so she wasn't taken aback by Holden's housekeeping regimen.

"Holden?" she said again, and then, "Gage?"

"Let's look around," I said.

I walked through the combined living room/kitchen and down the short hallway to Holden's bedroom while Diana checked the bathroom and the second bedroom, where Holden kept just about anything one could think of, except an actual bed. It was filled with cardboard and Rubbermaid containers packed with god knows what.

As I came up behind her, Diana called out, "Holden?"

If she was thinking there was enough mess in there for him to hide in, she wasn't wrong. She took two steps in, peered over a stack of business boxes, found no one lurking there, and came back into the hall.

She stepped into Holden's bedroom.

"Already been in here," I said. "Even looked under the bed. Not that anyone could hide under there, it's so jammed with stuff."

Diana moved across the room, stood in front of the closet, the louvered doors folded shut.

"They're not here. Let's go," I said.

But Diana didn't move. She stood there, frozen, like she was picking up something that wasn't on my radar.

FORTY-TWO

"Impossible," Holden said, taking the magazine from Gage and studying the address tag bearing his father's name. "I don't get it. I don't get how this could be here."

Still in Alicia's apartment, her body just steps away, Holden looked at the issue's date. It was from more than two years ago.

"Did Grandpa know Alicia?" Gage asked.

Holden slowly shook his head. "No, I mean, I don't think so. How could he? And even if they'd met, even if they were friends, why would one of his magazines be here?"

"He lent it to her? Gave it to her?"

Holden stared vacantly. "I mean, let's say he knew her, which I don't think he did, why would he give her this? Alicia wasn't even into cars."

"He came by? Brought the magazine with him?"

Holden just looked at Gage.

Gage raised his arms. "You got a better explanation?"

"Sorry. No." His eyes went back to the shreds of duct tape on the floor by the table, wondering if there could be a connection and coming up with nothing. But he said, "She didn't know my dad, but she knew *who* he was. I told her all about him, about Mom, about what happened. I told her about everything that went down that night. So . . ."

"So maybe she talked to him?" Gage offered. "Before what happened yesterday? She went to the house?"

Holden wanted to sit down, puzzle this out, but he was still mindful about touching anything. "What about those?" he said, pointing to some other magazines on the coffee table in front of the couch.

Gage moved them around with his knuckles, careful not to let his fingertips touch any surface. "There's a couple of *People*s and a *Vanity Fair* and *Us*. There's no address on them."

Holden moved nearer to the table, looked down at the magazines, needing to see for himself. He examined the car magazine again. "This issue is two years old. I mean, if she'd stolen my parents' mail or something crazy like that, it'd be a new issue, right? But this is one that had been sitting around, in a pile. My parents, they let magazines pile up, they can be months or years old before they toss them into the recycling."

Gage remained as baffled as his uncle. Finally, he said, "I guess it's a question for Grandma. Maybe she'll know."

"Yeah, maybe." He grimaced, then nodded decisively. "We're outta here. Bring that magazine."

They navigated their way around Alicia and the blood to the door. Holden pulled the sleeve of his jacket forward over his hand to turn the knob, peeked into the hallway to be sure no one was there, and stepped out, Gage following. Before heading for the elevator, Holden used his sleeve to rub the exterior door handle.

They went swiftly down the hall, Gage hitting the elevator button with his knuckle.

"You're learning," Holden whispered.

Once the elevator arrived and they boarded, Holden lightly rubbed the button he had pressed to come to this floor originally, but said to Gage, "A lot of people will have pushed these buttons before the cops get here."

They got into the Honda.

"I'll take you home," Holden said as they buckled up.

"No," Gage said.

Holden glanced over as he keyed the ignition. "You sure?"

Gage nodded. "I gotta know."

As they drove off, Holden became quiet, thinking. "I'm starting to wonder."

"Wonder what?"

"If Alicia . . . I really liked her, you know? Like, she was the best thing that had happened to me in a long time. We had a lot in common. But she kind of . . . she kind of leaned on me."

"Like, you mean . . ."

"Yeah. She could be, you know, manipulative."

Gage said nothing. He was thinking about something he'd learned when he'd visited Moira.

"There's shit I never would even have thought of if it wasn't for her," Holden said, more thinking out loud than actually talking to Gage.

"There's something I should tell you," Gage said.

"Yeah?"

"What she said? About her aunt getting shot in the bank robbery and the cops coming and shooting the robbers? All that?"

"Yeah?"

"There's nothing about it online."

"It was a long time ago."

"Right, I know. But there were still lots of other stories from around then. Like, some newspapers started putting all their archived stuff online, articles that were only in print before there was the net. So it should have come up."

"When did you do this?"

"Doesn't matter. Just listen. There was nothing about a Mary Zane getting killed. Searched for it all sorts of different ways."

"So maybe nobody covered it. There was no story."

"Something like that, it would make the news. My dad *worked* in news before he got downsized. He'd tell you this is not the kind of story that would fall between the cracks."

"You saying she made it all up?"

"Okay, so there's more. I looked up some other things today, when I got home, on my phone."

"Like?"

"Like Evelyn Corby."

Holden had told Gage what he'd witnessed that night when he was a kid, but he'd never told his nephew the name of the woman his mother shot. Holden himself had only learned it in the days following the murder, when his mother cautioned him that if anyone ever mentioned that name to him, he was to say he'd never heard of her.

But Gage had just heard it, from his parents. And that had prompted him, when he went up to his room, to do some quick online searches.

"This was the same time period when Alicia said her aunt got killed, but there were lots of stories about Corby," Gage said. "Like how they never solved the murder. But there was one detail that kind of jumped out at me."

Holden waited.

"Her niece was living with her at the time she got killed." Gage paused, then added, "Her name was Alicia."

Holden gripped the wheel a little tighter, pressed his lips into a thin line. "She had so *many* questions." He thought some more. "After that session, where I first hinted about what had happened, without getting into any real specifics, she was all, like, wanting to be friends, and gradually asking more and *more* questions, getting more details out of me about what Mom did that I was covering up for."

Gage's phone buzzed. He took it from his pocket. Another text from his mother, asking where he was. He put the phone away.

"We talked about it a lot. She was on my side. Agreeing with me that what Mom put me through wasn't right. That I had to do something. Like she wanted me to get even with her for all that."

"Like *she* was the one wanting to get even," Gage said, "but wanted you to do it for her."

Holden was trying to pull together the threads, put what he knew into some kind of order that would make sense.

"But who would kill Alicia?" he asked Gage. "Who would want to do that?"

Gage shook his head. "If I'd told you all this yesterday, I'd have said you."

FORTY-THREE

Crane left Alicia's apartment building and headed for his car. He popped the trunk with his remote, the lid yawning open as he approached. He dumped the box of magazines in there and vowed to get rid of them as soon as he saw a suitable spot. Got behind the wheel, brought out his phone, and did some basic research. It didn't take much time to come up with an address for Holden.

There was one hell of a mess to deal with. It was *Cleanup on Aisles Four, Five, Six, and Seven.*

People who couldn't keep secrets—either by deliberately revealing them or being too stupid to know how—were a liability. Catherine's blackmailer had been on that list, and Catherine's son Holden was on it from the get-go. That had been Crane's big mistake, not nipping that problem in the so-called bud. Should have killed the boy that very night back in 1999. He'd have never had the opportunity, years later, to tell Alicia Zane all about it, and, according to Zane, his nephew, Gage.

Catherine Chartwell's mistake with the magazines had now earned a spot on the list too.

She had to go.

At least Crane didn't have to worry about Brent Chartwell. Alicia Zane had evidently taken care of that. She'd have had little choice but to eliminate him after he'd witnessed her killing that Kennard woman. Thinking she was Catherine.

He found Holden's place and parked a few houses beyond it. There was no car in the driveway, but for all he knew Holden didn't own one. Crane wasn't worried about going up to the front door. Holden was unlikely to recognize him, not after all these years, and anyway, it was dark that night.

Crane knocked. Ten seconds later, he knocked again. When there was no answer, he tried the door. Locked. He glanced to be sure no one was walking past, then put his shoulder into it, giving the door a solid bump. It opened, taking some of the framing with it.

Crane quickly slipped inside and closed the door. He wasn't clear on his purpose here. Prove to himself, perhaps, that Holden wasn't home. Maybe he was passed out in his bedroom, or sitting in a bathtub. Either way, an easy target, and best not to pass up an opportunity if one presented itself.

But the house, he quickly determined, was empty.

Should he wait? Crane knew nothing of Holden's comings and goings. Maybe he had a job tending bar and wouldn't be home till midnight. He could be at a friend's. And he might walk through that door in five minutes. How long was he prepared to hang in and—

Noise out front.

He crossed the living room and peeked out the window. A man and a woman getting out of an old BMW. The woman got out of the car first, heading for the door, the man following.

Who the hell were these people? He didn't think the man was Holden. If it had been, he'd have pulled the car into the driveway.

At a passing glance, Crane thought he could see something of Brent Chartwell in the man. Something about the way he held his jaw. So not Holden, but the brother.

Would they walk in if no one answered their knock? Did they have a key? Not that they'd need one. He'd busted the door.

As he moved toward the bedroom, someone knocked. The woman shouted: "Holden! It's Diana!"

Then the man was talking, saying they should go, as Crane slid open the folding closet doors, hoping to hide in there.

The woman said, "I heard something."

The closet was so crammed with things Crane wasn't sure he could fit in. There were three cardboard banker's boxes on the floor, and Crane perched his butt on top of them. Felt them crush a couple of inches under his weight as he twisted sideways, pulling in his feet, and slowly pulling the door back into a closed position.

Slowly, quietly, barely breathing, he brought the gun out of the holster under his jacket.

He heard movement. They were in the house.

The woman, again, calling out for Holden, and then Gage.

Gage.

Through the slats, Crane could make out someone coming into the room. A man. He was there briefly, left, then returned with a woman. Made some comment about how no one would have been able to hide under the bed, there was no room. Okay, so that confirmed some things for Crane. This *was* the brother. Reece. And that had to be his wife. And Gage was their kid.

The woman was hanging around on the other side of the closet door. Crane's hand, gripping the gun, began to sweat.

He considered his options:

1. Kill them.
2. Find out from them where Holden and Gage were, and *then* kill them.
3. Listen and learn.

For the moment, he was sticking with Number 3. Clearly, Reece and his wife had no more idea where Holden and Gage were than he did.

Crane kept holding his breath.

Reece said, "They're not here. Let's go."

But the woman kept standing there, not two feet away from him. Like she sensed his presence.

Crane thought, *Looks like Option Number 1.*

FORTY-FOUR

The mall wasn't going to happen, but McCabe thought she might be able to make it up to her daughter if she brought home pizza. A pepperoni for herself, and a sausage and onions for Moira. McCabe couldn't handle the onions.

She set the two pizza boxes on the kitchen counter and called out her daughter's name.

"Dinner!"

She heard Moira thumping her way down the stairs. *So, still pissed*, McCabe thought. Maybe she should have bought a container of Kawartha Dairy's Death by Chocolate ice cream too. The pizza alone wasn't going to make up for the canceled outing.

Moira sauntered into the kitchen, opened one pizza box lid and then the other. Her stone face cracked slightly when she saw the sausage and onion.

"I didn't forget," McCabe said. "You wanna grab some plates?"

Moira went to the cupboard, got two plates, and put them on the counter. Transferred two slices of her pizza to one, two slices of her mother's to the other. Moira ate standing, while her mother took her plate to the table after grabbing a bottled water from the fridge. She put her phone on the table next to her food.

"Can you let me know how long the silent treatment's going to last? If it's going to be a while I'll turn on the news."

"You totally embarrassed me," Moira said.

Okay, here we go.

"I'm not five years old. You can't treat me like I am. All kinds of stuff goes on around me that I can't control. Kids are always drinking or smoking or doing whatever. Just 'cause you found me where people were doing something doesn't make me a crackhead."

"I know you're not a crackhead."

"You don't trust me."

McCabe sighed. "That's not the issue. You're just not old enough to know how to make smart decisions."

"So I'm stupid."

"I never said that. And you could have saved yourself the embarrassment if you'd come home when you were supposed to or had answered my texts."

Moira rolled her eyes. "I have to be this perfect kid because my mom's a cop. Kids are scared to hang out with me. I had to *tell* everybody it was okay to do whatever they wanted so they wouldn't think I was going to rat them out. I almost wanted them to get wasted so when nothing happened they'd know I was okay with it. And then what happens? You showed up. You can guess what they had to be thinking."

McCabe took her napkin and dabbed a drop of grease on top of a piece of pepperoni.

"I hear ya," she said and sighed. "Okay? I hear ya. Truce?"

Moira considered it. "I guess."

They each took a bite and were quiet for a moment.

"I heard you say Chartwell on the phone today," Moira said. "Before you went out."

"Okay."

"Gage is a friend."

"Gage Chartwell?"

Moira nodded. "It was his grandfather who killed that woman and then himself."

"Jesus," her mother said. "You know him."

A nod.

"How?"

"We have classes together."

It occurred to McCabe that she had neither spoken to, nor met, this Gage Chartwell. She figured he had to be the son of Reece Chartwell. Small world.

"He's pretty freaked about it."

"You *spoke* to him?"

One more nod from Moira. "I texted him, and he came by for a sec. He was really sad. He was at the party."

"The other night?"

"He left just before you raided the place."

McCabe was too tired to challenge her on her use of the word *raided*.

"Why are you telling me this?"

"Because me and my friends, we're all dealing with stuff. Some of it's not a big deal, and some of it's pretty huge. You have no idea the kind of pressure we're under, what we're dealing with. Like kids whose parents are dead, or maybe their parents have split up. Or their dad's in some crazy far-off place playing poker to make a living. So sometimes people need to unwind a bit so they forget all that. You know?"

McCabe nodded slowly.

Her phone started to vibrate.

"Shit," she said under her breath as she took the call.

"McCabe."

She listened. "Okay. Shoot me a text with the address." She ended the call and put the phone away.

"You're going out," Moira said, looking anxious, but also a little relieved.

"I'm going out," McCabe said, taking one last bite of her slice. "Gonna take two seconds and freshen up."

She excused herself from the kitchen, went quickly upstairs, and as she was heading for the bathroom, something caught her eye as she was passing her daughter's bedroom.

She stopped, took a step back, focused on what looked like the edge of a clear sandwich bag caught between the mattress and box spring of her daughter's bed. Stepped in, leaned over, got her fingers on the bag, and pulled.

It was, indeed, a small sandwich bag. And inside, what looked like ground leaves or, more accurately, weed.

McCabe opened the bag, gave it a sniff just to be sure, resealed it, stuffed it into her own pocket. Let Moira have a heart attack when she looked for it later, discovered it gone. McCabe was thinking, if Moira were in an interrogation room, this would be about the time when she'd be asked: *Would you like to change your story?*

She'd save that for later.

FORTY-FIVE

Reece

"What is it?" I asked Diana, still standing by the closet in Holden's bedroom.

Before she could answer, the cell phone that had not left her hand in the last thirty minutes started to ring.

"Gage," she said breathlessly.

She swept her finger across the screen to take the call, skipped a greeting, and went straight to, "Where are you?"

I caught her eye and mouthed the word *Speaker.*

Gage could be heard faintly until she moved the phone away from her ear, tapped the speaker icon, and held the phone out so the two of us could hear his end of the call.

"—with Holden," Gage said.

Background noise suggested they were in a car. Holden's Honda, most likely.

"Where?"

"We're going to Grandma's."

"What's going on?" I asked. "Did Holden pick you up?"

"Yeah."

Diana asked him to put his phone on speaker too. There was a pause, and then Gage said, "Can you hear me?"

"Yeah," I said. "Holden?"

"Hey, man. Hey, Diana."

Diana said nothing. I said, "What's Gage doing with you?"

"I needed to talk to somebody."

I wanted to remind him he had people at Sharnwood who could provide that service, at a more professional level, but held my tongue.

"What about Alicia?" I asked. "I thought she was your go-to these days for that."

A moment's silence, and then, "She wasn't available."

"Why are you going to see your grandmother?" Diana asked Gage.

Gage said, "Uncle Holden has some things he wants to say to her. And he wasn't nuts about this idea, but I thought maybe you should be there too."

That might be the smartest thing Gage had said in a long time. If Holden was planning to confront our mother about what she had kept from him all these years, about how he wasn't her biological son, that could go very wrong.

Holden said, his tone accusatory, "How long have you known, Reece?"

"A couple of hours."

"Liar."

"No," I said firmly. "Mom told me today. This thing with Leah Kennard, it brought everything out into the open. She was going to tell you."

"Yeah, well, I found out another way," he said, raising his voice to be heard over the sounds of driving. "Dad must've given Leah Kennard all these photos of me. She had an *album*. You know why? Because I'm her son! I'm her fucking son! And Mom—how can I even call her that?—kept me from knowing! Dad had been having an affair for years."

"No," I said. "Dad didn't have an affair with her, I mean, not in the beginning. It was a surrogacy thing. They hired Leah. Mom couldn't get pregnant."

"So where the hell did you come from then?" Holden asked. "Maybe you're adopted. Maybe you're not related to anybody in the family."

He said it like I deserved to be an outcast.

"I was a fluke," I said. "Look, let's not do this on the phone. And bring Gage home. This doesn't involve him."

This time, it was Gage who responded. "Uncle Holden's been setting me straight on this family. Stuff you guys don't even know."

"Like?" Diana asked. She beat me to that one.

But it was Holden who answered. "Alicia was part of it," he said, his voice shaking. "I'm trying to figure it out, can't see the whole picture yet. I think I've almost got it and then it slips away. Sorry about everything. Sorry for dragging Gage into it."

"What's this got to do with Alicia?" I asked.

"Evelyn Corby was her aunt."

Diana and I exchanged looks.

I said, "We'll meet you at Mom's."

FORTY-SIX

Crane waited a couple of minutes after Reece and his wife left the house, wanting to be sure they were really gone and not coming back, before sliding back the louvered closet door in Holden's bedroom and stepping out.

He'd listened carefully to the entire conversation. Everyone was heading to the same place. Made things a lot easier for him.

He smiled to himself.

To Grandmother's House We Go.

FORTY-SEVEN

It wasn't hard to figure out which room to go to.

There was a cluster of police officers in the hallway outside the apartment where the landlord of this apartment building had found a body. What McCabe had learned on the way over was that a tenant from down the hall had noticed blood seeping out from under a door, put in a call to the landlord, a Mrs. Harper, who used her key to open the place up. When she saw the dead woman on the floor, she immediately called the police and did not enter the room.

As McCabe came down the hallway, an officer she'd encountered at the Chartwell house the day before approached. The cop who'd been dumb enough to let Reece Chartwell leave the scene.

"Williams," she said.

The uniformed cop nodded.

"What do we know?"

"Not much."

"Neighbors on either side hear anything?"

"Away on that side, and woman on the other side's in her

eighties, needs hearing aids, didn't have them on. So, no. Here's the landlady."

Williams introduced McCabe to Mrs. Harper, a sixtyish woman with short gray hair who barely topped out at five feet.

"Nothing like this has ever happened here before," Harper said. "This is a good building. I mean, we get the odd neighborly disagreement, but they're not killing each other."

"You got a look at the victim?"

"I didn't get close. She wasn't moving."

"But you recognized her."

"Yeah, she's the one who lives there."

"Alone?"

"Yeah. No husband. Saw a guy here occasionally, but he didn't live here."

McCabe had her pad out, pen at the ready. "What's her name?"

"Zane. Alicia Zane."

McCabe started to write it down, but stopped. "Say again?"

"Alicia Zane."

McCabe had encountered it before. She'd seen it in the file she'd dug up on Evelyn Corby. The one she took with her when she talked to Maitland, that retired detective. She was Corby's niece.

"Excuse me," McCabe said, moving past the woman and the assembled uniformed cops. She entered the room, careful not to step in the blood that had already become tacky, and examined the victim. The bullet hole in her forehead, the way she'd fallen to the floor. The scraps of duct tape around the table. McCabe wondered whether Zane had been tied up before she was shot, but the strips of tape were too short to bind anyone, and there were no signs of leftover tape on the chair she appeared to have fallen from.

She went back into the hall, beckoned Harper with her finger.

"What do you know about her?" McCabe asked, tipping her head toward the open door.

"She was okay. She'd had some drug trouble. Not with the police, but she was in a program for a while. Missed her rent one month but I cut her some slack. I don't put people out on the street if they're a day late. You have to treat people like they're human beings. She had some shifts at the FreshCo, I think."

"Ever see anyone coming or going here, visiting her?"

The landlady shook her head. "I don't pay much attention to people's personal lives as long as they don't cause a fuss."

"Cameras?"

"What do you mean?"

"Security cameras? You have those?"

"Been thinking about it."

McCabe sighed. "Stick around."

She went back into the apartment, moving from the kitchen to the living area, then down the hall. Looking for anything that jumped out at her. Made a passing glance into the bathroom, then on to the bedroom, then stopped before going in. She backed up, looked again in the bathroom.

The toilet seat was up.

Alicia Zane lived alone. No husband. But the landlady had said there was a guy she'd seen around a couple of times. Maybe a boyfriend.

Well, if he hadn't been here recently, some other male had been, McCabe reckoned, although it was also possible the seat was up because Alicia or someone else had cleaned it. When she saw the forensic team, she'd have them scour this room. Prints, DNA, the works. Ditto for the rest of the apartment.

She returned to the main room, saw a purse, and picked it up in her now gloved hands. There was a cell phone inside, and she brought it out slowly.

The movement of the phone brought up a text that had been received, but not yet read. McCabe didn't need to get into the phone to know what it said and who it was from.

It read:

REALLY need to talk to you

It had been sent more than two hours earlier. From HOLDEN.

FORTY-EIGHT

Holden and Gage were the first to arrive.

He parked the Honda in the driveway, went up to the door, and rather than ring the bell, balled his hand into a fist to bang on it. A show of anger from the get-go. But as he had his arm raised, ready to pound, Gage grabbed his forearm.

"No," he said. "You need to get your shit together before you go in."

Holden appraised him, said, "Okay."

"Why don't you try the door."

Holden did. It was unlocked. He swung the door wide and the two of them stepped inside.

His mother was standing there in the front hall, a tumbler of scotch in her hand, as though expecting them. "Hello, Holden," she said. "Hello, Gage."

On the way over, Holden had been rehearsing in his head what he would say, the questions he would ask. Why had she never told him about his real mother, how he was the product of an arrangement with a surrogate? That someone had been *paid* to have him? Wasn't that something he was entitled to know?

And the big question: Did that make it easier? Was a child you'd never given birth to easier to threaten with a withdrawal of affection?

But what he ended up saying was: "Hi, Mom."

She looks a hundred, he thought as Catherine stood there before him. Could she have grown shorter in the last twenty-four hours? She had withered, her head hung low. That defiant chin was now hiding her neck.

She set the tumbler on a side table, came up to Holden, and gave him a hug. Unable to just stand there, he returned it. Then she turned to Gage and took him in her arms.

"Hi, Grandma," Gage said, hugging her in return. He had in his right hand the car magazine he'd found in Alicia's apartment. Catherine took no notice of it.

"Why don't we go sit out back," she said, grabbing her drink on the way.

As they followed her through the kitchen she asked whether either of them would like anything.

"I'm okay," Gage said.

Holden said nothing.

They went out onto the deck. Catherine flicked on an outside lamp as the sky now had a twilight glow.

She sat on one of the cushioned deck chairs and with a wave of the hand invited her two visitors to do the same. A half-full bottle of scotch rested on a small table next to her.

While Holden had his eyes on his mother, Gage looked out across the yard to the pond and the old, rotting rowboat that sat at its edge, tall grasses and flowers growing out of it, the family artifact overtaken by nature. The deck light reflected on the smooth surface of the water.

"You should have told me," Holden said.

"It wasn't my decision alone," she said, taking a long sip of her scotch. "A surrogate has the expectation of privacy."

"You didn't have to tell me her name."

"No, but once you knew of her, you'd have wanted to seek her out. Your father and I talked about it a number of times. When you got older, we'd say. When the time was right. But the perfect time never came along, and when you had your troubles, we worried that would only set you back more."

"Maybe it would have helped."

"How?" Catherine asked.

"It would have explained things. How it was different, between me and Reece."

"It was never different."

He looked at her the way one might view a child who denied breaking a window, hand still in the baseball glove, the ball inside the house.

"Of course it was. You'd never have said to Reece what you said to me. He's your own flesh and blood."

"You're wrong."

"Reece says it wasn't an affair."

"You talked to him."

"After I called you. He said he just found out and I called him a liar."

His mother nodded. "He didn't keep anything from you. He didn't know. And he's right. It wasn't an affair. Not then. She was hired. But a couple of years ago, she and your father ran into each other and things . . . developed."

"She had pictures of me," Holden said.

His mother shook her head wearily. "I didn't know about

that. She was . . . regretful, evidently. Wished she'd never given you up."

More to himself than to Catherine, Holden said, "She was my mother . . ."

His shoulders trembled as he struggled to regain his composure. Gage had gotten out of his chair and walked out into the yard, facing the pond, his back to the deck, but still close enough to hear their discussion.

Holden whispered, "I should have guessed. Figured it out on my own." He paused, wanting to take a breath before moving on. "Things were never the same between you and Dad after that night."

"No," she said. "But we were bound to each other by . . . shame and guilt. We were each other's alibi. They could never compel us to testify against each other, not as long as we were still married."

Catherine shot a wary look at Gage, hoping he was out of earshot.

"It's okay. He knows."

Catherine seemed to sink even further into herself. "He's not the only one you told. A woman."

"From Sharnwood," he admitted, "I kept your secret as long as I could. Alicia—" The name caught in his throat. "She's dead. Someone shot her in the head."

Holden had expected some glimmer of surprise, but there was nothing from Catherine.

"This was there," he said, picking up the magazine, pointing to the address label. "Right near her body."

Catherine paled.

Holden said, "If she'd died yesterday, or the day before, I'd have had to wonder if Dad did it. But she was alive this morning."

"How . . . you were there?"

"Gage and I went to her place. We found her."

Catherine fumbled her scotch, the tumbler hitting the deck and shattering into a hundred pieces, the scotch dispersing like blood the color of mahogany. She put a hand to her chest.

"Mom?" Holden said. She seemed to be struggling for air. Holden got up, knelt in front of her. "Are you okay? Mom?"

She'd lowered her head, and when she looked up, she couldn't meet his gaze but stared off into the distance, her eyes glistening. "I've done such terrible things," she whispered.

Holden had nothing he could say to make her feel better about that. But this was something new.

"What have you done?" he asked her gently, standing, towering in front of her.

"Your father . . . never knew that woman. He was never there."

"Then how could—"

"I filled a box with old magazines," she said. "That's what he said to do."

"Who? What are you talking about?"

Catherine got to her feet, slowly stepped off the deck, and walked out into the yard, past Gage and toward the old rowboat. She talked as she walked.

"She'd been calling me. Harassing me. Saying I'd pay for what I did." Her eyes narrowed when she looked at him. "Because you told her."

The words *I'm sorry* almost came out of Holden's mouth, but he didn't know for sure that he was. He wasn't the first domino in this tragic series of events. She was.

But it was all starting to make sense, how Alicia had played him.

His mother was still talking.

"Just threatening calls at first, that I was going to get what was coming to me. But then he said, offer her money, and she went for it, but it wasn't money, it was a box filled with old magazines to feel like it had money in it."

She had reached the rotting rowboat, resting one hand on the bow, its splintered wood surface rough on her palm.

"Who said to offer her money? Who followed her?"

His mother couldn't look at him. Her eyes were on the pond.

"Was it you? Did you kill her?" he asked, and added, "I know you've got it in you."

Catherine's head stayed down. "Not me. But I'm responsible."

"Who? Who did it?" He speculated. "The same man again?"

She nodded.

"So he's moved on from cleaning up for you. He'll kill for you too." His tone derisive, accusatory.

Catherine struggled to raise her head, to regain some dignity. She looked up at Holden and said with some defiance, "Maybe she had it coming."

Gage, only a few feet away, listened as Holden shook his head and said, "What are you saying?"

"She did it," Catherine said. "Came here and shot that woman and your father too. She thought it was me she'd shot."

Gage's jaw dropped. "What?"

"I don't . . . understand," Holden said.

She looked imploringly at her son. "That night, he knew what you saw. He wanted to kill you then, but I talked him out of it. I won't be able to do it a second time."

Now she looked at Gage, her eyes tearing. "He won't take any pity on you either."

"There has to be something we can—"

Catherine cut Holden off before he could finish. "You need to leave. Go. Just go. Get away from here and go away as far as you can. Once he finds out what you know—"

Inside the house, they heard a door open and close.

FORTY-NINE

Reece

"Mom? Holden? Gage?"

I had my key out, ready to use it to open the front door of my parents' home, but it was already unlocked, so I let myself in without bothering to knock or ring the bell. Given how the last couple of days had gone, I was dispensing with niceties. I stepped in, held the door for Diana, and closed it once she was inside.

"Back here!"

Gage's voice, and it sounded like it was a long ways away. We went through the house, slid back the screen door off the kitchen, and went out onto the deck. Diana nudged me, pointed to broken glass and a spilled drink.

Mom and Holden were standing down by the boat, but Gage came running.

He threw his arms around his mother first, then moved on to me.

"I'm sorry," he said. "Holden said he needed me and—"

"It's okay," Diana said, patting his back while his arms were still around me. "We're just glad you're okay."

He released me and looked at both of us, and now I could see the tears in his eyes. "Things are really bad," he said. "Really, really bad."

"What are you talk—"

But Holden was calling out to me. "Hey," he said.

Diana and I and Gage walked to within a few feet of the pond, where Holden had been huddled close to Mom. He moved away from her long enough to pull me into his arms. Then he turned to Diana, who for a second didn't look as ready for an embrace, but she took him into her arms just the same.

My mother had turned to observe us standing there, a group of four, all the family she had left, and there was a sadness in her eyes.

She said, "You all need to go."

"He's coming," Gage said.

"Who's coming?" I asked.

My mother looked at Holden, as if to say, *Over to you.*

Holden put a hand on my shoulder. "Brother, I know you think I was in the dark about some things, but the one who really needs to be brought up to speed is you."

I looked from him to our mother and back again. It was Mom who spoke: "All the things I did, they were to protect this family. Some of them a long time ago . . . some more recent. But I've only ended up putting you all in harm's way." The words *I'm sorry* seemed on the tip of her tongue, but what came out next was, "Leave. Leave now."

Diana wasn't ready to be ordered off the property without being given a reason. "I want to know what Gage has to do with this. I want to know—"

Holden said, "It's got nothing to do with Gage." He looked toward his mother. "It's got everything to do with her."

Gage said, "Mom, Grandma's right. We gotta go." He was shifting his weight from one foot to the other, like a five-year-old who needed to find a bathroom.

What the hell were they intimating? Who was coming? What had happened that would put us at risk? Diana and I were supposed to just believe this? Without any explanation? I'd reached my limit.

"No!" I shouted.

Everyone was, for a moment, stunned into silence.

I said, "Diana and I demand to know what's going on here." I glanced over at her, got a look of support, but not what I would call wholehearted. She was nervous. I could see it in her eyes.

Holden said, "You're closer than you know. Look, you remember what I told you about Alicia."

When we were having our phone conversation only a short time ago. That his friend from rehab was Evelyn Corby's niece.

"I remember."

"She's dead."

"What?"

"We found her," Gage said, barely able to get the words out. "She'd been shot. By the guy who's probably on his way here."

That left me momentarily stunned. Slowly, I formed a question: "How the hell does she fit into all this?"

"She wanted revenge," Holden said. "Her aunt was murdered. Evelyn Corby died right here, right where we're standing. I saw it all from there." He looked up at the window that was once his bedroom.

"I did it," Mom whispered. "I shot her. She was going to ruin us. All of us. Everything your father had worked for."

I had no words. I looked at Diana, who was equally shell-shocked. Gage didn't look surprised by this revelation at all.

"Evelyn's niece was blackmailing me," Mom said. "There was a man, someone who helped your father and me . . . hide what happened here. And I asked for his help again. I left the money for her in a dumpster. When she picked it up, he followed her, and . . ."

The man in the parking lot.

I was digging into my pocket for the card Detective McCabe had given me the day before. "I'm calling the—"

"There's not time," Holden said.

I'd rarely heard my brother say three words with more gravity. I glanced around at the assembled group. "Okay, let's go."

"No," someone said.

We all turned toward the house. I was right. Standing on the other side of the sliding screen door was the man I'd seen my mother talking to at the hotel.

But this time he had a gun in his hand.

FIFTY

Reece

"Mr. Crane," said my mother, greeting the new arrival with feigned cordiality.

She took three steps away from the boat, leaving Holden behind her, and was noticeably wobbly on her feet. It could have been the uneven grass, or whatever had been in that glass before it broke.

Or maybe she was crippled with fear.

"Where to begin," said Crane as he slid back the screen and stepped out onto the deck. His hand was raised, and the gun slowly waved from side to side, as though the weapon itself was trying to decide which of us to pick off first.

"Oh, put that away," Mom said offhandedly, like he was proffering a credit card to pay for a dinner that was on her. "Everyone, this is my friend, Mr. Crane, who handled your father's and my security concerns." To Crane, she said, "These are just some friends who came by to offer condolences. They were just leaving."

Hoping, clearly, that he hadn't been standing there very long, hadn't heard what we'd been talking about.

She slapped on a smile and looked at me and Diana, then our son and my brother. "Thanks for coming. I really appreciate you making the time."

Diana was quick to play along. "If there's anything you need, let us know, and again, so sorry for your loss."

"No one's going anywhere," Crane said, shaking his head sadly, as though this charade was wasting his time. He went through the group, nodding at each of us in turn. "You're Holden, you're his brother, Reece. You are *Mrs.* Reece, I gather, although I don't know your name."

"Diana," she said softly.

"Diana," he said, with a slight bow of the head. "And finally, this must be your boy, Gage. Only just heard about him today." Addressing him directly, he said, "I gather, from Alicia, that you know as much as anyone here. Perhaps more."

"No," my mother protested. "They don't know anything. Nothing. Nothing at all." Her denial sounded weak. I had little hope Crane would find it persuasive.

His eyes went from her to Holden. "Well, for sure *he* knows." He shook his head regretfully. "Of all the mistakes in my life, and there have been a few, you're the biggest. You couldn't keep it to yourself forever."

"Things have a way of bubbling up to the surface eventually," Holden said.

Crane looked at my mother. "It's too bad she got it wrong," he said. "Holden's rehab friend. If it *had* been you in that bed, we wouldn't be having all these problems now."

Holden and Gage exchanged glances. They knew something I didn't. Whatever it was didn't matter much to me in that moment. I was trying to guess Crane's intentions. Was he really going to kill us? Even if we didn't have a clue what was going on? I mean, *come on*. We were on the verge of a mass murder here, and that kind of thing just didn't happen in this town, not in Yorkton Hill.

And if that was his plan, would he really be able to get all five of us? He couldn't shoot us all at once. Not that there was a lot to be thankful for in this moment, but at least that wasn't an assault rifle in his hand.

If we all just ran off in different directions, where would we go? Crane was in the path of our only way back into the house. Fences erected at the sides of the property would slow any attempts to reach the street, but the woods beyond the pond could be a way out of this. If we ran quickly enough, we could get swallowed up by those trees.

But could any of us outrun a bullet?

We could do nothing, and all die. Or one of us could make a sacrifice in a bid to save the others.

Go down fighting.

Rush Crane, bring him down. He'd get off a shot or two, but if one of us could get even a half-second jump on him, maybe the others would seize the opportunity to overpower him.

I caught Holden's eye, as if I could somehow telegraph my thoughts to him. I felt that between the two of us, we might be able to do something. I'd charge Crane, and while he was fending off—maybe even shooting—me, Holden could tackle him.

Evidently, Holden read my message wrong.

He went first.

Crane was looking my way when Holden let out a scream. A simple: "Fucker!" I think he meant to startle Crane enough that it would slow his reaction time, that Crane wouldn't have time to turn the gun on him and fire.

But there was a gap of some ten feet between them, and it was going to take Holden a full second, maybe two, to close the distance, plenty of time for Crane to do what he had to do.

And he did it.

He trained the weapon on Holden and pulled the trigger. The gun was fitted with an attachment meant, I guessed, to silence the shot, but it still made enough noise to make everyone's heart skip a beat.

Holden wouldn't reach Crane before that bullet took him down. But it didn't hit him.

"*No!*"

The cry came from my mother. She leapt in front of Holden in time to take the bullet herself. As it entered her chest, she was thrown back into my brother's arms.

There wasn't time to take in the enormity of what was happening.

I shouted at Diana and Gage: "Run!"

They hesitated for a millisecond, then Gage grabbed his mother's arm and said, "Woods!"

A painful wail came from Mom as a dark patch began to blossom across her chest. Holden had his arms around her as the two of them sagged to the ground.

Standing as I was by the old rowboat, barely visible in the twilight, I saw something.

The top half of that paddle my father had angrily snapped in half so many years ago and left to rot. I grabbed it, a two-foot gray and weathered piece of wood with a sharp, jagged end.

Crane caught a glimpse of Diana and Gage running along

the edge of the pond for the cover of the trees, but he was more focused on Holden and my mother, thinking, I guessed, he would finish them off before he took me on and went into the woods after Diana and Gage.

I grasped my short spear with both hands and ran at him with everything I had.

He got off a shot, and I could swear, later, that I felt it whiz past my ear, but I was focused on other things at the moment, and before he could pull the trigger again, I drove the splintered end of that paddle into his stomach.

Crane staggered and hit the ground on his back, but the gun had not fallen from his hand. He started to raise it as I drew the paddle out of him—its sharp end black with blood—and drove it into him again, this time with more leverage since I was hovering over him.

There had to be a good six inches of it inside him.

He made a choking sound and the arm wielding the gun fell to the ground. Holden had gently put my mother on her back and dived on top of her like a platoon commander saving his outfit by jumping on a live grenade. Blood bubbled out of Crane's mouth and his head turned slightly to the side as life slipped away from him.

It didn't take long.

Holden, not wanting to take any chances, got a grip on Crane's arm where it met his shoulder, immobilizing it, then pried the gun from the dead man's fingers.

I called out to Diana and Gage, who'd effectively vanished, "It's okay! He's down! Call an ambulance!" Crane hadn't gotten to relieving any of us of our cell phones, so Diana or Gage could make the call while Holden and I turned our attention to Mom.

Holden sat on the ground and cradled her head in his lap.

"Hang in there," he said.

I was on her other side. "Help's coming. Won't be long."

Gage, approaching, phone in hand, said, "They're on their way."

"Go out front, watch for them," I said. He nodded and dashed off while Diana knelt down with my brother and me.

Mom's eyes were fixed on Holden. She reached up with a weak hand and touched his cheek.

"I'm so sorry," she whispered.

"Save your breath," he said.

"What I said . . ."

"It's okay."

"I didn't mean it. I would never have stopped loving you. You're . . . you're my son. As much a son as Reece . . ."

"Shh," Holden said. "Don't say anything. They're coming. You're going to be okay."

"Please forgive me."

Holden brought her closer to him, brought his face close to hers, and said softly, "I forgive you."

Mom had nothing else to say. Her eyes closed, and she was gone.

FIFTY-ONE

McCabe: Thanks for coming. Have a seat. I'm recording this, just so you know.

Reece: Yeah, sure.

McCabe: First, I wanted to offer my condolences again on the passing of your mother.

Reece: Thank you.

McCabe: It's been quite a tragic couple of days for you. Your father Friday, your mother yesterday. It's horrible.

Diana: Thank you.

McCabe: And Mr. Chartwell, I wanted you to know that I have already been in discussions with the Crown attorney, and I think she's going to find that you acted in self-defense. The likelihood of charges against you is very remote. When you attacked Dalton Crane, he had already shot your mother and was clearly intending to shoot the rest of you. That said, I would advise you to retain the services of a lawyer through the process.

Reece: Understood. I've already been in touch with someone.

McCabe: How are your hands?

Reece: They did a pretty decent job getting all the splinters out of my palms at the hospital. Some of them were in pretty deep.

McCabe: Lucky that old piece of oar was there.

Reece: Yeah.

McCabe: Wish I'd have gotten there five minutes sooner. If Crane hadn't died, if your mother had survived, there wouldn't be quite so many unanswered questions. But we're going to do the best we can to clear those up. That's why I want to talk to everyone while their memory is fresh. I had a long chat with Holden this morning. He's pretty shaken up. I was hoping he might be able to clarify a few things.

Reece: Was he?

McCabe: Yes and no.

Diana: What do you mean?

McCabe: Let's go back a bit. Holden has described for me what happened back in 1999, which I understand you were not aware of until recently. That he witnessed your mother fatally shooting Evelyn Corby, who worked with your father at Wiffel-Smith.

Reece: Yes. It was . . . a shock.

McCabe: And that your parents, with the assistance of Mr. Crane, covered up this crime.

Reece: Yes.

McCabe: Holden said that during his time at Sharnwood, he met Alicia Zane, that they formed a kind of bond, that he unburdened himself about what he had seen so long ago, something his mother had sworn him to never talk about. And even before Holden got into the details, this Ms. Zane was able to figure out that it was her aunt that your mother had killed.

Reece: But Holden didn't make the connection.

McCabe: No. He had no idea. He never realized there was any connection until she went to your parents' house and killed Leah Kennard and your father.

Diana: So that *is* what happened, then.

McCabe: That's Holden's *theory*.

Reece: You don't think that's what happened?

McCabe: There's a problem.

Diana: What problem?

McCabe: I could see his thinking about her motive. She had plenty of reason to want to kill Catherine Chartwell, and given that she had never actually met her, it's understandable that she might have mistaken Leah Kennard for her, and thinking she had shot her, it makes sense she would have to shoot your father, since he was right there and would have seen it happen. And maybe, just maybe, there's some way she could have figured out how to make it look like a suicide. But as I said, there's the problem of the gun.

Reece: The gun?

McCabe: The gun.

Diana: What's the problem with the gun?

McCabe: We'd already determined that the gun used to kill Ms. Kennard and Mr. Chartwell was the same gun that had killed Evelyn Corby back in 1999.

Reece: Right.

McCabe: So how was Alicia Zane in possession of it?

(long silence)

Reece: I don't know. What did Holden say when you asked him?

McCabe: He didn't have an answer for that one.

Reece: He had no idea at all how she might have come to have it?

McCabe: No.

Reece: Does my brother know what happened to the gun on that night? When he saw my mother shoot Evelyn Corby?

McCabe: He says he just figures your parents kept it. Which makes sense, since it was there on the floor in your parents' bedroom. But again, how did it get into the hands of Alicia Zane?

Diana: Maybe . . . Brent—Reece's father—was forced to hand it over?

McCabe: How would that have worked, exactly? Alicia comes to the house with the intention of killing Catherine Chartwell. She's been plotting this act of vengeance from the time she met Holden. But she goes to the house unarmed?

Reece: That does seem . . . unlikely.

McCabe: What happens when she walks into that bedroom and finds the two of them? She's not exactly going to ask politely to borrow a gun to commit the murder.

Reece: If my father had the gun in a drawer next to the bed—

McCabe: —then he could have grabbed it, and the one who was shot would have been Alicia Zane.

Diana: So . . . what *do* you think happened?

McCabe: I do believe Alicia was working on a plan to get even. We found a burner phone on Mr. Crane we believe was hers. It had her fingerprints on it. It had been used to make several calls to your mother, Mr. Chartwell. We found the calls on her phone too. Alicia was blackmailing her, but I don't see any evidence that she went to the house and killed her. We're right back where we started. You know the principle of Occam's razor?

Reece: The simplest explanation is often the right one.

McCabe: Right. I know you might find some small comfort in thinking your father did not kill Leah Kennard, that he did not turn that gun on himself. That it might leave you with a better memory of him. But I'm sorry to have to tell you that I think that's exactly what he did.

Reece: But why?

McCabe: There are some things we'll never know. We don't know what was going on between the two of them, what they might have been talking about. We don't know anything about your father's state of mind. The one thing we know for sure is that he didn't mistake Ms. Kennard for his own wife. I wish I knew more. You and your brother are in a better position than I am to try to guess what he might have been thinking.

Reece: I can't get my head around my father having a gun in the first place, or keeping it all these years. And all this time, it was there, next to his bed?

McCabe: And yet, here we are.

Diana: It's hard to accept.

Reece: I don't think I'll ever understand it.

McCabe: About your son.

Diana: Gage?

McCabe: Yeah. How's he managing? Last night, that must have been a horrible experience for him.

Reece: He was already having a hard time dealing with the death of his grandfather.

McCabe: My daughter knows him.

Diana: What? How?

McCabe: From school.

Reece: Teenagers. How do we ever get through these years?

McCabe: As teenagers, or as parents?

Reece: Both.

McCabe: I wish I knew.

FIFTY-TWO

Reece

When Diana and I were done being interviewed by McCabe, we stopped by Heffernan & Sons, where they were still holding my father. It seemed like a hundred years ago that I'd dropped off his suit at the funeral home, but it had only been yesterday.

I told them my mother would be joining him. When the police had finished the autopsy on her, the body would be sent here. We figured a joint funeral made the most sense, and we set it for a week from now. We promised to come by the next day to sort out all the arrangements. Did we want a private service, or one that was open to the public? We didn't know which way to go. My parents had a lot of friends in Yorkton Hill, especially my mother, with her friends on the arts council. But given the circumstances, would people even come? Or, equally concerning, would we be looking at a record turnout? And if the latter, did we really want to make small talk with all of them?

I was relieved when McCabe said I was unlikely to be charged in the death of Dalton Crane, but I was still pretty shaken by what had happened. Heffernan's would have had a lot more business today if I hadn't done what I did. My brother, Diana, Gage, and me. It seemed clear Crane was intent on killing all of us. Too many of us knew the truth, and the truth was ultimately very damaging for him.

Diana had already suggested I talk to someone. A counselor, psychologist, somebody like that. Maybe I'll take her up on that. Hell, we probably all need counseling. Maybe Sharnwood helped people with problems other than addiction. We could ask for a group rate.

My immediate concerns were for Diana and Gage, but my heart ached for Holden. A witness to what Mom had done, silenced by a threat of withdrawn love. He'd told our mother in her last moments that he forgave her, and maybe he was telling her the truth. I'm not so sure I would have.

I felt badly for Gage. His faith in his grandfather's sense of decency had been undermined by McCabe's conclusion that our initial take on what happened was right. Dad shot Leah Kennard and then himself. Diana was shaken too. She'd come around to Gage's way of thinking, that my father was not capable of such horrible acts.

When we got back from the funeral home we filled our son in on what the detective had told us. Alicia couldn't have been the shooter. It made no sense that she'd have had the same gun that had killed Evelyn Corby. She was still in her teens when Corby died. Alicia didn't know Mom, had never crossed paths with her, had no connection at all with our family.

Bottom line: Grandpa did it.

Gage listened. When we were done, he said nothing and walked out of the room.

***

The next day was a Monday, and as far as our family was concerned, it was a holiday without celebration. Diana didn't go to work, and Gage, with our blessing, skipped school. We all needed a few days before we resumed our normal lives, if they would ever really be normal again.

Diana set up her easel in the kitchen and tried to paint a landscape. I busied myself puttering around the house. I tidied my workbench in the garage. Not that much had been happening there. I was not much of a do-it-yourselfer. I didn't tackle household projects on my own. When a pipe burst, I called a plumber. When the lights flickered, I brought in an electrician.

When I was done in there, I took a partly filled garbage bag and did a run through the house. Kitchen, bathrooms, the wastepaper baskets in all the bedrooms. My last stop was Gage's room. He was outside doing something, probably wearing a path into the pavement with his skateboard.

As I was emptying Gage's trash into the bag, something caught my eye.

It was a crumpled piece of paper, with one word—FROM—visible in one corner. I snatched it up, uncrumpled it, and saw that it was a sheet of personalized stationery from a notepad. Across the top it read:

FROM THE DESK OF BRENT CHARTWELL

It was identical to the sheet of paper found on the bedside table in my parents' bedroom. McCabe had shown that note to me, asking whether the words written on it, where Dad took responsibility for killing Leah Kennard, were in my father's handwriting.

I'd concluded they were.

There was some writing on this sheet of paper, too, in that same handwriting. If this was indeed something my father had scribbled, this was what he'd had to say:

It's okay. I love you, Holden. Listen to Gage. Dad

I stared at it for a long time. Sat on the corner of Gage's bed, looking at that slip of paper, wondering what it meant.

It's okay. I love you, Holden. Listen to Gage. Dad

Where had this come from? Why was it in Gage's trash? I stared at it for the longest time.

It's okay. I love you, Holden. Listen to Gage. Dad

"You seen Gage?" I said, walking into the kitchen, where Diana was putting together some lunch.

"Last I looked, he was going up and down the street."

I went out front, and there he was. Zipping along on his skateboard. He was a bit obsessive about it today, going back and forth over and over again, but with no obvious sense of enjoyment. It was just something to do.

I walked to the end of the driveway and raised a hand as he approached. He came to an abrupt stop, one foot on the pavement, one on the board.

"What?" he said.

"Let's take a walk."

He tossed the board onto the lawn and joined me at my side as we strolled.

"Where we going?" he asked.

"Just walking."

I took the crumpled piece of paper from my pocket and handed it to him, not saying a word.

Gage stopped, looked at it, handed it back to me.

Said nothing for at least a minute. I waited.

"I was supposed to give that to Holden," he said finally. "And I never got to it and didn't see the point later. He knew."

I still said nothing, waiting for more. Gage bit his lower lip, looked away, struggling with what to say.

Finally, he said, "Uncle Holden held everything in, and it fucked him up."

"Yeah," I said.

"But sometimes, telling everything, that can fuck you up too."

"It can be a tough choice to make."

Gage's eyes began to glisten.

"You think we need to sit down someplace?" I asked.

He nodded.

"With your mom?"

Another nod.

The following, as best as I can put it together from what Gage told Diana and me, is what actually happened on that Friday.

FIFTY-THREE

Friday

"I'm gonna do it," Holden told Gage over the phone. "I'm gonna have it out with her, once and for all."

"I don't know," Gage said. "I don't think that's such a good idea."

"Alicia and me, we've been talking. She's been helping me through this. She says this is what I need to do."

"What? What is it you *need* to do?"

"Fucking lay it on the line," Holden said.

Gage could sense, from the sound of his voice, that Holden was on something. Gage had noticed this more often since his uncle had been hanging out with Alicia. He'd become more emboldened, but that change had not been matched by an increase in good judgment. Gage was worried he'd do something really serious, something he'd regret, and felt a duty to talk him out of it.

He considered telling his parents, or at least his father, that his brother was right on the edge, that he might have reached the point where he would actually harm his mother. That he'd been harboring all this anger toward her, for so long, and it had come to a boil.

said, that there be a verbal showdown between Holden and his mother.

"You need to do something that ends this, once and for all."

Gage was never present for those conversations, but Holden would tell him Alicia was pressuring him to do something he wasn't comfortable with. "It's not like I haven't fantasized about, you know, having it out with Mom once and for all, but that's just dark shit that happens in my head, not something I would do."

Gage had a bad feeling about what Holden meant by those comments, but he didn't believe Holden would actually harm his grandmother. If he'd thought Holden was actually going to kill her, he'd have broken his confidence, told his parents. What Gage didn't know at the time was that Alicia continued to lean on his uncle. It was the only way, she'd said, he'd ever be free.

And slowly, Holden began to come around. He even thought it might be the only way he'd ever be free of *Alicia*.

I'll do it if you get off my back.

He could see himself doing it. Walking up to his mother, pulling that trigger.

On that fateful morning, when he'd been up late the night before, getting high, he'd reached a decision.

This was the day.

He rose early. He got out the gun, made sure it was loaded. Maybe, he told himself, at the last minute, he wouldn't actually shoot her, but boy oh boy would he scare the living shit out of her. That might be almost as good. She'd never forget how he'd stood up to her.

His last words to Gage that morning over the phone: "This is the day, man! This is it! It's happening!"

Gage was scared.

He hopped on his skateboard and headed over to his grandparents' house, pushing that board faster than it had ever gone before. He wanted to get there before Holden arrived, talk him out of whatever it was he was planning to do, warn his grandparents if he could.

Holden's Honda was already there when Gage arrived.

He hopped off the board, ran up to the front door, and found it unlocked. Once inside, he called out: "Holden!"

"Gage!"

Not Holden's voice, but his grandfather's. Coming from upstairs.

"Gage, don't come up!"

But Gage was up those steps two at a time and followed his grandfather's voice to the master bedroom.

And came to an abrupt stop when he saw what was happening.

Brent Chartwell was sitting up in bed, propped on the headboard, sheets covering him to his waist and naked from there up. Beside him, a woman cowering under the covers, someone Gage had never seen before. She looked at him for a second, terrified, and then back at Holden, who was standing near the foot of the bed, on his father's side, gun in hand.

He didn't have it pointed directly at either his father or the woman, but nor was it down at his side.

"Who *are* you?" Holden said to the woman.

"Holden, please," his father said, keeping his voice very calm. "You need to put that down, and then we can all have a talk and—"

"Who is she?" he asked, this time looking at his dad. "What the fuck is going on? Where's *Mom*?"

"She's out, son. With friends."

"I wanted to talk to Mom!" He sounded like a child who'd just been told his trip to Disney World had been canceled. Again, looking at the woman, he asked, "Who *are* you?"

The woman raised her palms, not wanting to appear threatening. "Holden, my name is Leah. Leah Kennard. And . . . I'm your—"

Brent cut her off. "There are things we need to talk about, but we can't do it under these conditions. Why don't you go downstairs, we'll get dressed and come down, and we can all—"

"I don't understand!" Holden said. He was manic, waving the gun around.

"Hey," Gage said. He'd taken a few steps into the room and was only a couple of feet to Holden's left. "Come on, this isn't cool. You can't be doing this."

"Gage is right," Brent said. "We all need to calm down and talk."

"Give me that," Gage said, looking at the gun. He went to reach out for it, but Holden recoiled.

"No no no no," he said, the gun going up and down. "I had this all figured out! I have things I want to say!"

"I bet you do," Brent said. "And I want to hear them."

"Not to you!" he said. "And not to her."

"I want to tell him," Leah said, looking at Brent. "It might help."

"Not like this," Brent said.

Leah didn't look persuaded. She looked at Holden, who was still waving the gun, and said, "There's something you need to know. I'm your—"

"Give me that," Gage said to Holden.

For a second, it looked as though Holden was ready to surrender the gun to his nephew, but as he was about to hand it over, he reconsidered, drawing back. But Gage grabbed his wrist, got his hand on the gun.

Leah screamed and turned her body away, looking like she intended to drop off the side of the bed.

But in that moment when Gage pried it out of Holden's hand, his fingers scrambling for purchase, somehow the gun went off.

The trigger. You didn't have to draw hard on it.

Once the blast had passed, the room was stunned into silence.

It took a few seconds for everyone to grasp what had happened.

Leah Kennard had been shot in the back of the head.

Gage, struck dumb by his own actions, dropped the gun to the floor.

Holden said, "Oh fuck oh fuck oh fuck!" He had his hands on his head and was starting to turn in circles. "*Oh fuck!*"

At which point, he ran.

Gage watched him take off down the hallway, then turned to look at his grandfather, who hadn't moved. He was breathing shallowly, looking at Gage, then at Leah, then back at Gage.

Gage had yet to speak. He appeared to be in shock.

"It's okay," Brent said. "It . . . it was an accident. Gage, Gage, look at me. Gage."

Slowly, the boy focused in on his grandfather. "I didn't . . . I was just trying . . ."

"I know you were. Gage, I need you to look at me, and you need to listen very carefully."

"I . . . thought he was going to . . . I had to get it away . . ."

"Gage. *Gage!*"

Brent's tone was like a slap in the face. Gage took a breath before looking at his grandfather.

"There are things we're going to have to do," Brent said with forced calm. "You tried to do what was right, and you shouldn't be punished for that. You're a good boy, you've always made me proud, and I want to see you grow up to be a fine young man. We can't let what happened here do anything to stop that."

"But . . . it happened. It's . . . I'll tell the police I didn't mean it. I—"

"You won't have to tell the police anything."

"You'll tell them. You'll tell them I didn't mean it."

"I won't have to tell them either. But I'll let them know."

Gage looked at him, puzzled, not understanding.

Brent, thinking, said, "I'll leave them a note."

Gage slowly shook his head, still not understanding what his grandfather was up to.

"First, I want you to pick up that gun and give it to me," Brent said. "Grab it by the butt and be very, very careful. That's it, that's good."

Gage gave him the gun. Brent used the bed's top sheet to thoroughly wipe it down, erasing any fingerprints that might already be on it.

"Now, you have to listen to me," he said. "I want you to go into the bathroom and wash your hands and up your arms like you've never done before. Like a doctor getting ready for surgery."

Gage was wearing a short-sleeved T-shirt, no jacket.

"Why—"

"Just do that, and when you're done I want you to go into

my study and get me a pad, one of the ones that has my name on the top, and a pen. You got that?"

Gage nodded.

He went into the bathroom, did as his grandfather said, and lathered up. Once he had thoroughly washed his hands and arms up to his elbows, he dried off, then went to the study and found Brent's personalized stationery. He brought the pad, and a pen, back to Brent, who hadn't moved.

"That's good, that's good," he said. "You washed up like I said?"

Gage nodded.

"You know why I had you do that?"

"I think so."

"Okay." He wiped the pen with the bedsheet, just as he'd done with the gun, then did the same with the front and back of the notepad. With the pen, he wrote a short note, tore it off, and gave it to Gage.

"That's for your uncle. And you're going to need to catch up to him, tell him there's nothing to worry about. I'm going to take care of everything."

Then he started writing another note, which he set on the bedside table to be found later.

"I don't understand," Gage said, although he was starting to, and he didn't like where this was going.

"You remember what I told you when you stole those chips?"

Gage tried to think back.

"You said I was an idiot."

Brent smiled. "I probably did. But that's not what I'm referring to now. I don't remember exactly, but I told you I'd give my life for you if I had to. And I meant that."

Gage felt himself going weak.

"I love you more than anything in the world," Brent said. "I truly do. Right from when you were a baby. Loved going to those car shows with you. I don't know how they'll sort things out once I'm gone, but I'd like to see you end up with my Barracuda. It's a babe magnet. Maybe not for me, but for you? It'll work like a charm. Couple of years from now, you get your license, you'll be able to drive it."

"I don't want your car."

"So sell it, I don't care. Look, I've had a good run. You? You've got your whole life ahead of you. I don't want to see that messed up. And to be honest, part of me is ready. I'm tired of all the bullshit."

"No, wait, you don't—"

"What I wrote down there," he said, nodding toward the slip of paper, "that's no lie. This is all my fault. There were things I could have done, *should* have done, differently a long time ago, and if I had, we wouldn't be where we are now. Holden wouldn't be what he's turned out to be. None of what's happened here is on you. It's on me."

"Please, you don't—"

"But here's the deal. You can't ever speak of this. You were never here. And you've got to find your uncle, quick as you can, and tell him the same thing. Tell him it's going to be okay. Tell him I love him, and that he doesn't have to worry."

Gage was crying.

"Hey, pal, I'd give you a hug, but you might leave a tear on me or a hair or something. Can't go messing up the evidence, right?" Brent put on a cheerful face. "Live your life, kid. Now get the hell out of here. And don't steal anymore Doritos."

Gage backed slowly out of the room, turned and headed for the stairs. As he was reaching the front door, he heard the shot.

And then he went to my brother's house, told Holden what his father had done, that everything was sorted and it would be okay if they never spoke about this again, and then I arrived, and it was Gage I'd heard when I got there, slipping out the back door, leaving before he had a chance to give Holden the note his father had written just for him.

FIFTY-FOUR

Reece

Will we get through this? Honestly, I don't know. I don't see that we have any choice but to try.

I've only told this story to you because I trust you. Trust that you won't go to the police. We're not telling them. McCabe has her theory of how things went down and as far as she's concerned, the case is closed. We'd like to keep it that way.

Diana and I are very cognizant of what keeping something bottled up did to Holden. But we think—we hope—it can be different with Gage. He can talk to *us* anytime. As long as we're alive, we'll let him go over this again and again as often as he needs to if that's what helps. Better us than some therapist who might not feel bound by any oath of confidentiality.

Will he ever get over it? No. Just like I won't ever forget killing Dalton Crane. Or seeing my mother die in my brother's arms.

But you have to find a way to deal with these things.

This is the point we try to impress upon Gage when he's overwhelmed with guilt and considers calling Detective McCabe to confess: "Your grandfather made the ultimate sacrifice to protect you. Don't let him have done it for nothing. Make it count. Live your life. Make a difference."

We hope it sticks.

I'm not talking to Holden much these days. It's going to take a long time to forgive him for dragging Gage into this mess. I understand how he needed to unburden himself to someone, but it shouldn't have been our son. And it sure shouldn't have been Alicia.

It should have been *me*.

Whether I'll ever forgive him is an open question, but at the same time, I have to keep him inside the tent. He knows what happened in that room. That's his *new* secret to keep. At least he was smart enough when talking to McCabe not to mention how he'd found the gun in the pond and kept it all these years. He quietly disclosed that detail to me after Gage's confession. If McCabe had known that, she might have found a way to put Holden—and Gage—in the room, and we didn't want that.

Don't get me wrong about Holden. I'm not without sympathy. I can easily imagine what's eating him up this time, and it's as bad or worse than what was tearing him apart before.

Holden went there that day for a showdown with his mother. And through his actions, the mother he never knew he had died.

Try to get your head around that.

He never had a chance to talk to Leah Kennard. Never had a chance to learn what traits, what inclinations, what interests he might have inherited from her. We knew, from the album that she'd kept, that Leah very much wanted that connection, that she was a mother who wanted an opportunity to love him as only a true mother can.

That's a heavy load. I don't know whether Holden will be

able to carry it. So one of these days, I'll call him, see how he's doing. Find out whether he's using, if he feels another trip to Sharnwood might help. If he does, at least he won't be running into Alicia Zane again.

I saw him at the funeral, of course. Where we buried our parents together. I don't know whether that's what they would have wanted. We went with a family-only service.

Oh, and I've got a job interview next week, writing one of the evening newscasts. One of the stories about my mother's murder mentioned I'd been fired from WorldWide, and an old friend who works at the CBC called me up and said they had an opening. If I don't mess up the interview, looks like the job is a lock.

The estate is getting sorted, and my parents' house is on the market. My understanding is real estate agents may be obliged to disclose what happened there. The murder at the end of the last century, and the more recent tragic events. But hey, check out that beautiful pond. Surely that outweighs the negatives.

Dad's Barracuda is up for sale too. Gage said my father told him he wanted him to have it, that it would be his to drive when he turned sixteen, but Gage doesn't want it.

So, fingers crossed, we'll ride this out somehow.

But there are still nights, when Gage has a nightmare and cries out in his sleep, Diana or I will go into his room and hold him until the terrors subside.

ACKNOWLEDGMENTS

As I've said before, you don't do this alone. Okay, sitting in the study, staring at the screen, blood coming out of your forehead, writing the damn thing, *that* you do alone. But once you hit the SEND button and put that novel out into the world, there are teams of very smart people who make sure it gets into the hands of readers.

At HQ in London, special thanks go out to editor Kate Mills, as well as Kate Elton, Lisa Milton, Claire Brett, Alvar Jover, Sophie Rosewell, Joanna Rose, Georgina Green, and Becci Mansell.

At William Morrow in New York, I am in good hands with Liate Stehlik, Christopher Connolly, Dale Rohrbaugh, Kerry Rubenstein, and my editor Tessa James, who writes the best jacket copy in the business.

At HarperCollins Canada, I have a great team that includes Cory Beatty, Shamin Ali, Neil Wadhwa, Brenann Francis, Melissa Brooks, and Lauren Morocco, who could organize the invasion of a military installation if asked.

For all manner of support, moral and otherwise, I want to

give nods to Carol Fitzgerald, Tien Le, Rose Rillo, Leonard Szymanski, Tracey Chin, Jean Debos, and Tom Straw. For technical help, thank you to Vince Hawkes and Timothy Smith, and if I still got it wrong, it's not your fault.

For looking after my interests, thank you, Helen Heller. You, too, Jemma McDonough.

As always, a shout-out to librarians and booksellers. Lastly, a thank you to readers who recognize the difference between stories that come from authors' hearts and souls, and the slop that spews out from some AI blender. The world needs discriminating readers now more than ever.